Asking for Truffle

Also by Dorothy St. James:

White House Gardener Mysteries

Oak and Dagger

The Scarlet Pepper

Flowerbed of State

Asking for Truffle

A SOUTHERN CHOCOLATE SHOP MYSTERY

Dorothy St. James

CROOKED
LANE

NEW YORK

Published in the United States by Crooked Lane Books, an imprint of The Quick Brown Fox & Company LLC.

Crooked Lane Books and its logo are trademarks of The Quick Brown Fox & Company LLC.

Library of Congress Catalog-in-Publication data available upon request.

ISBN (hardcover): 978-1-68331-291-8
ISBN (ePub): 978-1-68331-292-5
ISBN (ePDF): 978-1-68331-294-9

Cover illustration by Rob Fiore
Book design by Jennifer Canzone

Printed in the United States.

www.crookedlanebooks.com

Crooked Lane Books
34 West 27th St., 10th Floor
New York, NY 10001

First edition: September 2017

10 9 8 7 6 5 4 3 2 1

In memory of Iona (2007–16), my beloved and feisty Papillon and the inspiration for the naughty pup Stella. Midway through the writing of this book, Iona left this world to romp in heavenly fields. My friend, my minion, my heart.

Chapter 1

The strange letter I'd received in the mail earlier today had me popping chocolate squares into my mouth as if they were candy. Well, to be fair, they were candy. But they were also chocolate. Expensive, organic fair-trade chocolate. Chocolate was supposed to be eaten slowly, each bite savored, not tossed into the mouth without noticing the dark, biting undertones in the exotic delicacy. Or so I told myself.

My nervous fingers unwrapped another foil-covered square, and I carefully placed the silky smooth chocolate into my mouth. That's when I realized my visitor was waiting for me to say something.

So much for savoring. I quickly chewed and swallowed before really tasting anything at all.

"This isn't the first time someone has tried to scam me," I said, staring down at the vanilla-colored envelope in my lap. It had arrived by special messenger that afternoon. "It won't be the last."

I looked up at the thin man seated across from me in the tiny living room I shared with Granny Mae Stoughton. Granny Mae, who wasn't really related to me, doted on me like any

1

loving grandmother should. She'd given me the bag of expensive chocolates a few hours after the envelope had arrived.

The thin man nodded in understanding before stretching out his long arm toward me. "Can I see it, Penn?"

I hesitated before handing it over. I'd only asked Craig "Skinny" McGee for help because Granny Mae had insisted I tell someone.

Skinny and I had been good friends during our prep school days. He got his nickname not because of his size—although he didn't have an ounce of fat on him—but because of the ability he'd had since childhood to use his mad computer skills to get the "skinny" on any situation.

In school we'd both felt like outsiders. As the tallest girl in the class, towering over nearly all the boys, I was all awkward knees and elbows. Skinny, on the other hand, was short and sort of scrawny. Plus, he was a computer nerd long before computer nerds had earned cool status.

It was during those tough teen years that we had grown close. We'd shared each other's secrets and adolescent fears. Like brother and sister, we'd protected each other. He'd even asked me to the prom when it looked as if no one else would.

As we grew up and moved on, I'd always felt safe with his friendship. Even though as adults we had little in common—if it didn't involve hacking or catching the next wave, it really didn't interest Skinny—our sense of trust in each other had never wavered.

I'd called him expecting him to tell me he was too busy to do anything. But he was in Madison on a short winter break to visit his father and was able to come right over.

"I was hoping you could use your computer to track down who sent this letter to me." I paused before adding, "Just so I'll know who I should be wary of."

He pulled out a letter that had been printed on high-quality, antiqued paper from the envelope I'd handed him. His dark-brown brows knitted as he read the gold-embossed script. "It says you won a trip to a beach in a contest?"

"A contest I didn't enter."

His thin mouth formed a funny little smile. "It includes cooking lessons at a chocolate shop. I'd think you'd be excited about that part. You should go." He tried to hand the envelope back over to me.

I resisted. "I don't enter contests. Can you—?"

"It's true. She never enters contests." Granny Mae swept in from the kitchen. The silvery mass of tight curls on the top of her head jiggled like an overflowing bowl of gummy worms around her pink headband. As she crossed the room toward us, she held out a tray with a couple of unrecognizable lumps on it, their edges blackened. "Have a chocolate chip cookie, Craig, dear."

"It's Skinny, ma'am. No one but my dad calls me Craig. And that's only when he's shouting at me." That was another thing I liked about Skinny. We were both the black sheep of our families.

"You should stay for dinner. I'm trying out a new recipe: cabbage croquettes." Ah, that would explain the sour odor that had followed her through the swinging door.

Skinny shifted in his chair as he frowned at the burnt offering in front of him. "Um, no thanks, I . . . I already have plans." He quickly switched his attention back to the letter. "So the prize to this contest you didn't enter is a trip to Camellia Beach in South Carolina?" He rubbed his scraggly goatee. "Why does that place sound familiar? Wait a sec." He tapped his phone's screen. After a moment, his quirky smile disappeared. The pink color fled from his cheeks. "Oh, that's why. *He* lives there now."

"Who?" Both Granny Mae and I asked.

"Nobody. Nobody. Just somebody I've—" He shivered. "Nobody. I've been to Camellia Beach once. It's a run-down beach community. No one ever goes there."

"Then why would someone send me this 'prize'?"

"Don't know." He reached over to the side table where I kept a glass dish filled with my dark chocolates. He unwrapped one and tossed it into his mouth. "Hey, look, this is what I'll do," he said as he chewed. "The town is about an hour's drive from Folly Beach. I'm already planning to be in Folly for next week's Ice Box Surf Championship. I could swing by after the competition and check things out for you."

"I don't know." The gnawing dread weighed even heavier on me. "I'd rather you'd just do your magic on the computer." I didn't want him to go out of his way or to get mixed up with the scammer. Doing so might be dangerous. "It's probably nothing. I'm sure whoever sent it is simply trying to con me into buying a time-share or something."

He sniffed the paper. "No, this isn't a mass-produced mailing. And now I'm curious about it." He gave the untouched cookies another wary look before rising from his chair. I stood too. "I'll let you know what I find out."

He was halfway to the door when he stopped and turned to me. "Hey, are you still dating that Cheese King?" he asked abruptly.

"Uh, yeah?" His question surprised me. "I—um—he's fun to be around," I answered, not sure why talking about the guy I was dating made my back stiffen up like a board. "And he owns a successful business, so I know he's not cozying up to me to meet my father like that last guy."

4

He started to say something in reply but clamped his lips together, which only caused my spine to bind up so tightly I thought I might tip over.

"Why did you ask about him? What do you know?" I demanded.

He stared at me a long moment but then shrugged and smiled. "Haven't *heard* anything. And as long as you're having fun, do it, right?"

"Are you sure you can't stay for dinner, dear?" Granny Mae asked as she followed Skinny the rest of the way to the door. "It'll be ready in a couple of minutes."

"Sorry. No." This time he didn't even try to make an excuse. He tucked the letter into the pocket of his baggy jeans and then pulled me into the circle of his boney arms to hug me tight. "Don't worry, Penn. I'm sure it's . . ."

* * *

"Nothing." Skinny had promised to call first thing in the morning. Two weeks had passed since he'd sat with me in my living room. I'd been eager to talk with him and hear what he'd discovered in Camellia Beach.

"Really? Nothing?" Granny Mae, dressed in a fluffy pink robe the color of cotton candy, with matching fluffy pink slippers, disappeared on the other side of the kitchen island to pull a tray from the oven. "I thought he said he'd call by now," she said, her voice bouncing around in the metal oven.

"He did." Whenever he was near a beach, "first thing" for him meant before the sunrise. After the sun came up, I could forget about getting in touch with him because his daytime hours were dedicated to surfing, or thinking about surfing, or planning his next surfing trip.

I dialed Skinny's number and listened to the rings. His voice suddenly came on the line telling me to leave a message. Again.

Last night he'd called my cell phone when I was in the shower and left an odd message: "Penn, I need to talk with you." He'd sounded out of breath. A car with a bad muffler must have driven past him because I could barely hear what he'd said next. "I know why you won that fake contest. I know who sent the letter. And it's really cool. No, I'm not going to tell you in a message. Don't want to miss hearing your reaction. I can tell you this—start packing your bags. You really need to come down here and see for yourself." He paused. I could hear the clop-clop of his clumpy stride. "Look, someone's following me. I've got to go. I'll give you a call first thing in the morning. We can talk then."

I'd tried to call him back right after listening to the message but had been sent to voice mail.

"He hasn't responded to any of the texts I've sent either." With a frown, I settled at the kitchen island where I usually drank my morning coffee.

"I'm sure he'll get in touch soon. And with a story to tell too. Have a scone. They're fresh from the oven." Granny Mae dropped a rock-hard lump of cooked dough onto a ceramic plate. The loud clang made Stella—the little fluff of a dog the Cheese King had given me—bark as if armed intruders had burst through the back door.

"I think I'll just stick with coffee." I loved Granny Mae to pieces, truly I did, but no matter how hard she tried, she could not cook, bake, or broil to save her life.

Nor could I, for that matter. The scone recipe was the same one she'd encouraged me to try last week. At least her attempt didn't smell as if brimstone had escaped from the depths of hell.

Despite the freezing temperature outside, I'd had to open all the windows to get rid of the stench.

In many ways we were two peas in a pod, which didn't surprise me. Even though Granny Mae wasn't really my grandmother, I'd known her my entire life. She was working as my paternal grandmother's personal assistant when I was abandoned as a newborn on Cristobel Penn's doorstep.

Ending up on that doorstep had actually been the second time in my short life that someone had abandoned me. First my mother, a fortune-teller who'd seduced and conned my father, had dropped me into my surprised father's arms earlier that day. My father, a junior in college, was unprepared for a baby, especially a baby born to a woman he barely knew. He drove straight to his mother's house and, without even coming inside, handed me to the butler. From what I heard, Cristobel had threatened to deny the relationship and take me to the local orphanage. It was Granny Mae who'd convinced Cristobel to let me stay. She'd even volunteered to take responsibility for my care.

Granny Mae hadn't had time for a baby, what with the work Grandmother Cristobel piled on her as well as researching and writing her dissertation. Even so, she did her best to make sure someone looked after me, even if she had to hand me over to the gardener, who'd smell of freshly cut grass, or to the cook, who'd often put me to work washing dishes. When she'd completed her first PhD and left Grandmother Cristobel's service to teach at the University of Wisconsin, Granny Mae kept in touch with frequent letters, phone calls, small gifts, and surprise visits.

She acted more like a devoted family member than any of my blood relatives. So when I was offered the position of chief executive of marketing for the Cheese King, Granny Mae had immediately invited me to stay with her in her vintage cottage in downtown Madison, Wisconsin. It had started out as a temporary living arrangement. Three years later, I still hadn't moved out.

"These scones will be perfect for dipping in coffee." Granny Mae picked one up and tapped it with her finger. She shook her head. The pink curlers in her hair clanged. The noise got Stella barking again.

"Hush." I couldn't think with that yapping machine running around my feet. Did I mention how the Cheese King had given me the dog? The jerk.

"You should give that thing back to Erik," she said, not for the first time since Stella had arrived last week. "Why would he give you a full-grown, nasty little dog like that in the first place?"

"He told me I needed a dog to carry around in my Gucci purse," I said absently. I was beyond worried about Skinny. Why in the world hadn't he returned any of my calls? And what had he been so excited to tell me?

"But you don't own a Gucci purse," she pointed out.

"Exactly. And I wouldn't carry a dog around in it if I did." The gift had been a wake-up call. I'd thought Erik had loved me for me and not for my trust fund or the billions my father had in the bank.

Was it only two weeks ago that I'd told Skinny how much I liked dating Erik and how I much I trusted him? I shook my head at how stupid I could be when it came to the men in my life.

To be fair, though, it wasn't like the Cheese King needed more money. He was the Cheese King, for heaven's sake. He owned a chain of touristy cheese shops all across Wisconsin. I'd been hired to develop and implement a PR campaign for his stores. That was how we'd met. With my help, a state newspaper had bestowed on him the title of king a few years ago. He'd introduced himself as the Cheese King ever since.

Until about three months ago, he saw me as a competent, valued employee and had treated me as just another member of the team. I saw him as a charismatic boss who just happened to look like a Nordic god with those chiseled cheekbones and icy-blue eyes. But he was my boss and nothing more until one day, quite out of the blue, he'd stopped by my desk and, instead of talking about the latest ad copy I'd been working on, asked me out on a date. And much to my own surprise, I'd accepted.

I'd been just as surprised this last Thursday when he'd thrust little Stella into my arms. The pup had promptly bit my nose hard enough that I'd bled. Ignoring my dripping nose, Erik had gaily explained how nice he thought the pedigreed Papillon would look in that Gucci purse I didn't own. Apparently, in his mind, all trust-fund girls carried little dogs in ridiculously expensive purses. It'd been a thoughtless gift. But at the time, I'd given him the benefit of the doubt. When we got to know each other better, he'd learn how I loathed touching even a penny of my trust fund and that I never (okay, rarely) spent frivolously.

The very next day at work, Gretchen, Erik's personal secretary, happened to overhear me talking on the phone with a friend about how Erik had given me the dog. She'd rushed over as soon as I'd gotten off the phone and boasted about how *she* was Erik's fiancée. The two of them had been dating for years, she'd crowed. She then announced—in tones as sharp as Stella's bites—that he was using me, since he loved *her*, not me. When he looked at *me*, he only saw dollar signs.

I didn't waste a minute. I marched right into his office and confronted him. The jerk didn't even bother denying his relationship with Gretchen. Instead, he'd agreed to call things off with her, totally ignoring the part where he'd been dating two women at the same time. And then, with that same breath, he had the audacity to suggest I invest heavily in his plans for a Midwest expansion of his cheese shops. Sure, it wasn't the first time someone had loved my money instead of me. But still, it stung.

"You really should give her back," Granny Mae said, interrupting my walk down that unhappy memory lane.

"I don't know where Erik got her. And she bites. No shelter will rehome a dog that bites." It'd be a death sentence. Though I might not like the little Papillon, I knew only too well how it felt to be put out of a home that didn't love you. I didn't have the heart to do that to her.

So I kept the little monster.

But I'd dumped the King.

I didn't want a dog. And apparently Stella didn't want a person. When she wasn't barking, she was nipping fingers, toes, and pretty much any piece of exposed skin she could find.

The little black, tan, and white monster was yipping and running circles around my chair. I told her to hush. Surprisingly she stopped and looked up at me. Her huge dark-brown ears tilted left and right. Her black eyes sparkled with mischief.

For a moment I thought she might obey. Silly me.

After a quick series of shrill barks, Stella jumped up and nipped my big toe. "Son of a—"

I jumped off the stool and chased after her. Even though Stella's legs were much shorter than mine, it didn't slow her down. Not one bit. We ran around the kitchen until I felt like a complete nut.

I finally opened the back door. With a happy yip-yip, the tiny Papillon hurried outside. Sometime during the night, a sparkly white blanket of Wisconsin snow had covered the tidy backyard. Stella wouldn't stay out long. It was too cold out there for a dog that could literally fit in my pocket. But she seemed to enjoy bouncing around the freshly snow-covered bushes.

I watched her for a moment before pushing the door closed.

"Oh, dear," Granny Mae said. While I'd chased Stella, Granny Mae had picked up her iPad. "Oh, dear; oh, dear," she said again and handed me the tablet.

On the screen was a newspaper headline:

Man Murdered in Vat of Chocolate

"What in the world is this?" I asked.

A consummate researcher, Granny Mae searching out articles about chocolate and chocolate shops didn't surprise me. Digging through information had been her way of helping out after I'd received that phony prize to an obscure chocolate shop on the beach.

I scrunched my brows and read the headline again. Murder by chocolate? The articles that usually caught her fancy were scientific discoveries, political opinion pieces, and human rights violations. Not sensational murders.

"What is this? I don't have time to read an article about some bizarre murder," I said and then checked my phone for the call that still hadn't come.

Granny Mae had three PhDs—one in biochemistry, one in astrophysics, and the third in journalism. Strange or sensational news simply wasn't her thing.

"*It's Skinny*," she whispered.

"What?" I dropped like a heavy weight into the nearest kitchen chair. A frigid cold that had nothing to do with the outside air settled deep into my bones. I read the entire article. *Skinny?*

"No. It can't be. It can't be him," I said.

Granny Mae bent down and enveloped me in her warm embrace. Together we cried loud, sloppy, hiccupy sobs, the kind I loathed. But with her holding onto me, making me feel safe and loved, I couldn't seem to hold back my messy emotions.

After I'd wrung myself dry, she handed me a tissue for my nose and then blew hers as well. "After we met with your friend, I subscribed to the digital edition of Camellia Beach's local newspaper, *The Camellia Current*. I was hoping the newspaper might help us learn more about the town and the chocolate shop that sent the prize letter," she explained. "It's a small-town paper. Most issues are filled with things like arguments about new land developments at the monthly town council meeting, surf contest results, and this scone recipe. But this morning's headline . . ." She tapped the iPad with the heavy scone she still had in her hand.

"I can't believe it," I whispered. It couldn't be true. But each time I read the article, the facts refused to change. Last night, Skinny McGee, *my* Skinny McGee, who'd promised to call this morning to tell me his exciting news, had been dipped head-first into a huge vat of semisweet chocolate in the back room of Camellia Beach's local chocolate shop, the Chocolate Box.

The Chocolate Box: the same chocolate shop where I'd won cooking lessons—cooking lessons Skinny had suggested I take.

I need to think.

I need to think.

But my mind, along with the rest of my body, had frozen up.

"Could you let Stella in? She must be a pupsicle by now," I murmured.

12

Granny Mae sniffed back tears. She grumbled about the little dog as she padded toward the back door and swung it open, letting in a blast of frigid air.

I looked at the article again.

"Start packing your bags," Skinny had told me. "You really need to come down here and see this for yourself."

Why? I silently asked him. *What did you find?*

A photo accompanying the article showed a pair of silver-haired ladies standing arm in arm in front of the now infamous chocolate shop.

Why would someone send me that gold-embossed letter informing me I'd won a trip and cooking lessons at their shop? I squinted at the screen to get a better look. The caption beneath the photo stated it had been taken last year at the shop's one-hundred-year anniversary celebration. Both women were wearing crisp, white aprons and grinning at the camera like a pair of giddy teens. The woman on the right, clearly the older of the two, had deep wrinkles around her eyes and etched in her forehead. The lines weren't unattractive. Rather, they suggested a long, well-lived life of experiences, of joys and sorrows. Though her shoulders were hunched with age, she had a tall, slender frame that made her blue gingham dress hang loosely as if it were still on a hanger. Her partner, an African American woman who wasn't nearly as tall, had much better proportions. Her body filled out her black-and-white suit dress and apron in a way that would make my fashion-designer half sister smile. Her dark skin nearly glowed as she leaned toward her friend. A broad smile creased the corners of her wide mouth. Her arm was wrapped protectively around the older, taller woman's, clearly providing support.

They looked so nice, so friendly—like the kind of women who could be trusted to the ends of the earth, like people I would desperately want in my life. Luckily, I'd learned a long time ago not to trust nice people. They could turn on you faster than a nest of hornets.

Could those two women overpower my friend and shove him into a vat of chocolate? He wasn't very tall. If they took him by surprise, they might have been able to—

Stella, soaked from her romp in the snow, shook her wet little self, splashing icy water on the legs of my flannel pj's. With a shiver, I jumped up from the chair and grabbed a towel I'd hung from a hook beside the door for just this purpose. She took one look at the towel and growled. I tossed her a doggie treat that was about the size of her head. While she happily chomped, I dried her off.

She was reasonably dry by the time she scampered off into the living room.

"Skinny had said I should go to Camellia Beach. Do you think I should go?"

"I don't know, Penn." Granny Mae refilled my mug with fresh coffee. The steam from this new pot perked up my senses with its sweet aroma. I inhaled deeply, savoring the rich scent from the shot of chocolate she'd added to the brew. She only did that when she was truly worried. The bittersweet flavor tasted like home and family. Well, not *my* home and my family, but the fantasy home and fantasy family I dreamed of one day finding.

I took another sip of the rich, chocolaty coffee and remembered how Skinny had died. Suddenly, the chocolate tasted more bitter than sweet. I gazed again at the photo of the two older women grinning at the camera.

My hand shook just a bit before I set the mug on the counter. It might seem crazy to think of those two shop owners as murderers. But what if my friend's life had been cut short because one of them had lusted after my money? Or rather, my *father's* money?

The old-lady angle—that was a new one.

I needed to be on guard. Heck, I needed to do more than that. I needed to stand up for myself and shout, *Enough!*

Yes, that felt right. It was time to act. I'd let the cheese kings and chocolate mavens and everyone else take advantage of me and my unfortunate birth for far too long. But not anymore.

I needed to do this for myself. More importantly, I needed to do this for Skinny. I owed it to him to find out who killed him and why.

I picked up my cell phone and dialed the number for the Camellia Beach police department.

Chapter 2

Was someone out there? Watching me?

Come on, Penn. Get a grip. I rubbed my hand over the nape of my neck to chase away the uneasy feeling creeping up my spine.

Skinny had told me I needed to be here, so despite my trepidation, here I stood, in the same town where he'd been murdered.

The gray, stormy stretch of Camellia Beach lurked outside the door of my tiny motel room. I padded a few steps into the powdery gray sand so I could get a better view up and down the shore. Before I had a chance to stop her, Stella bounded out of the room and scampered several yards past me to sniff where the tide had receded, leaving the sand damp.

She seemed to love the sand just as much as the Wisconsin snow.

"Hello? Are you even listening to me?" Tina, my half sister, shouted through the speaker of my cell phone. She sounded even more worried than usual. Perhaps she should be worried this time. I hadn't told her what I'd planned to do until this morning . . . after I'd arrived in Camellia Beach. For one thing,

16

she had the power to talk me out of coming. "I don't know why you're not letting Daddy take care of this."

"You know he's on his yearly rainforest sojourn. Which means no phones. No contact for the next month." Our father was the driving force behind Penn Industries, a multinational conglomerate that bought companies, restructured them, and sold shares of the rejuvenated businesses at large profits. He'd learned the business at the knee of his father, who'd built the business from the ground up. After his father had died more than a decade ago, he'd taken over and had expanded the company with holdings in twenty new countries. It was an exhausting job. When he took time off, he took time off from work, family, everything.

"Then the police. Good gracious, they should be investigating," she said and then huffed with frustration.

"I called them. The Camellia Beach officer listened politely and told me the women who run the chocolate shop are as gentle as a pair of lambs. He actually chuckled at the thought of one of them wanting to do me or Skinny harm. Then he told me that they found illegal drugs in Skinny's pockets and that his murder must have been a drug deal gone wrong."

"Was it?" she demanded.

"No. No! The police are wrong. Skinny didn't do drugs. *Wouldn't* do drugs. He said it messed with his ability to surf competitively."

"At least tell me you are going to ask Granny Mae to go with you. Perhaps she can keep you from doing something stupid and dangerous. Running after a murderer—that has to be the height of stupidity."

I didn't answer right away. Early this morning Granny Mae, who was still in Madison, had sent a batch of articles for me to read about the chocolate industry and Camellia Beach.

"Penn? Penn? Are you still there?" Tina shouted into the phone.

"Sorry, Tina. I'm still here. Granny Mae couldn't come. She has her classes to teach at the university."

"And you don't have a job that needs your attention?" was her quick reply.

"Actually, I don't. I quit."

"You quit?" she shouted. "What? Why?"

"It's a long, boring story."

"Penn? You don't have a job? Does that mean you're actually going to dip into your trust fund to pay for the trip? What about your foolish vow to never use it?"

"I never said I wouldn't use my trust fund. It's the confrontation with Grandmother Cristobel over my spending habits that I vowed to never have."

Tina was quiet for a moment. "She does seem to have an ugly chip on her shoulder when it comes to you."

That was an understatement. Grandmother Cristobel managed to find fault in everything I did.

"You don't have to worry about me. I have a savings account. Stella, don't go too far," I called to my little dog. She'd started to run toward a man dressed like a harbor seal with a surfboard tucked under his arm. Then I saw what Stella had spotted: the man's naked toes. Toes, unfortunately, proved irresistible for biting.

"Don't tell me you're already in Camellia Beach." Tina's voice grew shrill with alarm.

"Okay, I won't tell you. Stella!" That poor guy's toes were about to get attacked. I started to run toward him.

"You *are* already in that beach town. I can hear the waves. I can't believe you. You called me after you went and put yourself in danger?"

"I'm not in—hold on."

I shoved the phone into my jeans' back pocket and ran as fast as my spindly legs could carry me. It was one of the few times in my life I was glad my legs had grown so long.

"Look out!" I called in warning. Too late. Stella had already reached the poor surfer.

Stella growled. Then chomped.

"Ouch!" the man cried.

I scooped up my naughty dog. Frustrated that I'd taken her away from her new chew toy, she clamped down on my finger.

"Owww! Stella, behave."

Behaving was the last thing the silky little dog had on her mind. She wiggled and yipped and tried to take another chunk out of my finger.

"Do you need a hand with your dog?" the man asked.

"She's not my dog," I replied while still wrestling with the little monster. "Well, she is my dog. But I didn't—" I finally managed to get her tucked safely under my arm. "It's a long story. Is your toe okay?"

He shook his foot. "She didn't break the skin. But you really need to train that thing. It could hurt someone."

"I know. I'm sorry. She's—" I stopped myself from saying what had been on the tip of my tongue—that she'd been an unwanted gift. Yes, I knew she was just a dog, but I grew up in a household where family members talked about me as if I were an unwanted gift. The memories cut too deeply. "She's still adjusting to her new home. And then I brought her here. So she's pretty confused."

The corner of his mouth curved up a bit. "Picked one hell of a time to go on vacation. A nor'easter is blowin' in. It's supposed to rain like the devil all week. I hope you got a discounted price on the room." He nodded to the run-down motel behind us.

"I'm not on vacation. Not exactly."

"Business? Here? Not much happens on this spit of sand, at least not in February." He stuck the nose of his long surfboard in the sand and leaned against it. "I'm Harley."

Water droplets from the drizzly rain hung like tiny stars in his hair, which was dark with a few naturally sun-bleached highlights. His slightly-too-long hair curled at the ends. As I looked at him, my breath got caught in my throat. He had the sharply sculpted features that master artists have strived for centuries to capture in their artwork.

"Uh . . . hiya. I'm Penn." My voice squeaked. Embarrassed, I cleared my throat.

"Penn? As in Penny?" His smile grew. He was tall. Not many men matched my height, but with this guy, I had to tilt my head up just a bit to see that wry smile of his and to gaze directly into his stormy green eyes.

I scowled. Not at his good looks, but at my silly reaction to them. Heck, I was a smidge older than thirty-five. My stomach shouldn't jump around like it was filled with baby frogs. And my head definitely shouldn't fizzle with silly romantic bubbles. But I couldn't stop it from happening. Irritated with myself, I suddenly felt as prickly as a woolen winter sweater.

Not only that, but I'd always shied away from talking about my name. So instead of saying something witty or even *nice*, I said sharply, "No, my name's not Penny. Penn. Just Penn." Not the most intelligent way to start an investigation, I know, but I plowed on anyhow. "Did you happen to know the man who'd been murdered, Skinny McGee?"

He'd been relaxed, leaning against his board as if he had all the time in the world to stand in the cold drizzle and flirt with a stranger, until I'd mentioned my friend's name. His muscles suddenly tightened. He stood a little straighter. "Why are you asking about him?"

"Because he was murdered and—"

"Why are you asking *me* about him?"

"Because you're the . . ." I was about to tell him the truth—that I was asking because he just happened to be standing there, that he was the first person, other than the ancient, half-deaf clerk manning the motel's front desk, I'd met in Camellia Beach. But the way he'd clammed up when I'd mentioned Skinny set off several alarms in my head. He knew something.

So I leaned toward him and whispered, "Because you're the one who can tell me the most about him."

He recoiled as if I'd slugged him. "You can tell whoever told you that to tie an anchor around his neck an' go take a jump into the pluff mud. I'm not talking to anybody about that no-good loser other than to say he got what he deserved." He plucked his surfboard from the sand and dashed toward the angry waves. He plunged into the crest of a wave, emerging again several yards from the shore.

Well, that struck a nerve.

As I watched him paddling his board with an expert's skill through the rough surf, I stood there wondering about this Adonis of the waves—with his Southern accent and strained connection to my friend—until the rain started to fall in earnest.

Stella wiggled and nipped my hand, a gentle reminder (gentle for her) that I hadn't yet fed her breakfast.

Huddled against the wintry rain, I plodded back through the wet sand to my motel room. I glanced over my shoulder to watch the mysterious lone surfer.

What did he know about Skinny's death?

And how would I get him to tell me?

* * *

After taking care of Stella's many needs—feeding, grooming, crawling under the motel's very low bed to fetch her rubber ducky chew toy—I locked her in the motel's bathroom and braved the cold and wet conditions to explore Camellia Beach's blink-and-you'll-miss-it downtown. It wasn't quite the "best sunny days and wondrously warm winter weather that South Carolina has to offer," as promised in the travel brochure for the island. The brochure had also featured pictures of beautiful sunbathers on the sand, a line of pelicans soaring in the sky, and shrimp boats trolling along in the crystal-blue waters.

It had conveniently left out a picture of the pink run-down, one-story beachfront motor lodge from the 1950s that punctuated the end of Main Street, or the one-screen movie theater that played films from three years ago, or the shabby shops lining Main Street, with their creaky floorboards and slightly musty smell. Instead, the brochure had proclaimed the resort town a "scaled-down Miami, with all the glitter and none of the crowds." I'd been to Miami. It wasn't anything like this place. In my opinion, only a bulldozer could fix a town as broken as this one.

But I wasn't here for pleasure. My focus was on proving Skinny hadn't been murdered because of drugs. Honestly, I didn't want to be here. Despite his final request that I come to Camellia Beach, I'd resisted and resisted some more. Only after the local police and Skinny's family had written off his death as something he'd brought on himself did I change my mind and book a flight to the heart of South Carolina's Lowcountry.

How could I not come? After all, Skinny would have never set foot in this town if I hadn't shown him that phony letter and asked him to help track down the sender.

A sudden gust of wind rose up from nowhere and shoved me off the sidewalk and into the intersection of Main and East Europe Avenue. I pulled my windbreaker tight against my chest to hold off the biting cold while the wind swirled around me like eddies in the ocean. I felt as if I'd been caught in an undertow as the wind pushed me toward a mud puddle that had formed around a clogged curbside storm drain.

My fashionable, fleece-lined Timberland boots sank deep into a wet, dark abyss. I stood in the puddle, muttering angrily beneath my breath, when suddenly a black sedan careened around a corner. Its muffler screaming, it swerved left, right, and then jumped onto the curb. It was heading directly toward me!

In a spurt of self-preservation, I dove toward the first available door. It was the entrance of a shop located in a two-story redbrick building with three storefronts and what looked like offices above.

The bumper of the car brushed my khaki pants a moment before I burst into the store. A copper wind chime tinkled madly in the sudden gust of wind as I fell into a shop crammed full with all shapes and colors of crystals.

A woman about my age—with beautiful chocolate-brown skin and dressed in a vibrant silk dress with swirls of varying shades of purples and blues—made a surprised sound at the sight of me and hurried from around the shop counter. The shop's wood-plank floor creaked and moaned as she moved toward me. Her broad smile appeared warm and genuine as she approached.

She extended her hand to help me up from the floor. "Didn't expect to see anyone today. The weather is so awful, terrible for business. I almost didn't open. Now I'm glad I did. Can I help you find anything in particular?" The name tag pinned to her dress read, "Althea."

"Did-did you see that car?" I wheezed while bending over with my hands on my knees and struggling to catch my breath. "It-it nearly ran me down."

Althea went to the window and looked up and down the street. "Are you sure? The street is empty." She shrugged. "Some of our older drivers have trouble seeing in the rain."

"Who-whoever was driving was going too fast. I think the car was aimed right for me."

She looked out at the half-flooded Main Street in front of her shop again. "I'm sure that's not the case," she said but no longer sounded so certain. "Can I help you find something in particular? I have some lovely black tourmaline imported from Brazil in the back. Black tourmaline is one of the most powerful stones you can buy for protection."

I looked around. Though the crystals inside the shop sparkled like a miniature sky filled with tiny stars under the cleverly placed lights, I had no interest in them. It must have shown on my face.

"You're not shopping for crystals. The storm blew you in," she said with a small sigh. "Happens whenever the weather is like this."

"Don't forget the car. It pushed me toward your door," I reminded her. "I was actually looking for the chocolate shop."

"The Chocolate Box?" Her entire face lit up with pleasure again. "You're almost there. Go one more block toward the back of the island and take a right. It's the third building on the left on West America Street."

I could have thanked her and left. But my instincts told me to wait. A normal person in a normal town would have been horrified to hear about a near miss with a car. And yet she'd dismissed the incident, quickly blaming it on a careless elderly driver. I stepped closer to her and said, "I hear the chocolate shop has the best chocolate in the state."

"Oh, they do. Best in the world too." She nodded so vigorously, the three brass mandala pendants hanging around her neck clanged together violently. "Be sure to buy some of the sea-salted caramel chocolates. They are the finest I've ever tasted. And I'm not just saying that because my mom makes them. They really are the best."

"Does that mean your mother is Bertie Bays?" Bertie was the younger of the two women pictured in the newspaper article.

The salesclerk nodded again. "Do you know her?"

"No. I just arrived in town. I saw an article."

"Ugh, not *that* article." Her cheery disposition dropped from her face, pulling her lips into a frown as it fell. "You're not one of those ghouls looking to see where that awful man died, are you? If you are, you can turn around and leave now. And not just my store. I mean, you can leave this town. We don't need—"

"No, no. Wait." I held up my hands. "Really? People have been coming just to see?" Skinny would have hated that.

"A few." She sighed again. "It's really appalling. Bad for the town, the business association president is saying, which means bad for business. And our businesses can't take any more bad news. Deloris said three families cancelled their reservations at the Pink Pelican after the article came out."

"Deloris?" I asked.

"The desk clerk at the Pink Pelican Inn. She was telling me how the place is practically empty right now."

Althea looked so depressed about the state of her town, I felt as if I needed to say something comforting. "I'm sure it's the cold, wet weather that's scaring tourists away. They should come back once the sun starts shining again."

"No. They won't." Her dark-brown eyes turned nearly as black as the tourmaline crystals as she spoke. "Not unless . . ."

"What?"

"Nothing." She picked up a smooth, round crystal the color of the moon and turned it over in her hand. "Are you sure you aren't interested in buying something from my shop? I get the feeling you could use some positive energy in your life right now."

"Positive energy?"

"Our beach is located in the middle of an energy vortex, you know. The metaphysical powers swirling all around us super-charge these crystals."

"You mean like magical powers?"

"Strong natural magic." She smiled and nodded with enthusiasm. "There are also the island ghosts; many date back to the Civil War and earlier. They help charge the crystals too."

"Ghosts? Magic? I don't believe in mumbo jumbo like that," I snapped. "You shouldn't either. No one should."

It was a rude knee-jerk reaction on my part. But I had a reason to distrust people who talked about such nonsense. My mother—the woman who had seduced my dad—had been a fortune-teller. A con artist. A fraud who'd dumped me at my father's dorm room because raising a child got in the way of stealing money from those who are hurting, who are desperate, who are aching for answers to unanswerable questions, such as what the future will hold.

Althea's lips curled into a patronizing smile. "I won't try to convert you. You don't have to believe in anything to enjoy crystals. They have a beauty all on their own." She turned the moon-colored stone in her hand until a rainbow of colors reflected off its surface.

I knew it was time to thank her for the directions to the chocolate shop and leave, but still I hesitated. I'd flown halfway across the country to get answers. Even if it meant chatting and pretending to be friendly with a charlatan. A charlatan whose mother was part owner of the chocolate shop. A charlatan who didn't seem at all concerned—or surprised—to hear how a car had tried to run me over.

Was her mother involved in Skinny's death? Was Althea an accessory? Was she part of the scheme to lure me here and perhaps steal money from me and my father? Or worse, hurt me? This wasn't the time to lose my nerve and run away just because the thought of "magic" made my skin crawl.

"Did your mother know Skinny McGee?" I asked.

Instead of responding to my question, she took several steps back. "Because he died in their shop, they must have known him?" she demanded. "They must have been involved in his death? Is that what you're thinking?"

"Should I think that? According to the local police, your mother and her partner in the chocolate shop are both gentle as lambs."

"Of course you shouldn't be thinking they were involved in his death." Her words came sharp and quick. "Mama and Miss Mabel are innocent. That man came into this town to make trouble and got what he deserved."

"Got what he deserved? What do you mean by that?"

"The . . . um . . . drugs . . ."

She'd been quick to answer all my other questions. Why did she hesitate now? Was it because she was struggling to remember the tale she was supposed to tell when asked about his death?

Suddenly, her practiced answer seemed to click in her head, and she said in a rush, "Yes, the drugs they found on him. He brought those drugs into our town. And he brought his drug-dealing friends too. That's what I meant."

No. I suspected that wasn't what she'd meant at all. Perhaps that was what someone had coached her to say. Or perhaps she had trouble keeping her own lies straight among all her flaky, "magical" thoughts.

I had toyed with the idea of hiding my identity when talking with the townspeople about Skinny, but I swiftly changed my mind.

"I'm Penn," I blurted out. "Skinny was my friend. And I know for a fact he didn't use drugs. Since the police aren't willing to look beyond what's clearly a setup, I'm here to find out what really happened in your mother's shop."

Her eyes widened at the mention of my name. "Penn?" She set the moon crystal she'd tried to sell me back on the shelf with an inelegant clang. "Penn?" she repeated.

"Do you know me?" I asked.

"No, of course not. Skinny was your friend? I am sorry. I didn't know he had any. Friends, I mean."

"He had loads of friends," I said. But did I know that? We were both outsiders at prep school. As an adult, he seemed personable enough. We would meet up for drinks whenever he came into town. Yet I didn't know much about his adult life beyond his surfing obsession. "He didn't use drugs. He didn't."

He'd told me he didn't. His word was good enough. He had no reason to lie to me.

"I'm sure you're right." She kept looking at me and smiling.

"What?" I demanded.

"I'm so glad to meet you," she said. "We're going to become good friends, you know."

"Because some magic voodoo cards told you?"

Her smile held firm. "I don't think you want to know the answer to that."

"Oh, don't try to scam me." I'd had enough experience with scammers in my life—scammers who pretended to be my dearest friends—to know when someone was hiding the truth from me. I made an effort to narrow my gaze in an accusatory manner. "I know what your mother and her partner at the chocolate shop were up to. I know they wanted to lure me here." I actually didn't know anything. I'd simply said that because I wanted her to start telling me the truth. She'd clearly recognized my name.

Althea's cheeks darkened. She placed her hands on her hips. "If you already have all the answers, why are you here asking questions?"

"Because I need to know who killed my friend. Who killed him?"

"I don't—"

"I don't have access to the family money."

"Your family has money? Cool."

"I never had access to it," I said, not that it mattered. "Not really." There was the trust fund, but whenever I tried to withdraw anything from it, I'd have to get approval from the trustees who answered directly to my disapproving grandmother.

"Doesn't matter." Althea gazed out the large storefront window at the shabby Main Street beyond. "Hardly anyone has much of anything around here. You'll fit right in." The rain outside pelted the glass.

"But I'm only visiting. And only until—"

She reached up abruptly and touched my cheek. Her palm felt hot under my winter-cooled skin. I was too stunned to object. With the exception of Granny Mae, people simply didn't touch me. I'd spent many years building up a facade that kept everyone at arm's length. And I liked it that way.

"You'd better get to the chocolate shop. Miss Mabel will be near to bursting out of her skin waiting for you."

"Waiting for me? Why? What does she want from me?"

The hard look Althea gave me made me feel as if my world was about to be turned upside down. "She wants to teach you to cook."

Chapter 3

"Teach me to cook? Good luck with that," I murmured under my breath, even as goose bumps rose up on my skin. The goose bumps had nothing to do with the unrelenting wind or bone-chilling rain and everything to do with where I was standing. The two-story, white-painted clapboard building on West America Street looked as if it'd barely survived the last hurricane. The building listed to one side like a drunk in a strong wind, which made me wonder whether it was even safe to go inside.

A wide porch spanning the front of the building offered a refuge from the storm. There were two shops in the building. The first was the Drop-In Surf Shop. Posters of surfers challenging waves much larger than the building were plastered in the two windows flanking the shop's door.

The second shop, as Althea had promised, was the Chocolate Box. Written on the sign above the door of the shop was one word: "Chocolate." No games. Straight to the point. A shopper wouldn't have to guess what she was getting. I approved.

Handwriting on a piece of paper taped to the door announced, "Cooking Lessons: Inquire Within."

Althea had insisted I take those cooking lessons. "It's the reason you're here," she'd said after I'd protested the crazy idea that Mabel wanted to teach me to cook. No one would send out a phony prize letter simply because she wanted to teach a stranger how to properly melt chocolate.

I'd tried to get Althea to explain why her mother and Mabel Maybank had targeted me. But she'd refused to answer and had nearly pushed me out the door and back into the wet, cold weather.

It'd be insane to walk directly into their trap and actually agree to take their cooking lessons. But on the other hand, what better way to question them than to sign up for their classes? Of course, if Mabel and Bertie were indeed the ones who'd sent me the fake letter, they'd already know who I was and wouldn't be fooled by my attempts at subterfuge.

Perhaps I could use that to my benefit. With my mind made up, I squared my shoulders, drew a long, steadying breath, and pushed open the door. A copper bell tinkled a happy tune as I stepped inside the cozy shop and inhaled the warm, decadent scent of chocolate.

There were two other patrons in the shop: a woman who looked to be about my age with hair nearly as short as mine but the color of the midnight sky—mine was an arctic blonde—and a young boy around ten or eleven wearing a black wet suit with a heavy coat over it. The woman was scowling at the two white-haired ladies standing behind a glass display case filled with a symphony of chocolate truffles of every imaginable flavor. The boy, his eyes rimmed red, was scowling at everyone.

Mabel—I recognized her deep wrinkles and thin silver hair from her picture in the newspaper—glanced up and clasped her hands over her chest when she spotted me standing at the entrance. Her partner, Bertie, came around the counter to greet me.

"Welcome to the Chocolate Box," she said, her smile as broad as a river. While Bertie looked like an older, slightly plumper version of her beautiful daughter Althea, her fashion sense was completely different. Instead of flowing silks, she was dressed in a pair of worn blue jeans and a thick gray sweat shirt that proclaimed Camellia Beach to be "a heavenly island on Earth."

I bit my tongue before a laugh could escape at the sight of her sweat shirt. But really, it had to be a joke. No one would willingly call this wreck of a town heaven.

"What can we do for you?" Bertie asked.

"I came to . . ." I drew another fortifying breath and grew slightly dizzy from the swirling scents of chocolate candies. I'd been in chocolate stores before, but none had tempted me like this one. The aromas filling my senses were rich, deep, but not at all overly sweet. I grabbed onto the back of a wooden chair in the café area located at the front of the shop to steady myself. "I came to take cooking lessons," I finally managed to say.

"Did you hear what she said? She's here! And she's here to take the lessons!" Mabel exclaimed loudly and started to rush toward me. Bertie stopped her with a quelling look.

"You mean the sign on the door, Mabel? I think you're right," Bertie said quickly, as if she was afraid her partner might say something else, something that would give away whatever scheme they were planning against me. "Business has been slow because of the weather. We haven't had much interest in the classes. And as you can see, Mabel loves teaching about the special chocolates we use in the shop. Mabel, why don't you give Jody her change? I'm sure she has other businesses to . . . er . . . visit. And I bet Gavin is eager to get home and change out of that wet suit."

Bertie's energy level matched that of the storm raging outside. She just about blew across the room toward me, her smile now reaching every corner of her face. "I'm Bertie, Bertie Bays." She extended her hand.

I took it. "I'm Penn."

She nodded. "It's nice to meet you."

And with that, I was 100 percent certain these two were the ladies who had sent the letter. No, make that 110 percent sure.

Everyone, and I mean everyone, I met for the first time would ask the same question when they heard my name. Even that surfer had asked it.

"I'm Penn," I'd say.

"As in Penny?" is the response—unless the person already knows who I am.

Both Althea Bays and her mother Bertie had accepted my name without questioning its origin. The reason had to be because *they already knew* I simply went by my last name and that the mention of my first name made my skin crawl.

And yet neither of them mentioned the phony prize letter they'd sent or the cooking lessons that were included.

"I know what you've done, Mabel," Jody said. "You're not going to get away with it." She snatched a white bag from the counter.

"Does that mean your company won't fix our closet door? It sticks, you know," Mabel called out to the woman's retreating back. She grinned mischievously.

The tall woman huffed angrily but didn't rise to the bait. "Come on, Gavin." She grabbed the boy's arm and rushed out of the store without even glancing in my direction.

Bertie shook her head as she watched the woman leave. "That one needs to slow down and watch what she's doing if she knows what's good for her."

Was that a threat? Was the chocolate duo already planning another murder? Had killing my friend empowered these women to commit more?

"Penn, is it, dear? An unusual name for such a beautiful young lady." Mabel hurried over to me as soon as Jody had left. She grabbed both my hands and held them tight in hers.

I held my breath, waiting for her to mention the phony prize vacation. She didn't. Instead, it looked as if tears were swimming in her eyes as she looked me over from the top of my head all the way down to my soggy boots.

Could these two women, who looked about as sinister as newborn kittens, actually have committed such a crime?

Probably.

"Yes," I said and wrenched my hands free. "I'd like to take the lessons. How much do they cost? When are they offered?"

"Cost?" Bertie asked at the same time Mabel gushed, "Now!"

"Now?" That wasn't the answer I'd expected. "On a Sunday?"

"We're open for business, so why not?" Mabel said. "Follow me. Follow me." She tugged on my arm. "I have just the recipe you need to try."

"I don't cook." I'm not sure why I said that. It wasn't as if it mattered. I wasn't there to actually learn how to fix fancy chocolate treats. I was there to find out what involvement these women had in Skinny's death.

"Did you hear that, Bertie? She doesn't cook," Mabel crowed. "Good. Good. I have a clean slate to work with. So many people claim to know their way around a kitchen, but they do everything wrong when it comes to chocolate. They come in here thinking they can temper, and it's always such a disaster. Such a disaster."

As she led the way to the back of the store, she patted my hand. "Don't worry about the cost, dear. We'll work that out later. You pay what you think it's worth."

I'd heard that before from people who wanted more than just a simple payment for services. Erik, the Cheese King, had offered all sorts of free perks and acted as if he loved me before springing his idea of my investing and getting my father to invest in his expansion plans. By the looks of the chocolate shop's building, these women needed a steep influx of money to rebuild or, better yet, relocate to a new town.

But since I needed to know what connection they had to Skinny's murder, I took the bait and agreed to put myself in Mabel's hands for the afternoon.

Walking with her body slightly hunched, she took me down a narrow hallway and into the large back room with an extra long kitchen island in the center of the room. Burners lined two walls, and several sets of mismatched ovens covered the third wall. She flipped a switch, and the overhead florescent lights flickered on.

"Now"—she tapped her chin—"what should we make?"

"Something easy," I suggested.

She clicked her tongue. "Honey, it'll all come easily for you."

"Clearly, you haven't seen me cook," I muttered as I watched her move through the kitchen, opening and closing cabinet doors as if searching for something specific.

"What did you say?" She pulled a bag of powdered sugar from a cabinet and set it on the counter in front of me. Her kind eyes met mine. She stared at me as if the answers to the universe were printed on my face before asking, "You do enjoy eating chocolate?"

"Oh, yes," I said.

With a curt nod, she returned to rummage in the cabinets. "Dark chocolate?"

"Is there any other kind?"

She chuckled.

"We received a shipment of peanuts yesterday," Bertie said. She was standing at the doorway with her arms crossed over her broad chest. Her brows were furrowed with what looked like concern.

"We can do better than peanuts," Mabel said. Her eyes glittered with pleasure as she grabbed a bag of nuts from a pantry. "Here they are."

She dropped the bag next to the sugar.

"Filberts?" I asked as I read the label on the plastic bag.

"Also known as hazelnuts," Bertie said.

"They're the key to Christmas," Mabel said at the same time, her voice trembling with excitement. "With them, I'm going to teach you how to conjure the magic of Christmas no matter the time of year."

Conjure? Magic? Oh, dear, she sounded as nutty as Bertie's daughter. I held up my hands. "I'm simply looking to take a cooking lesson."

"Don't scare the girl," Bertie warned from the doorway.

Mabel smiled sweetly. "It's an old family recipe that I'm going to teach you. A dark-chocolate hazelnut truffle."

"I like truffles," I said, feeling my body relax.

"The flavors of this truffle remind me of Christmas. I hope they'll taste like Christmas for you too."

Only if they tasted like broken promises and time spent with the hired help.

She must have mistaken the pained look on my face for disbelief. "I know it sounds crazy, sugar pie, but you'll see. When the flavors come together, something amazing happens. The truffles truly taste like Christmas."

While Mabel finished gathering the rest of the ingredients, she had me mix together cocoa powder, sugar, and salt in a large metal bowl. We then moved over to the gas stove to melt bars of dark chocolate in a double boiler. I stirred while Mabel controlled the amount of heat. The air filled with an amazing chocolate aroma.

Once the chocolate had melted into a silky liquid, we poured the dry ingredients into the pot.

Mabel had been right. This wasn't a difficult recipe. I smiled as I picked up the wooden spoon and started to stir.

"Butter my biscuits!" Mabel grabbed my wrist to stop me from stirring. "What in tarnation did you do? The recipe called for a cup of powdered sugar, not granulated sugar." She frowned as she peered into the pot.

"I used powdered sugar." I frowned as I looked into the pot too.

She dipped her finger into the half-mixed ingredients and tasted it. "Salt," she said with a grimace. "How much salt did you put in?"

"A cup like it said in the recipe."

"Sugar pie, the recipe calls for a *teaspoon* of salt."

"A teaspoon? Oh, no! I've ruined it," I cried. All that delicious dark chocolate ruined. "I knew I couldn't do this."

Mabel grabbed both my hands in hers. "Listen to me," she scolded. "It's just chocolate."

"That I ruined."

She took the spoon and started scooping out dry ingredients that hadn't yet been mixed into the melted chocolate. "Go get the powdered sugar, the cocoa powder, and a measuring cup."

When I didn't move, she gave me a little nudge. "Go!"

With her guidance, I poured correct amounts of sugar and cocoa powder into the melted chocolate. Using quick strokes, she stirred everything together.

Once it was smooth and silky again, she dipped a spoon into the pot to taste it. "It needs more sugar," she said.

"It needs less salt," I corrected. "Or no salt."

"No, that's where you're wrong. The salt is necessary. It enhances the sweet. In cooking, just like in life, you need the salt in order to notice the sweet."

She added more sugar, tasted the chocolate, and then added even more sugar. Finally, she nodded. She dipped a spoon into the mixture and held it out for me to taste.

It was sweet—perhaps a little overly sweet—but surprisingly, I didn't taste the salt.

For the rest of the lesson, Mabel hovered, keeping a close watch on what I was doing, saving me from any further disasters. The way she worked with me, with an endless supply of patience, reminded me of cooking sessions with Granny Mae, but with one main difference: Mabel actually knew what she was doing in the kitchen.

When we were finished, we had filled a tray with perfectly rounded balls of chocolate with a nutty center. The truffles were coated in cocoa powder that was so dark in color, they looked as black as the night sky.

Smiling widely, Mabel used tongs to place two truffles on a fine china plate. She then held the plate out for me to take one. She took the other. Starving, I popped the truffle into my mouth. The delicate chocolate melted like butter in my mouth. The nuts had a satisfying crunch. I closed my eyes as the simple mixture of flavors hit me. Then I jolted in surprise as my mind conjured the soft chords of a Christmas carol, complete with organ music and a choir singing. The piney scent of Christmas trees tickled my nose.

I quickly swallowed and opened my eyes. My gaze scanned the kitchen, searching for a diffuser that could send the scent of the holidays into the air.

But there was nothing. And as soon as I'd opened my eyes, the music in my mind had stopped. The air no longer smelled of pine. What I found instead was Mabel watching me with her hands clasped over her chest.

"What do you think?" she asked.

"I think you're good." I wasn't sure how she'd done it. Perhaps it'd simply been the power of suggestion. Or perhaps Bertie and Mabel had worked together to time the scent of pine to fill the air the moment I'd closed my eyes.

Heck, it really didn't matter how they'd managed to fool me into thinking about Christmas when I ate the truffle. Christmas scams aside, the chocolate was delicious. At Mabel's urging, I happily agreed to come back the next day to learn how to perfectly temper chocolate.

As soon as I left the shop, I realized I'd gotten so wrapped up with the cooking that I hadn't learned anything useful about Mabel and Bertie and their plans for my money. I'd even forgotten to ask them what they knew about Skinny's death.

I promised myself to not let the lure of chocolate, no matter how delicious, distract me from investigating my friend's murder again.

Chapter 4

The next morning, a chilly Monday, I started the day with a series of phone calls. First I returned a call to my half sister, Tina, to reassure her I was safe. She'd left five worried messages the day before. "No, you don't need to jump on the next plane to rescue me," I told her. "Really, you don't." After I regaled her with tales of the quirky townspeople and bored her with a detailed description of my first chocolate cooking lesson, she finally relented. As long as I promised to keep in contact with her, she would stay in Chicago. I couldn't have been more relieved. Grandmother Cristobel would kill me if she thought I put her precious oldest grandchild in any kind of danger. (I might be Cristobel's oldest grandchild, but if you asked her, she'd readily tell you there's nothing precious about me.)

Next I called Granny Mae. "Holy cow, you're a lucky duck, Penn," she exclaimed when I told her about Mabel's chocolate shop and the delicious truffles she'd helped me craft. "If I didn't have these classes to teach, I'd be rushing to the airport to take those cooking lessons with you." She paused a moment. "That reminds me." I could hear her tapping on her iPad. "I just saw an article." She tapped some more. "Ah, here it is. It's about chocolate production. Did you know some plantations routinely use child labor and sometimes even slave labor? It happens mainly in Africa, but it sounded as if the practice and abuses were pretty widespread. Disturbing, disturbing. I'll send you a copy of the article."

I promised to read it when I got a chance. We then talked a bit more about what I'd learned yesterday, which wasn't much. "If I were you, I'd try to find out what questions Skinny had been asking before he died. What exactly was he doing? Who had he contacted? And what had he done to make at least two of the people you'd questioned yesterday visibly uncomfortable when you'd mentioned his name?"

It was sound advice. After I hung up with her and had taken care of Stella's needs, I paid a visit to the town's police chief, Hank Byrd.

"Drugs," he declared as he leaned back in his ratty desk chair. "Not from this town, mind you, but from the city of Charleston or perhaps North Charleston. The drug dealer must have followed your friend into town because we don't have a drug problem here. Never had. Never will." He leaned back even farther in his swivel chair and scratched his bristly chin.

I tried to tell him Skinny wouldn't use drugs, but the town's top cop stubbornly refused to listen. "Look here." He dug out a paper from beneath a towering pile on his desk and tapped on the printed list. "Marijuana."

I leaned forward and squinted at the page. The line his chubby finger had pointed to did say "marijuana" and had an amount written next to it.

I looked up at him. "What is this?"

"It's an inventory of what we found on your friend's body. And you can't argue with facts. We found marijuana in his pocket."

I glanced down the list, scanning the catalog of Skinny's clothing and wallet and their contents. I looked up at Byrd in confusion.

"He didn't have his phone on him?"

Byrd shrugged. "Likely stolen. Didn't find any money on him either."

"The fake prize letter I'd given Skinny isn't on the list either. What happened to it?"

Byrd shrugged again. "Don't rightly know."

"And this . . ." I tapped on the paper. "What in the world does 'fragment of Hodgkin DNA' mean?"

He yanked the paper away. "It's nothing. Just a torn piece of paper the coroner found in a pocket. Trash most likely. They have to list everything. Even pocket lint."

"Trash? Trash that had 'Hodgkin DNA' written on it? That's unlikely."

What was "Hodgkin DNA"? Was Hodgkin a person? A company? Had the police found a fragment of a DNA report? Why would Skinny have a DNA report on him?

My heart started to beat wildly.

A DNA report? Could that be what he'd wanted to tell me when he'd called the night he'd died?

With a spurt of nervous excitement, I told Byrd *again* all about why Skinny had come to Camellia Beach, and I reminded him *again* about the phony prize letter I'd been sent. Wouldn't sending fake prizes be considered a crime in his precious town?

I also reported the black sedan that had tried to run me off the road yesterday. Wasn't that a crime?

"Drugs." He beat his fist on his desk so hard, the desk jumped. "It was the drugs that caused your friend's death, not some convoluted plot involving mystery DNA reports or con artists or crazy drivers."

Nothing I could say, apparently, would change his mind.

I ended up stomping away in anger and frustration, vowing to bring enough evidence that even the closed-minded Byrd couldn't ignore it.

A few minutes later, I arrived at the Chocolate Box for my next lesson.

No one noticed my entrance to the shop even though the copper bell above the door had tinkled its sweet song. Standing a few steps inside the door, I breathed deeply to savor the dizzying aroma of rich chocolate that filled my senses.

Mabel was sitting at one of the café tables in deep conversation with a man with short dark hair. His wide shoulders filled out a well-used leather bomber jacket. Underneath he wore a hand-tailored white oxford shirt along with cargo pants and leather hiking boots. He looked like an action hero with his square jaw. There was even a weathered Indiana Jones–style fedora sitting on the café table next to his arm. Action hero or model. He looked . . . good . . . like a model on set for one of my half sister's fashion shoots.

I didn't see Bertie anywhere.

I took a moment to reflect on what I'd learned at the police department. The possibility that Skinny had died with a DNA report in his pocket had my mind reeling.

Was it possible? Did Skinny somehow find my mother? She was a drifter, a fortune-teller scam artist. No one knew her true identity. Had Skinny learned her name? If he had, I wasn't sure how it made me feel. Excited? Angry?

Did I even want to meet her?

My gaze traveled across the room, and I wondered if I'd somehow already met the woman. Was that the reason Mabel and Bertie had lured me here—to this dinky beach town—to reunite me with the con artist who'd given birth to me and then promptly abandoned me on another's doorstep?

Was that what Skinny had been hinting at when he'd left that cryptic message on my phone the night he'd died? Was that the secret that had gotten him killed?

So many questions needed to be answered. And suddenly, I felt less and less sure I wanted to learn what those answers might be. Would I be strong enough to hear the truth?

For Skinny's sake, I needed to follow this investigation through to the end, even if I didn't like where it would take me. I couldn't run, even though that's what I did best in life. I needed to find out what Mabel and Bertie knew and how they were involved.

Mabel leaned forward as she listened intently to what the man sitting next to her was saying. With a nod, he reached into a leather satchel and produced a photograph that made Mabel squeal with delight.

Not wanting to be caught eavesdropping, I cleared my throat.

"Oh, Penn! There you are, sugar pie. I didn't hear you come in. I was beginning to wonder if you'd make it for your next lesson. Come over here, girl, and join us." A warm feeling tingled in my chest as Mabel turned her bright smile in my direction. Her movements were slow as she rose from the chair. I rushed across the room to help her, but the man took her arm before I could reach her.

"You should use your cane," he said gently.

"I don't need a cane or your hands all over me, Cal. I might be old, but I'm not infirm. Now let go already." She batted at the hand cupping her elbow. But the action appeared to be more to preserve her own dignity than to really push him away.

All of a sudden, she crumbled in on herself as a coughing fit overcame her. The man deftly helped her settle back into her chair.

He then rushed over to the shop's counter to find a small pill bottle in her purse. He pushed a pill into her hand, which she willingly slipped under her tongue.

"Can I do something?" I asked as she still struggled with her coughing.

"Nothing that won't make her madder than a wet hen," he drawled in a low whisper. "Miss Mabel hates to admit weakness. Has for as long as I've been alive and I suspect for much longer than that, though I couldn't vouch for it. I'm—"

"Penn, dear, that whispering snake standing next to you is—" A series of dry coughs interrupted her introduction. "He's—he's a Dalton. Calhoun is his name. The Dalton boy who doesn't live here anymore. Both boys used to work in the shop," she said between gulping breaths. "And he's brought me some good news." With her finger, bent from years of work, she tapped the photograph that had made her so happy.

I moved toward the table to look at the photo, expecting to see a picture of a new baby or some other domestic milestone people about my age generally experience. What I saw instead was a photograph of a long concrete block building freshly painted white with rainbow stripes encircling it about a third of the way up the wall. A matching rainbow-striped door was opened a crack, and a small brown-skinned child peered out at the photographer.

"Is this from around here?" I asked. The type of construction wasn't that different from the concrete beachfront motel I'd been calling home for the past couple of days.

"No," Mabel said. Her energy and her ability to breathe smoothly seemed to return as she talked about the building in the picture. "It's the new school. The Chocolate Box funded its construction."

"This is a school in town?" I asked.

"No. No. No." She coughed again. "It's located in the village of Cabruca in Brazil. The old school's roof leaked so badly, it ruined all the computers we'd sent. Cal happened to be in the area for work and took an extra day to travel up the mountain to the village to take some pictures of the completed school. Isn't that wonderful?"

"You built a school in Brazil?" If the Chocolate Box had that kind of money, why in the world was Mabel trying to scam me? And why had she used her money to build a school in South America when she should have used it to shore up this building? After all, it looked like it was about to fall over. "Why would you do that?"

"We built the school in Cabruca because that's where our chocolate comes from. Oh, dear, I haven't told you about that yet, have I?"

"About what?" I asked. "Doesn't the chocolate you use come from a wholesale supplier?"

"Not Miss Mabel's chocolate," Calhoun said proudly. "Best beans in the world. Rare as the most precious diamonds. They come from Brazil. Hand harvested. And—"

"Hush now, Cal." She slapped the back of his hand. "You'll ruin my presentation. I'll tell Penn all about the chocolate during our class."

"So you're the student she's been talking about?" Calhoun's brows rose up into his hairline as he looked me over from head to toe with his piercing green eyes.

"I hope she didn't tell you how I nearly ruined a batch of truffles yesterday by adding a cup instead of a teaspoon of salt."

"Don't go on so; it wasn't that bad. We made it work."

Calhoun chuckled. His deep laugh sounded as smooth as a jazz singer's voice.

"I'm Penn," I said and stuck out my hand.

He looked down at my proffered hand and chuckled again before offering me a sturdy handshake. "Penn? Penn? Oh! You're the one I've been hearing about all around town. You've been asking questions about that strange fellow who got himself murdered."

My cheeks flamed at both his offhand comment about my friend and the way Mabel sucked in a sharp breath. What he'd said was true. I had talked with several residents about Skinny, including the police chief. But I hadn't yet asked Mabel about Skinny simply because . . . because . . . well, because she seemed like such a sweet old lady. And I didn't have the heart to remind her of how my friend had died in her store.

There's a good chance she's guilty as sin, my inner voice reminded me. I shushed it.

Since he'd mentioned the murder, I saw no good reason not to talk about it. "Skinny was my friend. I asked him to come here to do some research about an odd letter I'd received from someone in this town. And before he could tell me what he'd learned, he was killed. That's why I'm here."

Mabel grabbed my hand and squeezed it so tightly my bones creaked. "That poor boy was a friend of yours?" Her voice trembled. "Lord, I'm so sorry. So, so sorry," she whispered. "I wish I hadn't—"

"Miss Mabel, it wasn't your fault. A drug dealer broke into the shop, dragged the man inside, and killed him. You couldn't have stopped that from happening," Calhoun said firmly. He clearly loved her and felt protective of her, which was sweet.

All the same, I wished he had let her finish what she'd been about to say. Had she been on the verge of confessing that she'd sent me the phony prize letter? Had she been about to confess to murdering my friend in cold blood?

"Skinny didn't use drugs," I said through gritted teeth. "And why would some random drug dealer know where to find a huge vat of chocolate? What in the world was the shop doing with a vat of chocolate large enough to drown a man in the first place? It's not like I've seen you use it for your business."

"The police have it. Not that I'd use it again. Gracious, no. Not after . . ." Tears filled Mabel's eyes. Tears of regret? Guilt? "I'd purchased the cauldron for a charity event that had been scheduled for the next day."

"Everyone in town knew about the event," Cal added.

"It was going to start early in the morning, so I'd filled the vat with chocolate before leaving that night. Not melted, mind you. Waiting to be melted. The local schoolchildren were going to try to break the world record for making the most chocolate-dipped candies in a day. We were then going to sell the chocolates to their parents to raise money for new gym equipment. The equipment they have now is in worse shape than what the children in Cabruca are using. I wanted to help."

"I've been telling you all along, Miss Mabel, your heart is too big for that little body of yours." Calhoun kissed her on the forehead. He then turned to me. His deep-green eyes looked troubled. "I'm sorry about your friend. I hope you'll find some answers soon."

After promising to join her for dinner, he swept his hat up from the table and sauntered toward the door. He paused when he heard me say, "We could skip today's lesson."

"Heavens, no!" Mabel protested. "Bertie will be back in no time. I'm sure she won't mind demonstrating the recipe's steps while I explain the hows and whys. Please, Penn. Please, you must stay."

"I can help as well." Cal returned and dropped his hat back on the table. "One cannot disappoint someone as special as Miss Mabel, you hear?"

So I stayed. And I got so swept up in the act of creating amazing chocolate candies and laughing and talking with a charming man with a honey-sweet voice and two of the kindest women I'd ever met, I forgot to question their motives. Again.

Cal showed up again the following day. Together with Mabel, we cooked and laughed. The only rocky part of the day happened when Mabel started questioning me about my family. She'd wanted me to talk about my mother and father. I never shared stories from my rocky childhood or about what little I knew of my mother with anyone. I didn't even talk about it with Granny Mae, who'd been there and had witnessed what I'd gone through.

Thankfully, Cal had noticed my discomfort and helped steer the conversation back to chocolate.

Despite that one awkward moment, I couldn't remember ever feeling so alive or happy. During those hours of perfect chocolate bliss, I would have sworn those two sweet women had nothing to do with sending me that phony prize letter or causing my friend's death.

Deep in my heart, however, I feared I knew better.

Chapter 5

"You're late," Bertie scolded when I arrived on the fourth morning. Her small, round body moved with surprising speed as she pulled the door shut before the wet winter wind could sweep through the shop.

"I didn't realize there was a schedule," I replied and took a moment to enjoy the warm chocolate scents that had started to smell and feel like that mythical home I'd created in my imagination ages ago.

"Tut, tut, of course there isn't a schedule," Mabel said as she used tongs to fill a gold-foil box with an assortment of the shop's signature chocolate candies. "Bertie is teasing you. Aren't you, Bertie?"

Bertie harrumphed. The way she watched me with her narrowed gaze and her disapproving pursed lips made my insides wobble the same way they would whenever I had to deal with my grandmother. "Mabel has been pacing all morning. She's eager to show you one last recipe."

"Last recipe? This is the last class?" I asked, feeling a spurt of panic. This couldn't be the last class. I hadn't discovered anything important yet.

We'd only just begun taking a semisweet journey around the globe, learning about the individual chocolates grown in the tropics from South America to Madagascar and beyond. Mabel had told me how each bean variety had its own unique flavor. Some varieties were even on the verge of extinction. I had to learn more.

And I also still needed to find out how these two sweet but cunningly sharp old women were involved with scamming me and with my friend's murder.

"Won't Mabel agree to more classes? I'm sure she would for me."

Bertie raised her brows and shrugged.

So this was it, then? After this class, they planned to spring their costly trap?

While Bertie continued to keep an uncharacteristically chilly distance that morning, Mabel was all about the hugs. She couldn't seem to get enough of them. And when she wasn't hugging, she was asking all sorts of probing questions about my life.

Without Cal there to help deflect her questions, I felt exposed and vulnerable.

"Isn't Cal coming today?" I asked, looking around in the corners of the shop as if I'd find him hiding there.

"I told him you'd cancelled. I wanted to keep you to myself," Mabel said and pulled me into another tight hug.

Perhaps she was lonely or was simply displaying the warm Southern hospitality I'd heard about. At least that's what I told myself. Because, whatever it was, I shouldn't like it. But I did. Expressions of affection had always felt . . . strange. Especially from overly friendly strangers. I liked boundaries. They kept me safe. But whenever I tried to put up those boundaries with

Mabel, she'd bless my heart and walk right past them to hug me again.

And the odd part about her hugs was that I'd let her give them to me. Oh, these two ladies were experts at playing the con game.

Even though I'd come to their shop with my defenses on high alert, I suspected all Mabel needed to do was hug me like she really loved me one more time and I'd be handing over a blank check for her to spend.

"I worry about Mabel," Bertie came up beside me and whispered, her soft voice quick and cutting. "She's not well. She doesn't have the strength to get so worked up over her classes with you. I told her that at ninety-one, she needs to settle down. I told her that she's only making herself sicker, but she won't listen to me or her doctors or her family. She won't settle down."

"I'm here now," I said, patting Bertie's arm, "and I've been enjoying the lessons. Really, I have."

"What are the two of you whispering about?" Mabel demanded.

"We were whispering about how your fretting has been driving me wild all morning," Bertie shot back.

Mabel chuckled. "Bertie, you are such a tease," she said as she shuffled out from behind the display counter and grabbed my shoulders. After studying my expression for a moment, she wrapped her arms around me. This hug, like all her others, felt surprisingly warm for such a frail, skinny woman.

"You're too thin, dear," Mabel said, not for the first time. Her voice was muffled because she hadn't let go of me.

Bertie cleared her throat. "Go on, get started with the lesson."

Mabel squeezed me closer for a moment before stepping back. "Right, we do need to get busy. Are the ingredients ready?"

"All but the chocolate," Bertie replied.

The backroom at the Chocolates Box was large enough to accommodate a dozen students, but Cal and I were the only ones who ever showed up to take a class. With the miserable weather beating against the windows that looked out over a small patio and the marsh at the back of the island, I wondered why no one else came to the classes. Was the town's tourist industry really that dead?

Perhaps it was. The few people I'd met who were staying at the Pink Pelican Inn were elderly long-term residents who were using the motel as a retirement home. But surely the local residents would be interested in taking these chocolate-covered lessons.

Mabel was a master at her craft. Her passion for teasing the senses came through in everything she did.

A white truffle dusted with dark-chocolate cocoa waited for me on a bone-china plate in the middle of the counter. Mabel lifted the plate. My mouth was already watering. This is how most of the lessons began, with a taste of the finished product. When my greedy fingers reached for the small, round piece of heaven, Mabel pulled the plate back.

"This isn't what we are making today. Today is special," she said, holding the white chocolate truffle hostage. "We'll be making something rare and wonderful. In the Cabruca village in Brazil that I told you about, they call it the *Amar* bean. *Amar* is Portuguese for love. This is a special chocolate you cannot buy anywhere else in the world. The responsibility for it has been passed down in my family for generations." Her gaze went to a line of photographs on the wall. "My children . . ." her voice trailed off. She swallowed hard and shook her head.

"Don't fret over them," Bertie said as she entered the kitchen. Her gaze, too, lingered on the photographs. "They have their own lives and their own troubles. What child would want their future career decided for them before their birth?"

"The chocolate shop and these chocolates, especially the Amar, are part of their DNA," Mabel said as she slammed her slender fist on the counter's marble slab.

Their DNA? It made me wonder about my own half-missing DNA and the paper fragment found on Skinny's body. Yesterday, I'd contacted Hodgkin DNA, a testing laboratory that mainly catered to running paternity tests. But without an intake number, no one at the company would tell me anything.

I studied Mabel's face, memorizing each line and contour, wondering if her narrow nose resembled mine. Or was it my nose that resembled hers? Were we related? Or was I merely trying to see things, hoping against hope to discover I was somehow, even distantly, connected to these two talented women and their sweetly scented shop?

"But they are too stubborn to understand that," Mabel said.

I shook myself out of my overactive imagination. My mom was a con woman who couldn't be bothered with a baby, and that was really all I needed to know about her. Some people won the lottery when it came to parents. And others got stuck with what they got.

That was how life worked.

"I'm sorry. I seemed to have drifted off for a moment. What were you saying?" I asked.

"My children," Mabel said with a sigh. "They have no interest in the chocolate shop, and it breaks my heart into teeny-tiny bits. I might have been able to forgive them for that slight, but they've gone and poisoned *their* children against the shop as well. That I can never forgive."

I wandered over to the photographs. A yellowy print of five grinning towheaded children caught my attention. Three girls and two boys wearing matching blue cotton jumpers sat on a wide Victorian porch. The photograph was from a different time. Judging by the style of the clothes, I guessed it was taken around the time when my father was about the same age as Mabel's kids.

"Sometimes parents expect too much from their children," I said as I continued to gaze at the portrait of the happy family. Such portraits often hid the truth—and the pain. "We're hardly perfect."

"Did your father tell you that?" Mabel demanded, her voice suddenly sharp.

"Not in so many words." His absence from my life had spoken volumes. And what he didn't say, my grandmother had no trouble voicing. Nothing I did was ever good enough. *I* was never good enough.

"There's nothing wrong with you," Mabel insisted. "Nothing at all."

I knew that wasn't true, though it was nice to hear it, even if it was said by someone who didn't know me very well at all. And since I wasn't visiting Camellia Beach to discuss my troubles, I quickly brought the subject back to chocolate, which seemed to make Mabel giddy with approval. She discussed at length various flavor combinations before finally offering me the white chocolate truffle that had been sitting in the middle of the plate.

"It's supposed to taste like the tropics, but I've never traveled there. Do you think I pulled it off?" she asked.

I bit down on the truffle. The layers of coconut and vanilla flavors that exploded in my mouth made me think I was standing on a sugar-sand beach in the Caribbean. I could almost hear the steel-drum band playing in the distance and smell the sweet tang of body oil.

"Oh, it worked all right," I exclaimed, looking around for another piece.

Mabel clapped her hands and gave a toothy grin.

Bertie cleared her throat and cast a meaningful glance at the clock above the door.

"Yes, yes. It's time to get started." Mabel straightened her hunched shoulders.

Her hands may have been slightly swollen and bent from years of laboring in the kitchen, but they moved sure and true as she worked. She opened the doors of an oversized pantry. On the bottom of the pantry sat a burlap bag tied closed with twine. It had to weigh at least a hundred pounds. So when Mabel moved to lift it, I rushed over and took over the task.

"I just need it moved out of the pantry," she said. "I can do it, but if you insist on having your hands on every part of the lesson, I suppose it's a good idea for you to get a feel for the hard parts too."

The bag was superheavy, but I managed to slide the bag out of the pantry and onto the kitchen's pristine floor. Mabel then unwound the twine holding it closed and reached inside, where she retrieved a metal scoop.

"Fetch me that bowl over there." She pointed to a shelf crowded with metal bowls. I grabbed one. "No, not that one. The big one."

I carried the largest bowl I could find over to her. She then measured out three heaping scoops of blackish-brown beans into the bowl.

"Set that on the counter while I put the beans away," she instructed.

I quickly deposited the bowl and rushed back over to Mabel in time to manhandle the large bag back onto the pantry floor for her.

"What are we making?" I frowned as I peered at the unappetizing contents of the metal bowl. "Bean soup?"

"Bean soup!" She laughed so hard she started gasping for air and ended up having to sit down. "Bean soup! You are too funny, sugar pie."

I looked at her and then at the beans. "No, really. What are we making today?"

"Chocolate," she said as if offended that I needed to ask. "Could you be a dear and get that cask off the shelf for me?"

The large wooden box Mabel had indicated looked as if it was hundreds of years old. I ran my hand over its deep-red wood, worn smooth from years of use. It took two hands to carry the heavy cask to the counter in the middle of the room.

Mabel's face lit up at the sight of it. "The chocolate inside this box comes from the Cabruca village."

She lovingly stroked the top of the cask. "My father gave me this box. He used it to store the bounty from each year's special harvest. His father had used it before him. It had been given to my grandfather by a member of the Cabruca village who had carved it by hand. My family has served as caretakers of the Amar chocolate and the kind people who grow and harvest their special crop since before the turn of the last century."

She went on to explain in detail how there were three main types of chocolate beans. While there were offshoots of all the varieties, the Amar seemed to be in a class of its own.

"The trees that grow this special cacao bean are rare and sparse within the forest. The bean, you see, will only grow on one narrow slope deep within the rainforest. My father believed it was a combination of the harsh soils and the unique variety of cacao beans that produced a chocolate with the perfect mix of flavors. The villagers say their Amar chocolate beans originated from a mystical fruit gifted to them from the Aztec gods. And they have cultivated and protected it since the beginning of the ancient village's existence."

I leaned forward with anticipation as she pried open the wooden cask to reveal several thick bars of dark chocolate. A deep, rich scent that smelled almost like an expensive cappuccino filled the room.

"The Chocolate Box holds exclusive rights to the harvest of what is possibly the rarest chocolate in the world. In exchange, we provide the villagers with a fair living wage and full educational opportunities for their children."

She pulled out a bar and turned to me. Her blue eyes pierced me with a stinging glare. "For the candies we sell in the store, I add a quarter of the Amar chocolate to the more common Forastero chocolate the villagers grow on their plantations. I have to mix it. Otherwise, we'd sell out of the Amar chocolate in less than a week. And have lines out the door."

It was sweet that she'd think that, but I couldn't imagine her shop ever being the least bit crowded.

"But for special occasions," she continued, "I'll use the chocolate straight from this box to make my recipes. You'll soon taste the difference and understand why."

"I still don't know what we're making," I said, looking over at the bowl of beans again.

"We're making magic," Mabel breathed. For a moment, the old woman looked decades younger. "In this box is—"

"It's just chocolate, right?" My skin prickled at the thought of magic. There was no such thing as magic. I didn't want anything to do with magic.

"Yes, yes. It is chocolate. The young have no patience. I was trying to set a mood." As she heaved a deep sigh, her years returned to etch their marks on her narrow face. "As I already told you, the villagers call their chocolate Amar, or love. And scientists have proven that eating chocolate ignites the same pleasure centers that light up when falling in love. If that's not magic, I don't know what is. The Amar chocolate is very special. In it you'll find the building blocks of dreams. Whispered wishes carried on the wind end up mixed within the depths of these flavors. It is a magical sweet handed down directly from a god."

This woman is nuts, I thought to myself, and not for the first time. I'd long given up on believing in silly things like wishes and dreams. It wasn't as if Santa Claus or the Easter Bunny had ever convinced my father to take an interest in my life or had softened my grandmother's hatred despite years and years of wishing for just that. "So we're making a 'magical' truffle?" If it was half as tasty as the tropical truffle, she could call it whatever she wanted. Even so, the thought of magic made my stomach clench. Charlatans professed the use of magic only to leave you abandoned and heartbroken.

"Once you taste it, you'll see," Mabel said after a bit. But she didn't let me taste the chocolate bar she'd lifted from the cask. Instead, she put it back inside and closed the lid. "We need to sort the beans."

"The beans?" I asked.

"They're chocolate beans. Weren't you listening? I already told you that we're making chocolate."

"Oh, we're making chocolate. From beans. Isn't that difficult?"

She patted my hand. "I'll show you what to do."

Together we sorted through the beans much like I used to do with fresh peas in Grandmother Cristobel's kitchen. There were a few stones and leaves and pieces of wood that needed to be removed. Once they were clean, Mabel used a scale to measure out ten pounds of beans.

"This is a small-scale operation, so we do things a little differently than a large company would," she explained as I went to fetch several baking sheets. We laid the beans on the sheets, making sure they were spread out in one layer. They were then placed in the twin ovens. We roasted them until the room smelled like brownies and the beans started making popping sounds.

I kept looking over at the cask of chocolate bars, wishing I could have a sample. But Mabel was adamant that we complete our task before I got to taste the finished product. While we waited for the beans to roast, we cleaned everything in sight. Apparently cleanliness was an important part of the chocolate-making process.

After the beans came out of the ovens, we ran them through what looked like a large food mill to remove the husks from the beans. My arm felt like it was about to fall off after cranking ten pounds of beans in small batches.

Mabel then had me carry the bowl of cracked beans mixed with the hulls over to a large metal machine tucked in the far corner of the kitchen. Mabel poured the contents of the bowl into a chute and turned on the machine. In no time, the loose hulls were separated from the beans.

She handed me the bowl of the finished product. "These are chocolate nibs."

"This is chocolate?" I asked, dying to taste it.

"Not quite." She let me taste the nibs anyhow. The flavor was strong and dark and not at all sweet.

I wrinkled my nose. "Are you sure these are going to turn out? It tastes sour."

"Good, that's what we expect at this point."

Next we poured the beans into a grinder that Mabel called a melangeur. It had two granite wheels that spun around and around. She also had me add a carefully measured amount of sugar to the melangeur.

"How long do we have to wait for it to grind?" I asked.

"Oh, about three days."

"*Three days?*"

She laughed at my distress. "I'll not make you wait that long, sugar pie. I simply wanted you to get a feel for how the chocolate in the shop is created. The farmers send us the bags of beans, and we craft our own chocolates using a process that has been refined for centuries. There's a world of history in what we've just done."

She gave me one of her grandmotherly hugs and then removed two tiny squares of her special chocolates from the cask and placed them on the same white bone-china plate she'd used earlier.

After all that work, I was disappointed. There weren't even any nuts in it or any decoration on top. The plain squares of chocolate were kind of a letdown, knowing Mabel considered this my last lesson. I definitely needed to change her mind about that.

"I'm sure it tastes better than it looks." I grabbed one of the tiny chocolate squares and started to pop it into my mouth.

"Wait." She grabbed my arm with surprising strength. "You will want to savor each bite."

The muscles in my back tightened. *Okay, here it comes.* I figured she was going to have me taste the "magic" chocolate and then try to convince me to hand over wads of money to invest in expanding the village's production of their special bean.

Of course she would. She'd been carefully setting up the con for days now. First luring me in with stories of how the world is quickly losing the diversity of chocolate plants. Then by showing me the photo of the schoolhouse they'd built. She'd even admonished Cal for telling me information about the village before she'd felt I was ready to hear it. And during the classes, she had constantly tried to get me to talk about my family . . . my *rich* family.

Even so, I had a piece of chocolate in my hand. I wasn't going to walk away without eating it first.

I took a slow breath to steady my suddenly racing heart and then bit into the chocolate square that was so dark and bitter that it nearly bit me back. Flavors exploded in my mouth, a swirling symphony of sweet and bitter, smooth and creamy. "Hmmm . . ." I closed my eyes and groaned with a pleasure bordering on the obscene.

Mabel grabbed my hands and held them to her chest. "This flavor is my legacy and responsibility. And now it's yours."

If only that were true.

I swallowed the last of the chocolate. The memory of its smooth texture and swirling flavors left me feeling more than a little unsteady. It pricked at an ache that had long lived in my heart. An ache I never believed could be healed.

I wish . . . I wish . . .

What did I wish? What would heal that gaping hole in my heart?

A home?

A family who loved me?

More chocolate?

Yes, all that, but also something more.

I wish I had a place where I belonged, a place where, like Mabel, I can spend my days dreaming up new and exciting flavor combinations to tease the senses—a place where I have a purpose, where I'm more than someone's stepping stone or bank account.

I swallowed the last of the delicious chocolate and opened my eyes.

I then waited for Mabel to pitch her case. I waited for her to try to pry out of me a large portion of my family's fortune.

Without a word, the older woman released my hands and took a bite of the second piece of chocolate on the plate. Sparks seemed to dance on the air as she bit into it. Once she'd finished the decadently rich treat, a sad smile spread across her lips.

"My greatest regret, my dear, is that we didn't have more time together," she said before she hurried out of the room.

"Wait," I called after her. "It doesn't have to be over. I want to take more classes. I want to see what the chocolate mixture looks and tastes like in three days."

But it was too late. She was gone.

Chapter 6

That night, I woke up in the middle of a dream where chocolate beans were being hand harvested by hardworking
villagers in the depths of the Amazon rainforest and then deliv-
ered to me so I could craft them into something beautiful for
others to enjoy. I tasted the truffle I'd just made from the hand-
made chocolate and smiled. I'd finally found what I was meant
to do. I was finally happy.

Stella's high-pitched bark jolted me out of that decadently
sweet fantasy.

"Hush now," I said with a sleepy groan.

She kept barking.

"You're going to wake the neighbors."

She kept barking.

The room was dark. I fumbled for my phone so I could look
at the time.

"It's three in the morning. There's nothing out there. Settle
down."

This was the second time since we'd arrived in Camellia
Beach that she'd started barking like a mad dog in the middle

of the night. I yawned, then rolled out from under the motel's scratchy sheets to get down on the carpet, where she was running around in circles yapping.

"Stella, it's okay. It's just someone returning to their room. Remember? It's just like before. They're not trying to get into here. No one is trying to get into here."

She kept barking as if she expected an army of ninjas to break through the door at any minute. If I didn't get her to quiet down soon, someone would be pounding on the door. I certainly didn't want that to happen, since it would only prove to her excitable little mind that she had good reason to be on high alert in the middle of the night.

Tired of stumbling around in the dark, I flipped on the nearest light switch. That's when I noticed the door.

It was open.

*   *   *

Police Chief Byrd stood inside the small motel room. Instead of taking notes, he folded his arms over his pudgy chest and leaned against the doorjamb. His eyelids kept sinking over his eyes while I talked.

"Someone tried to break into my room," I reiterated when I'd finished walking him through the steps of what had happened. I shivered at the thought that someone had nearly succeeded in getting into my room.

"You said the door wasn't open much more than a crack?" he asked with a long sigh.

"Yes, but—"

"And that the swinging latch arm had been locked? So really, the door couldn't have opened much wider than that without force?" He woke up long enough to demonstrate how wide a crack the door had been opened.

"I guess, but that doesn't mean—"

"Ms. Penn, listen." He swung the door fully open, letting in a blast of icy winter wind that carried with it the salty scent of the Atlantic. With his beefy finger, he pointed to the lock. It was the old-fashioned mechanical kind of motel lock, the kind that used an actual key. Because the room faced the ocean, the lock and the metal strike plate around it were puckered with rust. "This is an old building. The locks can be tricky. Sometimes they don't turn all the way."

"I locked the door. I know I did." I hugged Stella close to my chest. If not for her and her maniacal barking, who knows what might have happened. Was it an attempted burglary? Or something more sinister? Had I been lured to this godforsaken beach town so the residents could hold me hostage until my father paid a fortune for my release? Was that how they planned to pay for the town's redevelopment? Or had the intruder broken into my room in order to kill me the same way Skinny had been killed?

I hugged my little dog even closer. Stella, who loathed cuddles, growled and wiggled and tried to nip my fingers. She desperately wanted me to set her down. I ended up closing her in the bathroom, where she barked and scratched to get out. Better have her do that than let her loose and risk having her attack an officer of the law.

"Ma'am, I understand you're upset." He had to raise his voice in order to be heard over Stella's barks. "But look at the door. If someone had picked the lock, you'd see signs of it. The rust would be flaked off. There's no sign anything happened here that couldn't be explained by regular use. Perhaps you thought you had locked the door, but with the rust and the wind, the door opened a bit while you were sleeping. It happens around here. Especially when a nor'easter is blowing."

"No," I insisted, "someone was out there."

"Because your little dog was barking? The same dog that's barking right now?"

"Yes, and because of the letter—"

"Let's not start with that again. So you won a contest that included a trip to our town."

"A contest I didn't enter. You don't seem to understand—"

"I understand you sent your surfer friend here to poke his nose around. And he brought his drug-dealing friends to town with him."

"He didn't use drugs!" I shouted in frustration. "Someone must have planted those drugs on him!"

The police chief took a menacing step toward me and then stopped himself. He drew a deep breath. "There is no crime in Camellia Beach. Sure, there might be a domestic disturbance now and again. And some kids from the city might think the road running along the length of the beach is a choice spot for drag racing. But there's no serious crime out here. People aren't robbed, scammed, or murdered. At least they weren't until you and your friend arrived."

"Are you saying we brought this trouble on ourselves?"

"I'm saying there's no serious crime in our gentle beach community, and I aim to keep it that way. Do something with that noisy dog of yours already." And with that, he spun around and marched out of the motel room, slamming the door behind him with enough force that the thin walls shook.

I suppose I should have been happy he didn't write me a ticket for disturbing the peace.

Before the police chief had arrived, I'd been ready to pack my bags and run home, thankful I didn't get hurt during tonight's attempted break-in. His dismissal of my problems and of my friend's death only made me that much more determined to find out what Skinny had found out about that phony prize letter and why it had gotten him killed.

*   *   *

Thanks to our harrowing night, both Stella and I ended up sleeping past nine the next morning. When I did finally start to stir in the bed, I felt awfully foolish. Had I overreacted to what I believed had been an attempted break-in? I'd probably overreacted.

I wiggled the doorknob on my way out to the beach to walk Stella. The lock did seem loose. Perhaps Chief Byrd was right. Perhaps the wind had blown the door open.

The first thing I noticed when we hit the wet sand was the subtle warmth in the air. The sun had managed to break through the heavy winter clouds. The wind had died down. The vast ocean sat nearly as still as a lake. Golden sunlight glinted off its glassy surface. For the first time since I'd arrived in Camellia Beach, the waves didn't look like angry hands trying to reach out and drown someone.

After Stella had finished her walk and gobbled her breakfast, I tried to lock her back into the bathroom. She refused to go inside. Instead, she looked up at me with those big brown eyes of hers, eyes that were almost too big for her body, and gave her tail a little wag.

"Go on in," I said. "I won't be gone long."

She didn't budge.

I squeaked her rubber ducky and tossed it into the bathroom. She gave a little woof, but she didn't chase it.

"You don't want to be left alone? Is that it?" I felt silly talking to the little monster. It wasn't as if she could understand me. But she did seem to understand that when I reached for the leash, she was coming with me. She only lightly nipped my fingers as I snapped the leash to her pink collar.

As we made our way down Main Street, she walked alongside me, barking at anyone she happened to see. I didn't know where we were headed until I neared the Chocolate Box.

Every morning, they offered fresh coffee and chocolate croissants, my favorite breakfast combo. Mabel and Bertie also had answers. Something I dearly needed.

So many questions bounced around in my head, I didn't quite know where to start. Yesterday, on the last day of my classes, neither Mabel nor Bertie had asked me to write a check or make an investment or even pay for the classes I'd taken.

Wouldn't they have at least asked for payment for the cooking classes? What if they weren't interested in my money? Then what were they up to? What had Skinny learned about them? And why would that information get him killed?

Did that information get him killed? Or was it something else? Like the letter from that DNA company?

Both Althea and that surfer, Harley, had said nearly the same thing about my friend—that he was a troublemaker who'd gotten what he'd deserved. That description sounded nothing like the somewhat shy Skinny I knew. He'd routinely go out of his way to help others, not cause trouble.

I needed to have a frank talk with Mabel and Bertie. Perhaps they could shed some light on Skinny's last days. I also needed to know why Mabel and Bertie had sent that letter telling me I'd won a trip to the beach. What did they want from me?

I came to the Chocolate Box looking for answers, but the only thing I found was a "Closed" sign on the door. That was odd. The shop opened at nine, and it was half past ten by the time I'd arrived. I stepped off the porch and looked around for clues that might tell me why the shop was closed. The white clapboard building looked just as run down in the bright morning sunlight as it had during the deepest part of the storm. Nothing jumped out at me to explain why the shop's interior was dark and the front door locked up tight.

Maybe I needed to talk with Althea again. She seemed to be just as involved in this scheme as her mother. My stomach growled, reminding me I still needed to find somewhere else to eat. I'd started to walk away when I heard my name.

"Ms. Penn?" a man called again as he hurried down a flight of stairs that ran along the side of the Chocolate Box's building. The stairs led to what looked to be apartments on the second floor.

"Yes?" At first I didn't recognize him. He'd traded his wet suit for a warm leather jacket with a crisply pressed white shirt and a conservative red-striped tie underneath.

"Harley, isn't it?" I asked even though I not only had remembered his name but also knew from talking with Deloris—the elderly motel manager—that Harley had walked away from a position at a high-profile law firm in Atlanta and had returned to Camellia Beach to take over his father's one-man law office.

Clearly Stella also remembered him from their first meeting on the beach and her successful toe chomping. With a happy yelp, she started a mad dash toward him. Luckily she was on a leash this time and could only get so far. She tugged at the end of the leash and growled. Her growls grew more ferocious as he approached.

"So you're really not a Penny," he said. Though his voice had that velvety-smooth Southern accent I could listen to all day, his green eyes were narrowed, and his handsome features had turned hard as rocks. He reached into an interior pocket in his jacket and pulled out an envelope. "Your name is Charity Penn?"

My entire body bristled at the mention of my full name. Charity. That's what my grandmother had named me, because it was an act of *charity* that the Penn family had taken me in after my mother had left me on my father's doorstep and my father had taken me to my grandmother's house.

When I was sixteen, I'd tried to change my name, but Grandmother Cristobel had blocked my efforts. No one, but no one, goes against Cristobel Penn. Anyone who tries pays a steep price.

Or, in my mother's case, I ended up paying the price for her having the nerve of becoming pregnant by Cristobel's darling eldest son. Since mommy dearest had run away, I took the brunt of Cristobel's anger.

"I suppose we should do formal introductions. I'm Harley Dalton," he said, his expression grim. "Mabel Maybank's attorney."

"Her attorney?" Why was he telling me this? Was she going to sue me? Was that her game? "I don't know what she told you—"

"She didn't tell me much of anything. Between you and me, I told her it was a bad idea."

"Well, tell her again." I would have said more, but the color started draining from his tanned cheeks at such an alarming rate I worried he might faint, topple over, and land on both Stella and me. "What? What's wrong?"

"You don't know," he said quietly. "No, of course you don't. Deloris never gets up this early. And who else would have told you?"

"Of course I don't know. I don't know anything." Stella, as if to emphasize my frustration, started barking and tugging at the end of her leash again. "That's why I'm here. I came to this wreck of a town for one reason and one reason only. To get answers. My friend is dead."

"Your friend? You mean Skinny McGee?" Harley closed his eyes and drew a long, slow breath. After all that, he uttered a rude word, which only urged Stella to bark louder.

I reached into my jacket pocket and produced a doggie bone for just this purpose. Eating muffled her barks, even when it didn't stop them all together.

While I tossed Stella the bone, Harley apologized for his foul language. "That was unprofessional of me. I didn't realize he was your friend. That's why you were asking about him the other morning?" He swore again. "Despite what you might have heard, I didn't kill him."

Actually, I hadn't heard that. People in this town seemed to be amazingly protective of their own. "But you know something. Are you ready to talk to me about it?"

He appeared to consider the question before shaking his head. He then held out the letter he'd been passing from one hand to the other. "She's named you as an heir in her will."

"What?" I took the envelope. It was identical to the one that had contained the "prize" trip. "Who named me as an heir? Mabel?"

Why was he telling me this now?

My gaze lifted from the envelope and traveled back to the "Closed" sign hanging on the front door of the Chocolate Box.

"*No*," I whispered. That couldn't be the reason. Not dear, sweet, *scheming* Mabel.

His color still hadn't improved. He shook his head. "I'm sorry to be the one to tell you. Miss Mabel passed away last night."

"No." I refused to believe it. She couldn't be dead. I still had so much to learn about the special chocolate beans she used in her shop and, yes, also about why she had tried to lure me to her shop in the first place.

Maybe she'd started having second thoughts about what she and her accomplices had done to Skinny and had tried to do to me. Maybe last night's aborted attempt to break into my motel room had been the tipping point for her. And when she'd tried to back out of whatever evil plan the town had hatched, they'd killed her.

"How was she murdered?" I demanded.

"Murdered? Mabel?" The idea knocked him back a few steps. "Are you serious?"

"Skinny didn't use drugs. And I didn't win a trip to take cooking lessons at some obscure chocolate shop."

"I don't know what you're talking about with the cooking lessons, but I do know Miss Mabel." He briefly closed his eyes. "*Knew* her. She hasn't been well for a long time. That she lasted so long . . . this . . . wasn't unexpected."

"Are you sure?"

"Bertie and I were both at her side the entire time." His voice cracked as he spoke, his words halting. "She said she was ready."

I nodded but was still unconvinced.

"And this?" I tapped the envelope.

He stared down at his leather loafers. "She was afraid you'd leave town, so she instructed me to set up the reading of the

74

will immediately. Today. This afternoon. The old gal loved to create dramatic scenes, and even more than that, she loved an audience."

I found it all hard to believe. Sure, he seemed upset by her death, but that didn't mean he didn't have something to do with it . . . that is, if she really had died.

The skin on the back of my neck prickled. My hand itched to shove the envelope back at him and run as fast and as far away from this town as possible.

The old me would have run.

But I'd stopped liking the old me—the wimp who'd believed nice people might actually exist in the world, the wimp who'd believed the Cheese King had loved her, the wimp who'd sent Skinny to his death instead of coming here herself.

"You seriously expect me to believe Mabel changed her will to include me after only knowing me for a few days?"

"No. That's not how it happened," he said. "She added you to her will about a month ago."

"A month ago?" Before the phony prize letter had even been sent?

My gaze narrowed with suspicion, which brought the hard planes of Harley's face into sharper focus. When we first met, he'd behaved as if he didn't have a clue as to who I was, acting as if he thought Penn was short for Penny and all. And yet today, here he was, telling me Mabel had added me to her will before she even knew who I was, a will he had drawn up and was now acting as executor of.

"What kind of sick game is this? Tell me the truth, because I don't believe a word of what you're saying. Mabel's not dead. She's not dead. You just want me to believe that so I'll let my defenses down and agree to hand over my money to you. And perhaps I'll even convince my father to hand over his money while I'm at it. Well, I have news for you and for Mabel and whoever else is involved. I don't have ready access to much more than the few hundred dollars in my savings account. And my father wouldn't pay you a cent, not even if I asked him to—*especially* not if I asked him to."

He touched my shoulder. "I'm sorry, Ms. Penn. I understand you're upset."

He couldn't begin to understand how upset I'd become in the last couple of minutes. The violent storm might have passed from Camellia Beach, but its fierce energy raged inside my chest.

"And what about Skinny?" I demanded. "He's dead. What do you know about that?"

"All I know is Miss Mabel passed away last night, and for whatever reason—one she didn't share with me—she wanted to include you in her will. I am sorry." He sounded so calm, so . . . professional . . . it made me want to yell and scream and jump up and down like a lunatic.

Why wouldn't anyone in this blasted place give me a straight answer?

In the midst of my panic, I remembered the way Mabel would wrap her arms around me. Her hugs felt like Granny Mae's hugs. They were all about love.

Had Mabel loved me? Or at least cared for me a little bit? Even if she'd wanted to take advantage of me, did she regret it?

Dear, sweet Mabel who could work magic—well, not literal magic, but the melt-in-your-mouth and I-think-I've-gone-to-heaven kind of magic—in the kitchen.

Was she gone?

I'd only known her for a few days. I didn't trust her. And yet I felt her loss like a gaping hole in my chest.

Did that letter from Hodgkin DNA have something to do with why she'd written me into her will? Was she a long-lost grandmother, the loving kind of grandmother my aching heart needed in my life every single day for the past thirty-six years?

Tears sprang to my eyes. Gad, I hardly ever cried.

I cursed under my breath and hastily wiped at those wretched damp things with the back of my hand, which only made me get embarrassing hiccupping sobs.

Harley made a low sound in his throat before gathering me into his strong arms. I immediately tensed up. Instead of letting go, he only held me tighter and whispered, "I know, I know, Penn. I'm hurting too."

I could feel by the way his arms trembled as he embraced me that he was telling the truth. His grief ran deep.

The prickly part of me started to fight off his unwelcome consoling. I didn't want or need his support and sympathy. What kind of jerk touches a woman just because she drips a few tears?

Another part of me, the little girl who grew up in a house where hugs were scarce and came mainly from the paid staff, longed to cling to him until all the hurt and anger in my life disappeared.

"Leave that poor girl alone, Harley. Can't you see you're upsetting her? Of course you can't see that. Get out of my way." Jody, the tall dark-haired woman I'd briefly met during my first visit to the Chocolate Box, shoved at the lawyer. Through brute force, she managed to wedge herself between Harley and me.

"Don't start with me, Jody. I'm only doing my job," Harley muttered. He quickly wiped his eyes with the back of his sleeve. "The reading is at four this afternoon in my office's conference room. The information is all in the letter," he said and then marched off down the street.

I watched him go, unsure how I felt about him. His embrace had given me an unexpected warmth that, now gone, my entire body missed.

"What a jerk," Jody said. She pushed a linen handkerchief into my hand. "Oh, what a cute dog. What's its name?" Without asking permission, she reached down to pet my little nipper.

"Um, careful," I said, pulling Stella away from her outstretched hand. "Stella bites."

"That little bitty thing? She couldn't trouble a fly. Besides, dogs love me." She tousled the fur on Stella's tiny head.

Stella might be kind to flies, but she really, really hates people touching her head. With an angry snarl, she snapped like a hungry alligator at the woman's hand.

"Uff! It bit me!" Her eyes grew nearly as wide and wild as Stella's. With a moan, she cradled her hand against her chest. Thankfully, it wasn't bleeding.

"Stella! No!" I scolded.

The little dog plopped her rear down and looked up at me as if she hadn't done anything wrong.

"I am so sorry. She bites."

"So she does." The woman gave a nervous laugh. "Funny, I've never met a dog who didn't love me. Never. There must be something wrong with it."

Though I might complain endlessly about my little beastie, it rankled me to hear someone saying something against her. "She's not used to her new surroundings. It makes her nervous," I said, even though it wasn't true. Stella would have nipped this woman's hand no matter what.

"Well, I can understand about that. I'm sort of new around here too." Her Southern twang had a bit more country to it than anyone I'd met so far in the beach town. "I'm Jody."

"Penn," I said.

"As in Penny?" she asked.

"No." I forced my lips into some semblance of a smile. "Just Penn."

"Well, whatever. It's nice to meet you, Penn." She lowered her voice. "You might have noticed there aren't too many women our age in town. And you'll soon see those who are our age are flakier than cornflakes and not really worth knowing."

"Is that so?" I said, wondering if she was talking about the crystal-loving Althea.

"You'll see." She tossed her arm over my shoulder. "But you, I can tell you have a solid head on your shoulders, even if you did team up with a vicious little dog."

"She's not exactly—"

"I suspect we're going to be the best of friends."

"Because of magic?" came my knee-jerk response. I hadn't forgotten how Althea had said just about the same thing when I first met her—that we'd be close friends while claiming that all sorts of mystical energies were at work on this island.

"Magic? Heavens, no. I already said I wasn't flaky," Jody said with a nervous laugh. "I think we'll be friends because I'm Harley's ex, and I distrust him as much as you seem to." She frowned as she looked warily up and down the street before whispering, "I know you've been asking around town about Skinny McGee's death." Her hot breath tickled my ear. "Did you know that Harley was seen arguing with him right before his death? It terrifies me to think this, but I think he killed your friend."

Chapter 7

Did I dare go in? My hand rested on the tarnished brass handle. I stood motionless outside Harley's law office.

With very little prodding, Jody had offered disturbing details of her ex-husband's violent streak. According to her, he'd fly into a rage with the slightest provocation. He was dangerous and most likely capable of murder.

Her warning to stay away from him repeated like a steady drumbeat in my head as I wondered what I should do. She'd cautioned me to never, under any circumstance, let myself be alone with her unstable ex.

"Sure, he might seem charming in public," she'd said.

"I didn't find him charming," I'd quickly replied. A lie. But then again, I had questionable taste in men. The Cheese King—need I say more?

"Just wait," Jody had told me. "Just you wait. If he takes the least bit of interest in you, he'll turn on the charm."

Charming men—I'd been learning the hard way—were slippery snakes lying in wait in the tall grasses to take advantage of women.

"Don't worry about me being attracted to him." His unwillingness to talk to me honestly about Skinny's murder was a major turnoff as well as a huge guilty red flag.

Except you'd practically melted into his hug, and what was with that giddy teen foolishness you'd experienced the first time you met him? a voice in my head chided.

I quickly dismissed those reproving thoughts. My emotions might run wild sometimes, but they never (okay, rarely) got the better of me.

So if I didn't have to worry about falling under the surfing lawyer's spell, why didn't I simply walk into his office?

Because of Skinny.

If Harley had killed my friend, it'd be beyond foolish to find myself alone with him. I didn't even know if the letter he'd given me about the will reading was true. Yes, everyone I'd talked with in the town had heard about Mabel's death. So I supposed he hadn't lied about that. But gathering the heirs together to read the will so soon after her death seemed wrong.

This had to be some kind of set up.

I took my hand off the doorknob and turned to leave, but my exit was blocked by Althea coming up the stairs, her brass mandala necklaces clanging with each step. She'd draped herself in flowing black silks. The only spot of color was the pale-pink ribbon tying back her long, curly black hair.

"Penn"—she took both my hands in her slender grasp when she reached the landing—"I'm so glad you came. Mama feared you wouldn't."

"I'm not sure why I'm here," I said. I quickly added, "I'm so sorry about Mabel."

She kept a firm grip on my hands as if she thought I might run away as she blinked back tears. "Thank you. We all knew this day was coming but . . ." She sucked in a deep breath. "Mama is taking it the hardest. It will be a comfort to her to see you here."

She draped her arm around me much like Jody had earlier that morning. As it had with Jody, my entire body tensed.

"I still don't know why I'm here," I said as I deftly slipped out of her embrace.

"Miss Mabel wanted you here."

"But why? Why me?"

"I don't know. She saw something in you she liked?"

"She didn't even know—" I started to say as Althea pushed open the door to the law office.

Stepping into the space located on the second floor directly above Althea's crystal shop was like stepping back in time. The lobby, if the tiny room could be called that, sported lime-green wallpaper with a spiraling design that made my stomach sort of queasy.

Behind a metal desk sat a woman who had to be in her eighties. A tall beehive—silver with a light-blue tint—wound around the top of her head. The area surrounding her smelled of Aqua-Net. When she spotted us approaching, she clicked her tongue and jumped from her chair with the bounce of a teenager.

"Althea," she crooned, "such a sad reason to see you today. The town has lost one of the great ones."

"Yes, it has," Althea answered, her voice cracking with every word. "It surely has."

"And you must be Charity Penn," the woman said after she and Althea released each other.

"Just Penn," I corrected.

Her silvery-blue beehive bounced on top of her head as she nodded. "Yes, yes. Harleston said to keep an eye out for you. I'm Miss Bunny. Follow me. They're waiting for you in the conference room."

"Harleston?" I asked.

"That's Harley's real name," Althea said. "Has my mother arrived?" she asked Miss Bunny. "I'm here to provide support. I hope it's not a problem."

"I can't see how it would be. Bertie must be devastated. The two of them have been bosom friends for as long as I've known them."

Before Miss Bunny could open the door, Harley emerged from the conference room. He smiled when he saw us. "I'm glad you came, Penn. I was worried you wouldn't." Althea had said about the same thing.

Before I could ask either of them what they'd expected from me, he ushered the both of us into a conference room that, like the lobby, apparently hadn't been refurbished since the seventies. Cheap wood paneling covered the walls. Many of the thin panels had buckled. A few of them had sprung loose from the nails holding them in place. They rattled as I walked past them, making me wonder if they might crash to the floor at any moment.

The laminate top of the long conference table had also buckled and warped. The room served as just another testament to how much this town needed a sudden and steep influx of money. In all my life, I'd never seen a lawyer's office furnished like this—with less than the best.

As soon as we entered the room, five pairs of eyes turned toward us. Several of the conference table's burnt-orange chairs squealed as their occupants shifted to look at me.

"It's four o'clock. You'd said we'd start at four," complained a woman who resembled a washed-out version of Mabel—sharp chin, high forehead, and all.

Harley checked his watch. "We're waiting on Bertie. She said she'll be here in about five minutes. We'll get started then."

"And who in Hades is this woman?" A man in his late fifties with thinning blond hair wagged his finger in my direction.

The man seated next to him tugged on the vest of his dark three-piece suit and shifted impatiently in a squeaky chair. "Yes, who is she?"

Harley moved a bit closer to me and stood a little taller as he faced the unhappy crowd in his conference room. "I'll make introductions while we wait."

A collective grumble arose from the five people at the conference table. Apparently, they all felt as if they'd waited long enough already.

Harley cleared his throat. "Let me introduce Charity Penn."

"Just Penn," I said automatically.

"She answers to Penn," he added. "And I believe you all know Bertie's daughter, Althea."

Harley then began to introduce the five people seated at the conference table. The washed-out version of Mabel was Florence Corners, Mabel's youngest daughter. Peach, her older sister, sat next to her. She was dressed in a deep-purple tailored suit. Her strawberry-blonde hair had been styled in a sophisticated French twist that suited her sharp features.

Sitting next to Peach was the man with the thinning blond hair. Harley said his name was Derek and that he was Mabel's youngest son. Next to Derek was the unhappy man dressed in a natty three-piece suit. He was Edward, Mabel's oldest son.

I silently repeated the names of Mabel's children: Florence, Peach, Derek, and Edward. None of them looked at all happy to be there. Edward looked downright furious. I reminded myself that anger was a stage of grief.

Finally, Harley introduced his brother, Calhoun Dalton (the one who reminded me of a swashbuckling action hero) at the far end of the room. His hair was slightly disheveled. His red-streaked eyes met mine. A corner of his mouth lifted slightly.

I nodded.

"Harley, I think it's crass that you demanded we all come here for the will reading less than a few hours after Mother's passing," Derek said, breaking the silence. "Your father wouldn't have—"

"This is how she instructed me to handle her affairs," Harley said tightly.

Edward barked a loud laugh. "Just like Mother to drag us all out to this damned place with no warning. Had to cancel six meetings just to make time to get out here."

"I hope you would have cleared your day anyhow," Peach said quietly. "Mother died last night."

"Yes, well." He coughed. "Unlike some of you, I have a business to run. Don't know why she didn't ask me to act as executor of her estate. Would have made things so much simpler. We could have all met at my office in downtown Charleston instead of driving all the way out here."

"Excuse Miss Mabel's family, Penn. They're not always like this," Cal said.

"We're never at our best during stressful times," I said.

"I still don't understand who you are, young lady, and what you're doing here." It'd been quite a while since anyone had called me a young lady. I didn't know if I should be offended or thank Edward for the compliment.

"Ms. Penn was a friend of your mother's and is named in the will," Harley answered before I had a chance to decide what to say.

Edward grumbled something that made Cal's cheeks turn red. The older man crossed his arms over his chest just as Bertie rushed into the room. She was breathing hard. Her gaze bounced from person to person, not staying long on anyone.

"Sorry," she huffed.

"Any luck?" Harley asked.

She shook her head. "None. Sorry."

"I hadn't expected . . . Oh, well, it was worth a try." He helped Bertie, who was dressed in a stylish black frock, into a chair next to where he'd set up all his paperwork.

Harley then held out a chair for me on the other side of Bertie. I took one look at it and then crossed the room to sit beside Cal. The ancient desk chair with burnt-orange upholstery had broken springs that protested loudly when I sat. "I'm so sorry for your loss," I said to Cal. "I could tell she was a dear friend."

He squeezed my hand. "Thank you."

Unlike the four Maybanks seated at the table, he looked genuinely upset over Mabel's death.

That's when it suddenly hit me. Mabel had died. She wouldn't be in the shop waiting for me. She wouldn't be giving me any more intrusive hugs. And she wouldn't be around to fleece me out of my fortune.

Althea gave me and then Cal an odd look before taking a seat next to her mother. The newer chairs must have been at the head of the table, since hers didn't make a sound when she sat. Bertie stared at the linen handkerchief balled up in her hands.

"Now that we're all here . . ." Harley started to say after he'd settled into the chair at the head of the table.

"Except for Carolina," the elegant Peach said.

"You thought that ungrateful girl would turn up just because Mother died?" her sister Florence snapped.

"She's been missing for nearly half a century," Edward practically wailed, showing his first sign of grief since I'd entered the room.

"Yes, um, well, let us get started." Harley shuffled through the stack of papers until he produced a handwritten document. He then slipped on a pair of narrow glasses and started reading. The first part of the will consisted of a bunch of legalese, which I pretty much ignored.

The next part concerned Mabel's children. "I provided you with love and everything I had to give. You had an abundance of everything growing up. I hope over the years you have learned that the important things in life have never been about money. And yet sadly, I'm sure some of you are sitting here thinking about nothing but money. Edward, I had already gifted you the house in Charleston. Florence, Peach, and Derek, my dear children, you received your share of the family fortune when you each turned twenty-five. Only my dear eldest child, Carolina, didn't receive—"

"Because she ran away," Florence interrupted. "Ungrateful, selfish—"

"Not now," Edward snapped.

Harley cleared his throat yet again. "Anyhow, it says that because Carolina didn't receive her share of the money on her twenty-fifth birthday, Miss Mabel and your father had invested it. The money in that account will go to either Carolina or her heirs. If she or her heirs cannot be found within two years from this date, the money will be split equally between Florence, Peach, Derek, and Edward."

"How much are we talking about here?" Derek asked.

Harley dug through his papers and then quoted a number that made even my jaded eyes widen.

"That's a total amount?" Florence asked.

"No," Harley said. "That's what each of you will receive if Carolina or her heirs cannot be located."

Cal whistled. I shook my head with disbelief. If Mabel had that kind of money, why hadn't she used it to fix up her shop?

The old woman had also bequeathed to each of her children specific pieces of jewelry and antique furniture. Harley read through the list. Mabel's children seemed somewhat indifferent to the gifts. Edward actually groaned when he heard he'd inherited Mabel's kitchen table.

The next part of the will concerned Bertie. Mabel wrote quite eloquently of the great love she had for her longtime friend and how she was indebted to her for serving as a trusted nursemaid in the past decade. She left Bertie several pieces of jewelry and a small amount of money.

She also left specific pieces of furniture to both Harley and Cal. Cal chuckled when he heard he'd inherited a corner curio cabinet.

"You didn't mention anything about the shop," Edward pointed out when Harley had finished that section.

"No. Not yet. That's coming up." Harley turned the page and looked suddenly uncomfortable, like he'd been dreading reading this part of the will.

Mabel's family members, who seemed bored with the entire proceeding, leaned forward with anticipation.

"As you know," Harley read, "the chocolate shop has been in the family for three generations. As much as it pains me, none of my children are the least bit interested in continuing the tradition. Because of that, I have decided to place the shop in the hands of someone I trust will take good care of the building and keep the shop open. To that end, I leave the building and the shop along with a small stipend to Charity Penn."

What?

She left it to me?

No.

I shifted. The chair's springs protested. That's when I noticed everyone had turned to stare. At me.

Harley then read the amount of the stipend. And yes, it was small, especially when compared with what I'd noticed, just on the surface, the building needed in repairs alone. Why in the world, if Mabel apparently had a large fortune at her disposal, would she not give more for the repair and upkeep of her supposedly beloved shop?

"Charity? You mean to tell us Mother gave her shop to a stranger?" Edward's voice boomed.

My cheeks heated with embarrassment. By all rights, Bertie should be inheriting the shop, not me. After all, she was Mabel's business partner. How could Mabel cut her out like that?

My gaze flew to Bertie.

I expected to find her looking as angry and shocked as I felt. Instead, she was sitting back. Her hands were folded calmly in her lap as she watched the explosion of emotions taking place at the conference table. Her eyes locked on mine.

And she smiled.

Harley held up a hand to try to quiet Mabel's angry children. "Miss Mabel anticipated that some of you would be upset by her decision. But I assure you she was of sound mind when she wrote her will."

"Coerced to write it, more like. Who are you?" Florence demanded of me. "What did you do to con my mother out of her fortune?"

That wreck of a shop hardly constituted a fortune. But I decided not to say that, since Mabel's children seemed to think they'd lost out on a great deal of money. And besides, the idea that I'd con someone out of his or her money was laughable.

"I don't want—" I started to say only to have Harley say loudly, "Ms. Penn had nothing to do with the decision. I assure you she is as surprised as you must be to learn of the inheritance. Your mother wrote each of you a letter."

He rifled through the papers in front of him and produced a stack of envelopes that matched the one that had contained the fake prize vacation. He handed one to each of Mabel's four children, one to Cal, and one to Bertie.

He then stood and swung open the conference room's pressed-wood door. "If you have any questions or wish to discuss what was spelled out in the will further, please don't hesitate to make an appointment on your way out."

"Oh, we'll contest this all right," Edward announced as he left. "There's no way I'm going to let some outsider steal what is rightfully ours."

"Ms. Penn," Harley said before I reached the door, "if you have a moment, I'd like to have a word?"

As everyone else filed out, I sat back down at the table. The orange chair once again made a loud squeak. When we were alone, Harley closed the conference room door.

My heart thumped nervously in my chest. Jody had warned me to never be alone with him. But we weren't alone—not really. Miss Bunny was only a few steps outside the door.

"Here comes the kicker," I said dryly. "It's money, right? I need to shell out a small fortune in order to keep the shop open."

"No. That's not why I asked you to wait. I . . . um . . ." He came around the table and sat down in the chair next to mine.

Somehow he managed to sit without making the orange relic shriek and whine. "Like the others, Miss Mabel had written you a letter. I can only assume it explained why she picked you to inherit her chocolate shop. The letter was sealed, and as far as I know, no one but her had read it."

"Super, give me the letter. I can't wait to find out what in the world she was thinking."

"That's the problem. I can't."

"Can't? Why not?"

He shifted in the ugly chair. This time the springs did squeal. "Someone broke into my office last night and stole it. Nothing else was missing. Just the letter she'd written to you."

"Someone tried to break into my motel room last night as well. And my friend Skinny, as I've already told you, had volunteered to visit this horrible little town to find out why someone—Mabel, I assume—was trying to lure me to come here. And he was killed."

He frowned at that. When he finally spoke, his voice was tight. "Has anything else happened?"

"No." But then I remembered the near miss with the car on that first morning. I told him about it and how I'd managed to run into Althea's crystal shop to avoid getting hit.

"What kind of car was it?"

"A black sedan."

"Was it a Ford, Chrysler, BMW?"

I shook my head. "I was too busy running for my life. Althea assured me that it had been a bad driver. She said the island is filled with them."

Harley took off his glasses and tapped them on the conference table. "I don't want to scare you."

"Yeah, well you shouldn't have started out by saying that because that alone scares me."

"Sorry. I'm not great at this kind of thing. My dad was." He kept tapping his glasses against the warped tabletop. "I'm only just learning to fill his shoes. But here it goes. I'm worried about you. I know you don't realize it, but the land underneath what you're calling a wreck of a building is worth a small fortune. And it sounds as if someone wants that land so badly that they might be willing to kill to get their hands on it. I'm worried, Penn, that your life could be in grave danger."

"But if I inherited the shop, how would killing me help someone else get it? If I die, Granny Mae inherits all my assets. And if she's not alive to inherit, my estate goes to a list of ten charities."

"Your estate?"

"You really don't know who I am?"

He shook his head. "Sorry. Should I?"

"No, you shouldn't. But most people I've met in town seem to already know everything about me."

"That's small towns for you. Anyhow, back to the will and how it might have put your life in danger. Yes, Miss Mabel listed you as heir to her shop. However, and this is a big one, in South Carolina, if you die within the next five days, you won't inherit anything. Your heirs won't inherit the building or the shop either. It'll all go to Miss Mabel's family." He looked at the closed conference room door.

"So you're saying you think one of her children wants me dead?"

"I'm not ready to go that far. But if someone is trying to get to you because of the inheritance, they'll have to act within the next five days."

Chapter 8

"That was one hell of a show in there," Cal said. He fell in step with me as I hurried away from Harley's law office.

"I can understand why Mabel's children are upset. They don't know me. And here I am getting their family's shop."

"No, I meant Miss Mabel. She has these wild schemes. Or rather she did. And she never considers who it might hurt. You don't need to take the shop, you know."

"It is rather like the plot from *Charlie and the Chocolate Factory*, isn't it? I won the golden ticket. I even received a prize letter embossed with gold print. She picked me without even meeting me. Did you know that?"

He shook his head. "I've been traveling for my work. If I'd been here when she'd written the will, perhaps I could have stopped her. Or at least she might have explained to me what was going on in that quirky head of hers."

I needed to talk with Bertie. Certainly she had some idea why Mabel decided to write me into her will.

Cal followed along as I made a mad march away from Harley's office. I wasn't quite sure where I was heading. The Chocolate

Box was closed. I didn't know where Bertie lived. And the motel and the beach were in the opposite direction.

I stopped suddenly and looked up. The late-afternoon sun had decorated the sky with streaks of reds and oranges. A squirrel rustled the fronds of the palmetto tree above me. A gentle sea breeze flavored the air with a salty tang.

"What are you going to do?" Cal asked.

That was a good question. I'd told Harley before I left his office to let Mabel's family know I wouldn't take the shop. I didn't want it. Even if I did, it wasn't worth getting killed over. Let them fight over the land among themselves.

While Harley had said he'd get the paperwork ready so I could sign the shop and land over to Mabel's family, he'd urged me to take some time to think about it. But really, what was there to think about?

My gaze traveled up and down Camellia's short Main Street. The dilapidated concrete-block motel capped the street on one end. A bridge to the mainland served as the gateway to the town on the other end. And in between were aging brick buildings and weathered clapboard shacks.

This town was a wreck in search of a wrecking ball. It definitely wasn't a place I wanted to call home.

"I don't think I'm safe here," I said and proceeded to tell Cal everything I had told Harley about almost being run over by a black sedan, the break-in at the motel, and now the stolen letter Mabel had written to me to explain why she'd left me the shop.

He grew unusually quiet when he heard about the car coming over the curb to try to hit me. "A black sedan? And you think the robbery and the near miss from the black sedan is related to your friend's death?" he asked.

"How can I not think that? He was here because of me. And now I'm here because of his murder."

A great blue heron cried as it glided on its stunningly large wings toward the marsh and river at the back of the island.

"I don't want it," I said as I watched the bird. "I don't want the shop."

Cal smiled. "Who would?"

"I told Harley that I wanted to sign the property over to Mabel's children. He said he'd put together the paperwork, but he also wanted me to think about it. But what's to think about? I don't want the shop, and I don't want someone to kill me over something I don't give two figs about."

"Let me tell my brother to put a rush job on those papers, or better yet, I'll tell Edward. He'll help you sell it or do with it whatever you think is right."

I gave a curt nod. So that was that: I would give it to Mabel's family. Or sell it. Or do something that didn't involve my staying in Camellia Beach.

"Good," I said and resumed my mad march, but this time I headed toward the ocean.

"Where are you going?" he called after me.

"Home."

* * *

"What a silly thing to say." That was one of the many things I liked about Granny Mae. She never stopped herself from telling me exactly what she thought.

"But it only makes sense," I protested.

I'd called her shortly after I'd taken Stella for a walk on the beach. I tossed the little dog a treat. I then dropped my suitcase onto the motel's lumpy bed and started throwing clothes into it. It was time to go home.

I dearly wished I was back in Madison having this conversation with Granny Mae in person. Actually, I didn't want to have this conversation. I simply wanted to be back in Madison. Then I could move on and not think about Skinny's or Mabel's deaths or the Chocolate Box anymore. That was something I'd learned to do well in my life—not think about the nasty bits.

"It's not silly. What else can I do other than give back the shop and go back home?"

Home. Granny Mae had been right. As usual. That had been a silly thing to say. Although I enjoyed sharing a place with Granny Mae, it was her home, not mine. Quite honestly, I'd never had a place that felt like home. I'm not sure I'd even know what a home felt like.

"I'm not saying you shouldn't get on the next plane and fly back here," she said quietly. "I don't want to see you get hurt. But—" She sighed deeply. "These past several days when you'd call me to tell me what you learned in the chocolate classes, I heard something in your voice—a lightness, a happiness I've never heard there before."

"It was the chocolate. Scientists have proven it has the power to simulate the feeling of love," I said, repeating what Mabel had told me.

I could hear Granny Mae nodding. Her earrings always clattered against the side of the phone when she nodded during conversations.

"Mabel picked you. Out of all the people in the world, she picked you. From everything you've told me about her, it sounds like she was one smart cookie. She must have had a good reason for leaving you the shop."

"My money," I grumbled.

I wished everything in life wasn't always about my money.

"Lots of people have money, dear. But she picked you. There has to be another reason. Why did she think you deserved to get the one thing that meant the most to her in the world?"

"But that's the thing. I don't deserve it. I don't possess any cooking skills. I'm not related to her. Unless that's what Skinny had discovered. And I don't even want it." Gracious, I needed some chocolate.

"Skinny knew why she gave it to you," Granny Mae reminded me.

"Yeah, and look what happened to him."

I stared at my hastily packed suitcase and swore under my breath. How could I leave with everyone believing the worst about my friend? He wasn't a drug user. And he would never sell drugs either.

"I'll talk to Bertie. She must know something. But then I'm hopping on the next flight home."

There was that pesky word again: *home*. If only I had a place like that, a place where I felt like I belonged.

"Good. Good. Book the flight," Granny Mae said, her earrings clanking against the phone again. "You should be safe here."

Yeah right, that snide voice in my head jeered, *I should be safe in Madison because murderers never fly on airplanes.*

* * *

According to Deloris at the motel's front desk, I could find Bertie at Mabel's house. She'd then leaned partially over the desk and shouted in what I suppose she'd thought was a whisper, "Several of Mabel's children are also there."

The long-term residents hanging out in the lobby started murmuring after they heard that. "She's the one who got the shop," a white-haired woman dressed in a bright-pink kimono said to the man in a seersucker suit sitting next to her.

"Does Jody know?" the man replied as he rocked in a wicker chair.

"Imagine she does by now," the woman said. Her rocking chair's movement matched his.

"That's going to cause a heap of trouble." He nodded.

I hurried over to them and demanded, "Why would Jody care who inherited the Chocolate Box?"

The woman frowned as she leaned toward me. "What?"

I repeated the question.

Both of them nodded. "Word around town is that Mabel's kids all wanted to sell. And Jody has been badgering Mabel to sell the building," the man said.

"What did Mabel want to happen with the building after she was gone?" I asked.

"What?" the lady asked.

I repeated the question.

"Oh." The woman's eyes, yellowed with age, lit up. "To keep it in the family, of course."

"But she didn't keep it in the family, did she?" the man said, shaking his head. "She gave it to you."

"She had to do something drastic. Those ungrateful kids of hers were trying to sell it out from under her even before she died," the woman said.

"What about Bertie?" I asked. "Why didn't Mabel give the shop to Bertie?"

"What?" the woman shouted.

I repeated the question.

The two of them laughed. "What would *she* want it for?" the man asked.

I couldn't get much else out of them because the lobby bunko game was about to start, and they were eager to get to the nearby game table. The man did, however, pause long enough to direct me to Mabel's house.

Actually, it wasn't a house but one of the two apartments in the same run-down building that housed the Chocolate Box.

The "Closed" sign still hung on the Chocolate Box's front door. The sight of it made my heart drop even farther into my already queasy stomach. That sign would remain there indefinitely unless I changed my mind and removed it.

I wasn't going to change my mind.

The stairway leading to the building's second-floor apartments snaked around the side of the building. It was the same staircase Harley had used that morning. I kept a firm grip on the railing as I climbed the rickety wooden treads. Many of the boards were rotten and in need of replacing. Like the rest of the building, it would take a complete rebuild to make them safe.

I wasn't going to rebuild them, because I wasn't going to change my mind. I wasn't going to keep the business or the building.

The stairs led me to a second-story porch that spanned the building's entire length. The view from there caught me by surprise.

Instead of a dirty, muddy marsh with a sluggish river beyond, the scene spread out before me reminded me of one of those gaudy photographs that were too good to be true—the colors too bright, the inspirational saying along the bottom too cheery.

But this wasn't a photograph. This was nature at its best.

Or pollution.

It had to be pollution. I'd read somewhere that pollutants in the air created stunning sunsets.

Heck, it didn't matter what had caused the scene. I stood transfixed, peering beyond the scrubby oak trees as the water in the river spilled over into the adjacent marshes. It sparkled with flecks of golden sunlight. Deep-red hues rose up into the twilight sky, where a full moon sat like a ghostly ball.

A sleek gray dolphin performed a graceful backflip in the middle of the river, sending a spray of the sun-kissed water flying into the air.

I supposed if you looked hard enough, breathtaking scenes like this one could be found anywhere, even in dilapidated little backwaters like Camellia Beach. Another dolphin joined the first one. The two jumped and sprayed water as they played in the river. I could have stayed there watching the show forever, but my cell phone chimed.

Bitch. I won't let u ruin me, the message said. I immediately checked who'd sent it. And groaned.

The Cheese King.

Don't know what u r talking about, I texted back.

U have a week to get back here and fix things or else.

I don't work for u, I texted back and then blocked his number.

Was that what was waiting for me in Wisconsin? Great. Just great. My life was crumbling even faster than the Chocolate Box's walls. I didn't have a job. Some nut had given me her family's legacy. Another nut was going around killing people and may have tried to kill me . . . *twice*. And now the Cheese King was threatening to come after me, and I didn't know why.

With a sigh, I turned away from the beautiful scenery and faced the decaying building that would never be mine.

Two red doors opened up onto the upstairs porch. One sported a magnolia wreath dotted with red and orange blanket flowers. I figured that must be the one that led to Mabel's apartment.

Before I could knock, Bertie swung the door open wide. "Penn, what a surprise. I'm so glad you're here. Come in. Come in."

"Inspecting your ill-gotten gains?" Florence, the pale imitation of Mabel, said as I entered the spacious living room. It looked as if she was on her way out. But as soon as she saw me, she set her Coach purse down on a nearby side table. "Don't get too used to the idea of owning the Chocolate Box or this building. I'll have you know Edward is already putting together the paperwork to contest the will."

"Florence, your mama taught you better manners than that," Bertie scolded. She latched onto my arm and pulled me deeper into the room, where I spotted Peach perched on a floral sofa. Althea was sitting in a matching armchair, sipping on tea. Small platters of chocolate truffles were scattered on end tables and on the coffee table.

"I don't want the shop or the building," I told them as I scooped up a truffle. "I've already asked Harley to start working on the papers to—"

"Hush now," Bertie scolded. "You can't go around making hasty decisions like that."

I wasn't able to tell her that I could and had, because I'd bitten into the dark-chocolate raspberry truffle. The chocolate treat practically exploded in my mouth with a tropical symphony of bitter and sweet.

Love. Mabel had said chocolate triggered the same parts of the brain as love. And oh, boy was she right. I was in love with these chocolates. It would be a shame to see the shop close.

No! I was not going to change my mind.

The truffle I'd eaten hadn't been made using the regular chocolates Mabel used for the shop. No, these truffles must have been made using her special chocolate. The Amar chocolate. The taste of *pure* love.

Before yesterday, I'd never tasted anything like it. It was a flavor I'd remember—and crave—for the rest of my life.

Part of me sorely wanted to stay and take Mabel's place and experiment with flavors that could thrill people like this truffle had for me.

"Certainly someone in your family wants to keep the shop going. If not one of you, one of Mabel's grandchildren?"

"The shop is a relic from the past," Peach said in that gentle voice of hers. "You've seen this town. It's coming down all around us. The best thing we can do is sell the land to a developer who has the power to breathe new life into the place."

"Someone like Jody?" I said.

Peach smiled. "You talked with her?"

"You can't sell to her. We have an agreement with her already," Florence snapped.

"No, you don't." Bertie had remained at the open door. Her hand tightened on the knob. "Up until yesterday, Mabel had complete control over the building. And she would not sell. Not to Jody or to anyone."

"Because she was too sentimental to see what's best," Florence countered. "If we don't tear it down, the next storm will do it for us."

"It's stood for over a hundred years. I think it can last a little longer," Althea said. "Besides, everyone knows the coastal fairies have always liked and protected your family's shop."

Fairies? She couldn't be serious.

I laughed.

No one else did. Instead, they stared at me as if I'd lost my mind.

I tried to cover with a cough—a lame move that I'm sure no one bought.

"Thank you for dropping by, Peach and Florence. You are welcome to come back tomorrow or another day to pick up your mama's personal belongings. Now, if you'd excuse us, I'd like to have some words with the new owner," Bertie said.

"She's the new owner over my dead body," Florence said as she thundered out.

"It was nice to meet you." Peach took my hand in hers. "I'm sorry it had to be under such sad conditions. Hopefully we'll see you around."

"I am sincerely sorry about your mother. She seemed like a . . ."

A con woman who'd tried to trick me into coming to this town?

A murderess who'd killed my friend?

Or simply a nice old lady who'd treated me with kindness?

Tears filled Peach's pretty blue eyes as she nodded. "She was," she said. "She was."

Chapter 9

As soon as I found myself alone with Bertie and her woo-woo, crystal-loving, fairy-believing daughter in Mabel's apartment, my entire body started to tremble with anger. Anger at the situation. Anger at them. Anger at Mabel.

"Why in the world didn't she give you the shop?" I demanded. My hands coiled into fists at my hips. Had someone killed Skinny because Mabel had left me her stupid shop in her stupid will?

"I'm an old woman, Penn." Bertie sounded so calm, so sure of herself. It only made me ache to scream even more.

"Give me a break! You're not that old. You must be at least twenty years younger than Mabel."

"Fifteen. But still, I don't want the shop. Don't get me wrong—I'll gladly help until you get your feet under you. But then I'm retiring."

"Forget that. I don't want it. I'm not keeping it. If not you, why not let your daughter run it?"

"I have to take care of my crystals. I'm providing an important service to the community," Althea said with a straight face.

Bertie rolled her eyes. "She has her shop."

"And why did the three of you—or was Harley involved too—send that phony letter telling me I'd won a prize to this stupid place?"

For a long time, neither of them said anything. Finally, Althea spoke. "Harley didn't know anything about that." She carefully placed her teacup down and pushed up from the chair. She crossed the room to stand shoulder to shoulder with her mother in the kitchen. "It was Miss Mabel's idea. But I sent the letter."

"Your trickery got Skinny killed!" I shouted. "Don't you understand that? My friend is dead because I asked him to come here and investigate why you sent that letter."

Shouting accusations—not a smart move on my part. Mother and daughter, one or both potentially killers, stood within arm's reach of a set of lethal kitchen knives.

In case I needed to make a run for it, I edged toward the door. "Did you kill him because you were worried he'd tell me the truth?" Though I tried to get my emotions under control, my voice kept getting louder and louder. "Did he find out you were scheming to thrust this money pit on me? Did you think I'd be grateful when I found out? Did you think I wanted this?"

I'm not sure what I'd expected after my emotional explosion. Shouting? Denials? One of them to grab a knife? Or what my family usually gave me, the silent treatment?

What I hadn't expected was the hug Bertie wrapped around me like a warm blanket. "I'm sorry, child. So, so sorry," she crooned. "Let it out. Just let it out." She held me tightly and simply stood there in the middle of Mabel's living room until it felt as if all my broken pieces had been pressed back together.

I drew several unsteady breaths before pulling away. "I'm leaving in the morning," I announced.

"I wish you wouldn't," Bertie said. "Mabel wanted you to—"

"I only came here to prove Skinny wasn't a victim of a drug deal gone wrong. And I haven't even managed to do that."

"Please, sit down," Althea said. "I've brewed a pot of chamomile tea."

"Because it's got some kind of magical powers?"

"No, because it's soothing. Please." She indicated a spot on the sofa closest to the door. "You came looking for answers. Don't run away before getting them."

That's what I did best, though. Run. Hide. Forget.

"Please." Althea motioned to the sofa again.

I perched on the edge of the seat and took a tentative sip of the tea she'd poured into a dainty bone-china cup.

"You can relax. No one in this room wants to hurt you," Althea said. "Yes, we did try to trick you into coming here by sending that letter. And I'm sorry for that."

"Why did Mabel pick me?"

Bertie shook her head slowly. "Child, I honestly don't know. But I do have something to show you." She ambled over to an old pie cabinet in the spotless but outdated kitchen. She opened the front to reveal a stack of magazines. I recognized the issue she took from the top. It was one of those gossip magazines, the kind that warped the truth. On the cover, a pop star who'd faded into oblivion years ago smiled like she owned the world.

My gut clenched at the sight of it, because I knew what was inside.

"Mabel saw something in this article." Bertie flipped open to a page near the back. "I don't know what it was exactly that caught her eye. But she must have read it a hundred times."

There I was on page 213, smiling like that stupid pop star on the cover. A professional photographer had snapped the picture. He'd made me feel special, like I'd meant something. And then a slippery reporter had written *the article*.

"Penn Industries' Bastard Black Sheep Speaks," the headline screamed. Both my grandmother and my father had been furious with me for agreeing to the interview without consulting with them first. I'd embarrassed them. My place was in the shadows, not in the magazines, Grandmother Cristobel had repeatedly told me while waving the magazine in my face.

And though their words had hurt, what had hurt more was that I'd trusted the reporter who'd contacted me. He'd said he'd wanted to do a story about my achievements at college. And I'd believed him. I'd been about to graduate at the top of my class. An article in a major magazine would have helped me land one of those impossible-to-get jobs at a Chicago advertising firm. Wouldn't that make my father proud?

I'd been so eager. And so painfully naïve.

The reporter had written a much different article than the one he'd promised. It was an article about my bastard birth and upbringing. Instead of focusing on my achievements, it detailed how I'd been shuttled from boarding school to boarding school, occasionally raised by my grandmother's housekeepers in their homes; how I'd been the only member of my father's growing family to be excluded from Penn Industries parties and events; and how I'd never even made it onto a family Christmas card portrait.

"This article came out more than fifteen years ago," I said, refusing to take the magazine from Bertie. "She's held onto it that long?"

"No, honey, she found it in her cardiologist's waiting room last year. You know how they never change out their magazines. After she came home with it, she started this file." Bertie returned with a manila file folder crammed with papers.

I flipped through the pages, pages that were my life. A copy of my birth certificate—no mother listed. Lists of places I'd lived. Jobs I'd held. She even had the article I'd written dubbing my now ex-boyfriend the "Cheese King."

"This is creepy. She hired someone to gather this information . . . on me?"

"She was pretty savvy on the computer. She did most of this herself. And after she'd collected this information on you, she changed her will." Bertie handed me a chocolate truffle, as if that could make everything they did seem okay.

I ate it. Not because I thought it would help but because, hey, it was chocolate. Excellent chocolate.

"She learned about my sorry life and took pity on me? Is that what she was thinking? Because if she was—"

Bertie lifted my chin. "No, baby. I'm sure she saw your strength."

"My strength?" I snorted a nervous sort of laugh. "There are much stronger people in the world. Why didn't she give one of them her shop?"

Bertie gentled her voice even more. "I think Mabel saw in you a kindred spirit. She trusted you'd do the right thing."

The right thing.

"You don't think . . . you don't think she picked me because she thought that I might"—my mouth suddenly turned dry—"that I might be somehow related to her?"

Bertie frowned as she sat down next to me. "If she did, she didn't say anything to me about that."

I searched her face, wondering if she was lying. But why lie? Wouldn't finding out something like that only increase the chances that I'd follow Mabel's wishes and keep the shop?

"Then why send me the fake prize letter? What was the purpose of that?"

Althea was the one who answered that question. "Miss Mabel desperately wanted to meet you."

That made sense, I supposed. What woman, crazy or otherwise, would want to give her beloved shop to a complete stranger? Of course she'd want to meet me first.

I took another sip of the tea. Althea had been right about the tea. It soothed my jangled nerves. I let my body sink into the sofa's soft cushions. I then told them about both the near miss with the car right before I'd met Althea for the first time and the break-in at the motel.

Bertie pressed her hand over her mouth in horror. "Did you tell the police?"

I nodded. "I talked with Police Chief Byrd. He suggested I was imagining things since, other than my friend's pesky murder, there's absolutely no crime in Camellia Beach."

"That Hank Byrd doesn't know anything about anything, and he doesn't know the first thing about how to handle a crime as big as a murder. The Charleston County Sheriff's Office is handling the investigation. That's who you need to go talk to."

"Really?" That was good news. "I'll call the sheriff's office after I get settled back in Madison." I set down the empty teacup. "I'd better get back to the motel and feed Stella. I am sorry about Mabel. I wish she had lived long enough to warn me about what she'd been planning. That way I could have politely refused her offer."

"You need to tell her," Althea said to her mother as I started toward the door.

I paused with my hand on the door handle. "Tell me what?" I reluctantly asked.

"Mama didn't tell you about the—"

"About the break-in," Bertie said a little too quickly. "Yes, I should warn you that Mabel had another file folder on you. When I went through her things today, it was missing."

"No, Mama, I meant about the—" Althea said.

"She knows all she needs to know. There's something funny going on here in Camellia Beach," Bertie said firmly. She turned back to me. "I think it's best for everyone if you go back to Wisconsin."

Chapter 10

That night my dreams flowed from one chocolate-scented nightmare to another and another. *"You can never leave,"* came an eerie whisper. *"You can never leave. You'll die here."* Mabel's ghostly arm grabbed me. And tugged. And tugged.

I woke with a start to find I'd somehow gotten myself completely tangled up like a mummy in the motel's scratchy sheets. Stella growled and tugged at a corner of the sheet that dangled off the bed.

She growled and tugged again.

"I'm coming," I said sleepily right before my head fell back on the pillow.

Stella ran to the door and started to bark loudly enough to wake the dead.

"I'm coming," I said again and actually managed to roll out of the bed. With a yawn, I looked at my phone.

No messages.

What I saw instead on the tiny screen hit me like a splash of icy water. The time.

Crud.

I'd overslept. My flight was scheduled to leave in a little over an hour. Nothing short of a miracle would get me to the airport before they closed the boarding gate.

Skip the shower. Skip breakfast. You've already packed. You can do this. You're not going to be stuck in this place for even one more day. You're not going to die here.

I hopped around the room as I brushed my teeth while pulling on a pair of black leggings. I tossed a thick navy wool sweater dress on over a white turtleneck. That should be warm enough for whatever crazy weather Wisconsin decided to throw at me when I landed.

I grabbed my bag, Stella's travel case, and my purse and was halfway out the door when Stella growled at me.

"I haven't forgotten about you. You can do what you need to do while we head over to the lobby. I need to order a taxi," I said to the little dog as I snapped the leash to her pink collar.

Her nubby little teeth clamped down on my hand hard enough to leave an angry welt.

"I'm walking you, you ungrateful beast."

With my arms loaded down with bags and a leash, I stumbled out the door and into a blast of frigid air.

What I saw shocked me. A light dusting of snow blanketed the sandy beach beyond the motel's narrow concrete breezeway. I rubbed my eyes. I couldn't be seeing what I was seeing. This was the South. It didn't *snow* in the South.

"It looks like you could use a hand," a man said.

I jumped and whirled and found myself standing face-to-face with Mabel's surfing lawyer, Harley Dalton. He pushed up from where he'd been leaning against the wall next to my motel room's door.

"What are you doing here?" I unlatched Stella's leash. She gave a happy yip and ran off to play in the sandy snow.

Harley watched the small dog push a small pile of snow with her nose before answering. "You'd said someone was trying to hurt you."

I stared at him. He had a full day's growth of stubble. His cheeks and nose were bright red. His lips were slightly blue. He stood a bit hunched, like he was trying to huddle within the full-length wool coat he was wearing. He shivered and gave his knit cap a tug until it completely covered his ears.

"You've been out here all night? In the cold?"

He shrugged. "On and off."

From the looks of it, I guessed "mostly on."

Did he seriously expect me to believe he'd guarded my door last night because I'd told him I was worried my life was in danger? Well, I didn't believe it. Not for an instant.

Instead, I suspected he'd been watching my room to make sure I didn't ask the right questions and find proof that he killed Skinny. And yet the way he was looking at me, with his green eyes flooded with concern, I kind of wanted to believe he'd spent an uncomfortable night in the cold just to protect me.

"Are you for real?" I muttered. Oh, heck, it didn't matter. I was leaving. I thrust my bags in his direction. "I need to get to the airport ASAP. Can you drive me there?"

"Sorry. No can do."

"You have a car, don't you?"

"Of course I have a car."

"Then what's the problem?"

"The bridges are closed. The airport too."

"What? Why?"

"It's the snow," Harley's brother, Cal, said as he crossed the beach toward us. He looked as if the cold didn't affect him. Sure, he was wearing his Indiana Jones leather coat. But he hadn't even pulled up the collar against the frigid ocean wind. He shook his head with dismay when he saw the two of us and then smirked in his brother's direction.

"Here," he said and handed me an insulated tumbler. "After the day you had yesterday, I thought you might need a pick-me-up this morning."

I took a sip and sighed with real pleasure. "Hot chocolate?"

He flashed his perfect pearly white teeth. "I suspected you were a fan."

"Am I ever," I said and took another sip. The thick, rich flavors almost made me forget all about the flight home I was about to miss. "Is this from the Chocolate Box? Did Bertie open the shop after all?"

He jammed his hands in his khaki pockets. "Sadly, no. This is something I brewed this morning."

"You have talent. Serious talent."

"Give me a break," Harley growled. "He opened a packet and poured in some milk. Anyone could do it."

"No." I savored the thick, bitter drink in my mouth before swallowing. "No, this isn't a mix. This was made with melted chocolate, am I right?"

Cal nodded.

I took another sip. "Maybe even some of Mabel's special chocolate?"

"I'm impressed. It is her chocolate. She gave me some bars. It's a recipe I picked up in Brazil." He smiled with true pleasure. "Unlike you, bro, I appreciate the finer things in life," he said without taking his eyes off me. It made fluffy things dance around in my belly.

Harley grunted.

"Can you get me to the airport?" I asked Cal. Certainly a world traveler like him wouldn't be afraid to drive in a dusting of snow.

"Would love to, Penn. But the bridges are closed. We can't get off the island. And even if we could, the airport is shut down," Cal said, repeating what Harley had already told me. Still, I had trouble believing what they were saying could be true.

"Everything is closed because of this?" I whined. "It's just a dusting. Not even a dusting. I can still see the ground in most areas."

As if to mock me, a fat snowflake floated past my nose.

"This is the South, Penn," Cal said with a chuckle. "Winter storms rarely happen. But when they do, everything shuts down at the first sight of the white stuff. Might as well decide to enjoy the day, because no one is going anywhere."

"If that's true, how'd you get onto the island?" I asked. "I thought you lived in Charleston."

"Stayed in Dad's old beach house." He hooked his finger toward a row of newer mansions lining the ocean a block south of the motel. At the end of the impressive row sat a small shack. I guessed that was his dad's old beach house. "With everything that happened yesterday, I decided to stay on the island last night. I'm glad I did."

"Things should open up by tomorrow morning," Harley said. "I can drive you to the airport then."

"You mean in that black sedan of yours?" Cal asked with a raised brow.

"You drive a black sedan?" I demanded. "The car that had tried to run me off the road was a black sedan."

"He does," Cal said. "A beat-up BMW. Come on, Penn. Let me buy you breakfast. I know a place that'll serve your dog too."

*   *   *

I still hadn't given up hope that I'd be able to catch a flight home today. Once the government officials who'd foolishly closed the bridges and airport looked at the sky and saw it wasn't really snowing, they'd open everything back up again. Wouldn't they?

With that in mind, I left my bags with Deloris in the lobby and then went with Cal to find some breakfast. As we walked toward the small downtown, Cal looped his arm with mine and pulled me snug against his side. He was so close I could feel his body heat through his leather coat. I wasn't sure how I felt about him invading my personal space like that. On the other hand, I'd left my coat packed in my suitcase, so I appreciated the warmth.

Much to Stella's delight, it seemed as if most of the residents of Camellia Beach were on Main Street, bundled up like Eskimos, as they watched the "snowstorm." She barked and growled at everyone we passed.

Cal led the way to a newly renovated one-story building located smack-dab in the center of the island. The concrete-block structure had been painted a bright blue. The wooden trim was an equally bright shade of green. Despite the dusting of snow topping its asphalt roof, I liked the building's bright island colors. A small signed beside the door featured a silhouette of a howling dog. Below it in fancy script was written, "The Dog-Eared Café."

"It's hard to believe this building started out life as a laundry mat," Cal said. "A group of surfers recently got together and renovated the heck out of the place. Jody helped finance it."

"It looks nice." It looked as if it belonged in the Caribbean. "If only the rest of Camellia Beach looked as cute as this. Tourists would come by the busload."

"That's what Jody has been saying. It's the stubborn residents who won't work with her. They say they don't want change. And yet they want more tourists. She keeps telling them that they have to make some adjustments to their so-called perfect island life if they want to attract outsiders to come and spend their money here." He stopped on the sidewalk in front of the café and turned toward me. "It's too bad you're not staying. Jody could use someone else on her side."

I hadn't forgotten how Jody had argued with Mabel that first time I'd met them. "She wanted Mabel to sell the shop."

He grunted. "Sweet as that old woman was, if you look up 'stubborn' in the dictionary, you'd find a picture of Miss Mabel. She was more set in her ways than a live oak."

"I can see her attachment. Sure, her building looks like it's about to fall over, but didn't she say it's over a hundred years old?"

"And yet it doesn't have any historical value. Not really."

"If Mabel had so much money, why didn't she use some of it to fix up her beloved building? I feel tired just thinking about the amount of work it needs," I said.

Cal shook his head. "She was an odd bird. From what I could tell, she gave away every dollar she could get her hands on to various charity projects. You'd rarely see her in a new dress. I don't think she even saw the disrepair of her own place. Those last years of his life, my dad did the same thing. The beach cottage was falling down around him, but all he saw was how the place looked in happier times. He resisted our efforts to make repairs or change anything."

"I can't believe she didn't see the rot on the stairs going up to her apartment or the way the building lists to one side. It needs so much work."

Cal agreed. "Jody could do so much for this town. She's got this fantastic vision of what it can be. You should talk with her."

"Are you sure you want me to do that? She's your brother's ex, after all. How does Harley feel about your supporting her?" In my family, exes—and there were plenty of them—quickly found themselves persona non grata and in a position nearly as bad as mine. Their pet charities would lose support from the Penn Foundation. They'd lose any board positions they might have held in social clubs and groups. And forget about getting a coveted invitation to one of Grandmother Cristobel's family holiday celebrations.

"He hates it, of course," Cal said. "Says I should be supporting him by speaking out against her crazy ideas. But her ideas aren't crazy. Her development plans are exactly what this town needs. We could have high-rise condos and high-end shops in less than two years if Jody had some cooperation with a few key property owners. Property owners like you."

"Like me?" I shook my head with such vehemence Stella started barking. "No. Not me. I'm not keeping the property. You should talk with the townspeople, Cal. They should listen to you. You grew up here."

"I wish they would listen, but they won't. I'm not Harley. I didn't take over Dad's law practice. Once you move away and make your home in some other place, even if it is just thirty minutes away in downtown Charleston, you no longer get to have a voice. I've become an outsider."

"I'm an outsider too," I reminded him.

He nudged me toward the café. "Yeah, but Mabel gave you the Chocolate Box. Her vote of confidence will put you on the fast-track to being accepted in Camellia."

We walked up the few wooden steps. "But I'm not staying." Why didn't anyone seem to believe me when I told them that? "I'm not keeping the shop."

"But you're here now. And that's all that matters in some people's minds. You'll see." Cal pointed to the spacious covered area that spanned the front of the building. The bright-purple wooden porch looked like a newer addition. "Since you have your dog, we'll have to eat out here. I'll let the server know we're taking a table."

Cal disappeared into the café, which by the looks of it was packed. Many of the residents on the island who were wandering around in the snow must have decided to go out for breakfast.

Portable heaters had been set up on the café's wide porch, creating a comfortable bubble of warmth within the space. Like the rest of the café, the porch was crowded with locals . . . and their dogs.

Stella took one look at the collection of pooches dining with their owners and froze. She hunched down and growled a warning to any invaders that might come her way. And she refused to move. I scooped her up as I crossed the porch to a small round table in a corner where hopefully Stella could feel safe.

"Cute dog," a woman said as she passed by the table. She stopped and stooped down to get a closer look.

"She's not exactly friendly," I warned, questioning the wisdom of taking Stella with me to the café.

The woman held her hands up and smiled. "I'm not usually friendly either. So I think we'll get along," she said to my little monster.

Stella seemed to like her tone of voice and that the woman wasn't reaching down to pet her. She wagged her tail.

"You look familiar," she said to me as she stood again. "Have we met?"

"I don't think so. I'm just in town for a few days. Actually, I was supposed to leave today, but then that happened." I nodded toward the few fat flakes that were still floating around on the wind.

"Crazy, right? It's a freaking winter wonderland out there. I haven't seen snow in years. Makes me wish I owned a sled."

I wouldn't consider the spots of snow on the ground a wonderland or sled-worthy, but I figured if you weren't used to seeing the white stuff, it would be exciting.

"Are you from around here?" I asked. "Does it really never snow like this?"

"Born and raised," she said, her words bursting with pride. She gave her blunt cut, shoulder-length hair a flip. Her dark hair had a purple rinse. At least a dozen braided friendship bracelets hung from her wrists. Metal hoops and studs stood like tiny soldiers up and down her ears. She was dressed casually in a fluffy white wool sweater and jeans. "I'm Izzy. This is my café. Well, it's me and two guys, but they prefer working in the kitchen. So I end up being the face of the place."

"I heard the owners are surfers. Do you surf?" My heart started to beat a little faster. "Competitively, I mean?"

"I do." Her easygoing smile widened. "Now that we've opened the shop, we're limiting ourselves to competitions that aren't more than a day's drive from Camellia. We're even trying to bring a competition here. Why? Are you a surfer?"

"Me? No. But a close friend of mine was. Perhaps you knew him? Skinny McGee?"

"Skinny?" Her tan cheeks paled a bit at the mention of his name. The smile disappeared.

"He was my friend," I said again. "I came here to find out what happened to him, what really happened."

"You were his friend?" Her shoulders dropped. "I am sorry. It's a terrible thing that happened."

"He didn't use drugs," I said, feeling suddenly defensive.

"Definitely didn't," she agreed. "He was all about the surfing." Her pencil-thin brows flattened. "But not this trip. He'd been asking all sorts of questions. Every time I saw him, he was talking with another member of that Maybank family."

"He was?"

"It was weird. He seemed to be obsessed with them, which didn't make sense."

"It didn't?"

"You know, I'd never known him to hang with rich brats. He was like us: poor as dirt and down to earth. Looked down his nose at lazy rich kids. Especially old, lazy rich kids."

"Like the Maybanks?" The McGees, Skinny's family, could buy and sell a family like the Maybanks. His surfer friends really didn't know that?

Even though I knew why he'd come to Camellia Beach, I asked Izzy, "Why do you think he was talking with them?"

"I'm not exactly sure. It almost seemed like he was investigating them, you know?"

Finally, I found someone willing to talk to me about Skinny, someone who didn't automatically write him off as a drug user. "Can you take some time to sit down with me and answer a few questions about Skinny's last couple of days?" I asked. "Please?"

She looked around at the crowd on the porch. The loud rumble of conversations floated out the door from the indoor seating area.

"I suppose the place won't burst into flames if I sit with you for just a moment," she said and slid into the chair next to mine.

"He'd come to Camellia Beach to look into a strange letter I'd received from someone here. Did you know that?"

She shook her head. "I just figured he'd followed Jody here. The two of them have a history."

"A history? With Jody? You don't mean a romantic history?" For as long as I'd known Skinny, I'd never known him to date. He was the nerdy outsider in prep school. And then, well, to be honest, after that, I didn't think about that side of him. He never expressed an interest in women—or in men, for that matter.

"Some say he's the one who broke up Harley and Jody's marriage. Don't know if that's true or not. Skinny and Jody were together a few years before she hooked up with Harley."

I leaned forward. "Really? Are you saying Harley stole Jody away from Skinny?"

She laughed. "Have you met Jody? She goes exactly where and does exactly what she wants. I'm sure she's the one who made the decision to move on from Skinny."

"But then she went back to him?"

"That's what I heard. When he got here, he had some heated words with the Dalton boys. As you might imagine, he and Harley hated each other. At the surf contests, it sometimes seemed like they'd try to sabotage each other, like getting in the other's way to cause a wipeout."

Sabotage? That didn't sound like the Skinny I knew. But then again, everything I'd been hearing about him made me think I didn't know my friend very well at all.

Izzy lowered her voice and nearly whispered what she said next. "The night your friend died, Skinny and Harley had gotten into a bitter argument at the Low Tide Bar and Grill. Nearly everyone there that night heard Harley shouting, 'I'm going to kill you.' Not that long after, Skinny left. And, well, I suppose you already know the rest."

"I'm afraid I do." Since I needed time to digest all this new information, I dug around in my purse for my card. It was an old one from when I still worked for the Cheese King. But it listed my cell number. I handed it to her. "Please give me a call if you can remember anything else that that happened that night."

She stood while she read the card. Her eyes grew wide. "Penn? As in *Charity* Penn? The new owner of the Chocolate Box? That's where I know you from. Your picture was on the cover of this morning's *Camellia Current*."

"It's just Penn," I corrected. "And I'm not keeping the shop."

"But you have to. Without the Chocolate Box's involvement, our first annual Sweets on the Beach festival won't happen. As you might have noticed, the downtown is mostly a ghost town. Even the locals go off island to shop. We need to bring people to Camellia, or none of the businesses will survive much longer. Mabel came up with the idea. She was the driving force behind its planning. It's her signature chocolates that are supposed to get people to drive out to Camellia Beach and spend their money for the day."

"This is the first I'm hearing about a festival. And I'm sorry I can't help out. As soon as the snow clears, I'm leaving."

"B-but," Izzy stuttered, "you can't. You can't abandon us. Camellia Beach needs the Chocolate Box. We need *you*."

Chapter 11

You can't abandon us. Izzy's words haunted me long after I'd left the café. It didn't help that while I'd breakfasted with Cal, Izzy had paraded the president of the business association and various shop owners by the table to pitch the case for keeping the chocolate shop open at least until after the inaugural Sweets on the Beach festival, scheduled for the next weekend.

Her pleadings had led me to the Chocolate Box.

"I don't have a key," I said to Cal, who'd followed me to the shop. We both stood on the front porch staring at the closed sign.

"I can get you in through the back door," Cal said. With a little wiggling of the knob, the lock on the back door popped open. I stared at Cal and then the open door with surprise.

"That must be how the murderer got into the shop the night he killed Skinny. We need to find out who else knows about the broken lock. I could use that information to create a list of suspects for my friend's death."

Cal shrugged. "As far as I can tell, pretty much everyone who's a local knows about the shop's broken lock. Anyway, there's not much crime out here, so people rarely worry about locking up their houses or their cars."

Had Chief Byrd also known about the broken lock? Was that why he hadn't felt a need to suspect either Mabel or Bertie of murder?

Did *I* still suspect them?

No. How could either of those sweet old ladies have killed Skinny?

It had to be someone else who knew about the faulty back door. Even though Cal thought everyone in town knew about it, I doubted that was precisely true. I needed to make a list of who really knew. And after talking with Izzy, I had a bad feeling Harley would show up at the top of that list.

He'd threatened Skinny. Jody suspected him. And apparently his own brother harbored doubts about his innocence. Cal had, after all, been the one to point out to me that Harley drove a black sedan.

Of course none of that automatically proved he did the deed. Anger can make us say all sorts of stupid things. I needed to make that list of suspects. And I needed to start finding clues—the kind of clues I could take to the police.

Did that mean I'd decided to stay? Would it be safe to stay? I'd told everyone I'd met today that I wouldn't keep the shop. As soon as Harley drew up the paperwork, I planned to sign ownership over to Mabel's family. With that done, who would have reason to want to hurt me?

Perhaps with Bertie's help, I could keep the shop open just long enough to help make the Sweets on the Beach festival a success. At the same time, I could keep investigating Skinny's murder. I'd left a message with the detective on the Charleston County police force, asking him to contact me. Hopefully

I could gather enough information to convince him and the police chief to look in another direction in their investigation.

Would they then look in Harley's direction? Maybe.

While Cal unlocked the shop's front door, my gaze roamed around its interior. Long shadows seemed to reach across the space and seep into the corners, hiding secrets. The air felt still, as if the building was holding its breath in anticipation of some disaster. Perhaps it already knew *I* was the disaster.

What did I know about making chocolates? Although I thoroughly enjoyed every moment of Mabel's classes, I'd barely managed to make anything edible this past week. And that was with Mabel's close supervision.

With a shiver, I started turning on the overhead lights. Wait a minute. Where had all the chocolates gone? Someone had emptied out the display cases. Would I have to start from scratch and make an entire inventory of sweets in a matter of days?

I couldn't do that.

What was I thinking? I couldn't do any of this. I couldn't make Mabel's magically delicious chocolates. I couldn't find Skinny's killer. I didn't even know the right questions to ask. Only a fool would think she could do these things. And I wasn't a fool.

"Knock. Knock." A lanky man in his midfifties poked his head through the front door. I'd seen him before but couldn't figure out where. "I saw the lights were on," he said.

"Come on in, Derek," Cal called out as if he ran the place.

Upon hearing Derek's name, I froze. While I may not have remembered his unremarkable face, I definitely remembered the name. Derek Maybank was Mabel's youngest son.

He was an unassuming sort of guy. The kind people tended to forget immediately after he left the room. He wasn't short or tall, fat or thin. He wore expensively made, but bland, tan clothes that seemed to match his bland complexion. Even his winter overcoat was tan. His thinning hair, graying in spots, looked more tan than blond.

As he stepped fully into the shop, Stella rushed forward and started barking. Good thing I still had my hand on her leash or she might have ripped a hole in his pricy tan pants.

"I-I wanted to . . . um . . . to apologize . . . for yesterday," he stammered as he closed the shop door behind him, the bell on the door tinkling a happy note. "I was in shock, you see. I never expected that she'd—" He drew a long breath. "I behaved badly. We all did." His eyes, eyes identical to his mother's, bore down on me. "Can you forgive me? And let us start over?"

"I'm not keeping the shop," I blurted out. Yep, that's me: always cool under pressure.

He seemed taken aback by my abrupt pronouncement. He held up his hands much like Izzy had back at the café after I'd warned her that Stella bites. "I'd heard you'd decided to go back home. Where are you from again?"

Now it was my turn to stumble. Where was I from? As a child, I'd been shuttled from place to place, from boarding school to boarding school. Where was my home? Was Granny Mae's tiny house my home? I'd only moved there temporarily when I took the job for the Cheese King. And I didn't even have that job anymore. "I'm going back to Wisconsin," I finally said.

"Wisconsin, eh? So people actually live there? I thought it was just one of those states that had nothing but cows." His eyes, wrinkled at the corners, had his mother's mischievous spark in them.

"Yep, people live there," I said dryly. "And not just farmers. My former boss made cheese."

He hooted a sharp laugh. "I like you, Penn. You don't take yourself too seriously."

My spine stiffened, which was my normal reaction to someone saying he liked me. I'd learned time and again that such statements weren't compliments but traps. He hadn't come all this way to apologize. He wanted something from me.

"How did you get out to the island?" I demanded. "The bridges are closed."

He rubbed the back of his neck. "Yes. Well. After yesterday's shock, I went straight to the Low Tide for a drink and . . . er, um . . . it got late. I ended up bunking in one of the rooms at the Pelican."

"Don't you remember? He was sitting at the table next to ours at the Dog-Eared this morning," Cal added.

I hadn't noticed, which made me wonder what else I hadn't noticed since coming to Camellia Beach. Despite years of watching detective shows and reading every mystery novel I could get my hands on, my sleuthing skills seemed to be about on par with my ability to cook.

Derek rubbed the back of his neck again. "I had another reason for sticking around. After hearing how you didn't plan to keep the shop, I knew I needed to talk with you."

I crossed my arms and waited to hear what he needed from me. Money? Did he think I'd sign the shop and property over to him and cut the rest of his siblings out of the inheritance?

"Well?" I said when he hesitated.

"I know it's a lot to ask." He spoke with great care. "And I know you're not interested in keeping the shop open, but the Sweets on the Beach festival was a pet project of Mother's. I was hoping"—he turned away from me and stared into the empty display case—"that you might consider staying and keeping the shop open. Just until the end of the festival."

He *wanted* me to keep the shop open?

My jaw dropped.

"It-it would mean so much to Mother if you did at least that much. I could help."

"Can you make the chocolates? Did Mabel teach you?" I asked.

The look of horror he gave me almost made me giggle. It was an embarrassing habit—I giggled whenever I was on the verge of making an utterly stupid decision, like deciding to stay in Camellia Beach to run a chocolate shop.

"Mother tried to teach me, but it didn't take. She was such a perfectionist when it came to her chocolates. She'd slap my hand if I made even the slightest mistake. She'd make me too nervous to think. I can man the counter and the register, though. I have tons of experience with that. Mother used to make us all work here after school and every summer."

"It'd just be temporary," I said.

I looked at Cal, who shrugged.

"I'm not keeping the shop," I warned.

I looked at Derek, who nodded.

Was I really going to do this? A tiny giggle escaped.

"I'll need all the help I can get."

I needed Bertie.

Chapter 12

"Of course I'll help." Bertie's face immediately lit up when I told her I planned to keep the Chocolate Box open. Cal and Derek both nodded in agreement.

I'd called Bertie immediately after deciding that I'd keep the shop open just long enough for the festival. She'd promised to come right over and had rushed through the Chocolate Box's front door so quickly, I suspected she'd come from Mabel's apartment just upstairs.

She bounced on the balls of her feet as she started listing what needed to be done. A few minutes into the list making, she sobered. "Are you sure you think it's safe to stay?"

"I'll only keep it open temporarily. Just until after next weekend's Sweets on the Beach festival. And I'm telling everyone who'll listen that I'm not keeping the shop."

Bertie nodded thoughtfully. "If you're not leaving right away, we need to get you out of that motel. I know!" She clapped her hands. "You can stay in Mabel's apartment. It's perfect since it's right upstairs from the shop. And as long as you hold off signing over the building to her family, the apartment is yours. All this is yours."

I cringed at the thought of staying in a place where I felt like an interloper. But I'd been going through my savings pretty quickly on this trip. And since I didn't have a job to go back to, I needed to economize.

"I suppose Mabel's apartment will work." *As a temporary arrangement*, I silently added. It would only be temporary. "So what do we need to do?" I asked, looking around the shop. "Where do I begin?"

"You open the shop," Bertie said as if it were as easy as that. She'd peeled off her winter coat. I followed like a lost puppy as she went and hung it on a hook in the small office where I'd put Stella.

The little dog lifted her head and gave a little woof before snuggling back down into the warm nest I'd made for her out of a pile of tablecloths I'd found in an old maple cabinet in one of the back storage rooms.

Bertie sniffed when she saw what I'd done. "Those are for the display tables. If you're going to let your dog nap in them, you'll have to have them laundered before Friday."

"I can do that." I might not be overly fond of the little dog the Cheese King had given me, but I wasn't going to punish her for my ex's bad judgment. If I had to lock her away, she needed a comfortable spot to rest.

Bertie nodded and then dropped a crisp white apron on over another one of her silly sweat shirts. This one had a fat orange cat sunning itself on the beach with "Camellia Beach" scrawled across the chest. She'd paired the sweat shirt with black jeans and black loafers that were designed not for looks but for comfort.

I felt so out of place as I followed her around. She went straight to a cooler in the back of the store where she unloaded several trays of the chocolates I'd feared were missing. After putting them in the display case, she turned over the sign on the front door from "Closed" to "Open." Finally, she powered up the ancient cash register. It sounded like a small plane taking off as it warmed up.

"Doubt we'll have many customers on a day like today," Bertie said. "The wretched weather will keep most of our regulars indoors."

Derek cleared his throat several times. I jumped. Honestly, I'd forgotten about Mabel's bland son. "I know how to get customers into the shop," he said. "Mother's done it before on cold, miserable days. She sells hot chocolate."

"We always sell hot chocolate," Bertie snapped.

"No. No, you don't understand. I remember when I was nine or ten, it had snowed like this. She put a sign on the street, added her special chocolate to her regular recipe, and the line was out the door."

"You should charge at least triple if you're going to use Miss Mabel's special chocolates. Call it your gourmet blend," Cal suggested. He leaned against the display counter as if he had nowhere else in the world to be. A slow smile spread across his lips as his expressive green eyes met mine. "Could make you a nice pile of money."

"I'm not interested in making money. I'm simply sticking around to help the town," I argued. "Besides, I couldn't leave even if I wanted to because this teeny storm has apparently shut down the entire state."

"Everyone is interested in making money," Derek said with a chuckle.

"Not me." I'd seen firsthand the ugliness that went with large fortunes. "As long as I have enough to get by and have done the best job I can do, I'm happy."

"They say you come from money." Derek waggled his finger as he advanced on me. "More money than even my family has. Naturally people who have money also have the luxury of denying they need it."

I started to tell him that I'd never had free access to my family's money, not like my half brothers and sisters, but he didn't give me the chance. "I also know possessing a great deal of money creates a hunger in the belly, one that cannot be sated." His tan cheeks took on a pinkish hue. He waggled his slightly crooked finger at me again. "I know. I've seen the results. It's ugly. You should be careful. You need to recognize how money can threaten you instead of pretending it doesn't play a role in your life."

I stepped back. "I'm sure you're right. Triple the price, and let's start making hot chocolate. Bertie, do you have a recipe?"

"You know I do. We can do hot chocolate shots as well."

"What's that?" I asked.

"You'll see," she said, imitating Mabel's dramatic flair. "You'll see."

Bertie produced a chalkboard sandwich board from one of the storage rooms. On a napkin, I quickly jotted down snappy ad copy that emphasized the use of Mabel's special Amar chocolates. Cal volunteered to write it on the board. Derek volunteered to man the front counter and run the register while Bertie and I went back into the kitchen to brew the hot chocolate.

Once in the kitchen, she handed me one of the student aprons to wear. The melangeur Mabel and I had set up two days ago to grind the beans and sugar together was still churning away. I peeked into the grinder. Surprisingly, the mixture had turned into a silky smooth liquid.

"That's the chocolate liquor," Bertie said as she moved around the kitchen, pulling out pots and supplies. "It'll need at least another several hours of conching and refining."

"Conching?" I asked.

"Just a chocolatier's fancy way of saying grinding." She hefted a large bag of sugar onto the main counter.

Mabel had warned me that the process of making chocolate—really good chocolate—took time. So I tried my best to forget about the churning melangeur that contained Mabel's final batch of Amar chocolates and went to help Bertie.

Instead of using cocoa powder, she took Mabel's cask of special chocolate off the shelf and carefully removed three bars. As she unwrapped the silver foil from the dark-as-midnight bars, the room filled with that deep espresso scent I'd already come to crave.

She directed me to put a large pot on the stove. In it, I heated a mixture of milk, corn starch, and dried milk to a low boil. While Bertie kept an eagle eye on my progress, correcting me whenever it looked as if I might burn the concoction, she deftly whipped up a bowl of heavy cream until it resembled summer clouds.

"When do we add the sugar?" I asked, quite certain the sugar had slipped her mind. When I made hot chocolate, I always doubled the sugar called for in the recipe.

"This isn't a children's drink," she said as she chopped the chocolate bars into small chunks.

"But won't it be bitter?" I didn't want to waste three of Mabel's rare chocolate bars to make a bitter drink no one would buy.

I could tell Bertie was getting irritated with me. She drew a long, slow breath. "Let's make it my way. If you don't like how it tastes, we can always ruin—I mean fix it with your sugar idea."

Once the milk had started a slow, roiling boil, she turned down the heat and added the chocolate chunks. With a quick, skilled hand, she whisked the concoction until it became a thick, deep-reddish-brown liquid. The rich aroma released from the melting chocolate made my head spin.

She took a white demitasse cup from a shelf and ladled a shot of the thick drink into it. "Taste it."

I took a tiny sip. Though it had the explosion of flavors that left me picturing the wildness of the Amazon forest, it wasn't right. "This isn't hot chocolate. It's hot syrup."

Bertie took another deep breath. "We'll sell these as the chocolate shots."

She took another large pot and started heating more milk. Once it was boiling, she added half the thick chocolate syrup to the milk and whisked until it was a frothy light-chocolate color. She then grabbed a larger mug from the shelf and poured.

I hesitated before taking a tentative sip. I had a feeling that if I didn't like it, Bertie and I would have a real problem on our hands. I swirled the drink in my mouth, letting the milk chocolaty flavors touch every taste bud. "It tastes like Easter."

"Is that a good thing?" she asked somewhat tersely.

"It's a very good thing."

A wide smile spread across her face. "Are you sure you don't want me to add sugar?"

"Don't you dare!"

*   *   *

Derek hadn't been exaggerating. By the time we emerged from the kitchen with the two large pots of hot chocolate and steaming chocolate shots, the line for the pricy specialty drinks snaked through the café area and was on the verge of spilling out the door. I have to admit, my heart skipped several beats at the sight of all those people and at the thought of how many hot chocolates we were looking to sell on that chilly Saturday morning.

Residents and business owners who'd come to purchase hot chocolate stayed to shake my hand, thanking me for keeping the Chocolate Box open.

"It's only temporary," became my refrain. "I'm not keeping the shop."

"You'll change your mind." The towering Bubba Crowley, president of Camellia Beach's business association, thrust out his meaty hand and grabbed mine to shake it with the enthusiasm Stella uses when she shakes her rubber ducky. "You'll stay. Everyone who spends any time on our little spit of sand falls in love with the place. How could they not? It's paradise. Just you wait and see. You'll fall in love too."

I seriously doubted that. But I smiled, nodded, and managed to get my hand back.

The only person who didn't appear thrilled at the prospect of my opening the shop was Jody. She sipped her hot chocolate and scowled as if it had left a bad taste in her mouth. Concerned, I crossed the room to her.

"Is everything okay with your drink?" I asked. The first lesson I learned in marketing was the importance of customer service. You could have the best campaign and a top-notch product, but subpar customer service would run off the buying public every time.

She took another sip and kept on scowling. "It's all right, I guess," she said with a shrug before abandoning the mug on the nearest café table. That scowl didn't ease one bit when she turned and started to walk away.

Was she upset—as the long-term residents at the Pink Pelican Inn had predicted—that someone other than a family member had inherited Mabel's shop? Well, if that was what had her in a snit, I knew a simple way of fixing that. "I'm not keeping the shop," I told her.

She stopped. Her shoulders tensed. "Then why did you open it? Why are you running it? The newspaper—"

"The newspaper doesn't know anything," I said, even though I still hadn't had a chance to read what they'd written. I was sure Granny Mae had already e-mailed me a copy. Oh, dear, I needed to try to catch up on reading the mountain of articles she'd already sent.

I told Jody what I'd been telling everyone: The shop would only remain open until the end of the Sweets on the Beach festival. Afterward, I planned to close up. Pack up. And forget I'd ever heard of the place.

"Are you sure you're not going to change your mind?" Jody's voice, still sharp and shrill, started to attract the attention of those around us. "Everyone is saying you've been bitten by the same bug that had attacked Mabel. A stink bug, if you ask me."

"Really, Jody. What would I do with a chocolate shop? I need to get back to Madison." To what? I had no clue. But still, I felt the pull to go back to the safe, the known.

The jobless.

"I-I can't stay here," I said with a rush of panic. "This is where my friend died. It'd be too painful to face that day after day while wondering if his death was somehow my fault."

Jody's shoulders dropped . . . just a bit. The tension around her mouth loosened. "I suppose I can believe that." She tossed her arm over my shoulder. "I'm sorry I gave you a hard time just now. The hot chocolate is excellent." To prove it, she started looking around for her abandoned mug.

I handed it to her.

"Thank you." She took a long, slow sip. "You really are a good friend, Penn. Like the sister I've never had. Makes me wish you weren't leaving."

"Thank you," I said and then asked, "Why does it matter to you if I keep the shop or not? Cal told me you intended to redevelop the property. But this is a fairly large island. Certainly, you can find another parcel—"

"The company I work for has already paid a large deposit on this building." I could feel the tension in her arm coil as she answered. "We paid that money in good faith, mind you."

"Who did you pay? Mabel? I thought she refused to sell."

"She did refuse to sell," Bertie said as she came up from behind us. She removed Jody's arm from my shoulder. "The town doesn't want or need the kind of megadevelopment you're proposing."

Jody sighed dramatically and said, as if talking to a child, "You don't know everything, Bertie. Thank you for the hot chocolate, Penn. I'll be at the Low Tide tonight if you want to talk some more." And with that, she moved on to chat with Bubba Crowley, who enveloped her slender body in a huge bear hug.

"You don't think Mabel took the money from Jody's company to pay for the new school in that Brazilian village, do you?" I asked Bertie.

"She'd never do that," Bertie replied tersely.

"Then who do you think Jody paid?"

Bertie shrugged. "Probably no one. That girl is stuffed full of lies."

I made a mental note to ask Jody the next time I saw her. Perhaps I would go to the Low Tide Bar and Grill tonight. All my questions seemed to revolve around that place.

With that bit of trouble handled, I returned my attentions to the rest of the public who'd crowded themselves into Mabel's tiny shop. Many of the residents, after finishing their drinks, had ended up staying. Soon the morning hot chocolate sale turned into an impromptu wake for Mabel Maybank. She was much more than a business owner in the town. I was quickly learning how she'd contributed to the community, donating hundreds of books to the local library, providing scholarships for graduating high school seniors, and mentoring young business owners like Izzy at the Dog-Eared Café. The picture the townspeople painted didn't mesh at all with the picture I had of her: a woman who had tried to scam me into dumping piles of money into her shop . . . and her town . . .

Wait a blasted minute . . . those two pictures *did* mesh.

She knew she was dying, and she needed to find someone with deep pockets to take her place. A dupe like myself, who found it hard to walk away from lost causes.

But she was such a sweet old lady. And I'd only reopened the shop until next week. So you couldn't say I'd been duped. Not really.

The cash register dinged from another sale. Derek grinned and gave me a thumbs-up from across the room. The day was unfolding better than I had ever hoped, and the money that was coming in would help fund the supplies we'd need to buy for next weekend's festival.

Speaking of the festival, I needed to take an inventory of what we had on hand so I could start making a list of what we needed to purchase. Since everything was under control out front, I headed down the narrow corridor toward the back rooms.

For the first time since arriving in this wretched place, I felt truly happy. I even had an extra bounce in my step. I could do this for a week. It was going to be fun.

I'd barely finished that last thought when a hand snaked out from a storage closet and grabbed my arm. Before I could react, someone pulled me into the closet's dark expanse.

Chapter 13

In a move learned from years of self-defense classes I'd taken to improve my self-confidence, I swung. Despite the almost complete darkness, my fist landed as intended, striking my attacker squarely on the nose. The viselike grip holding me hostage immediately released my arm.

"Oww!" a low voice cried before I managed to scream. "I pull you aside to have a word with you, and you hit me? What did you do that for?"

"Harley?" I asked, squinting into the darkened storage room. "Why did you grab me like that, you creep? You don't go around grabbing women and dragging them off like a caveman." My fists were still raised as I moved toward him.

He retreated, throwing himself into a shelf on the back wall. There was a crash as several items fell.

"Everyone is telling me how you have anger management issues, how you're dangerous to be around," I said. "So I'm wondering, am I safe here? Should I scream?"

"No! Heck no. Don't scream. Please. That would bring everyone running this way."

I had to laugh. "That's the whole point of screaming."

He started to chuckle. It ended in a moan. I flipped on a light.

Harley must have found a place to thaw out. His skin had lost the pasty-blue twinge it had the last time I'd seen him. His nose, now cradled in both his hands, dripped blood onto the concrete floor. Littered all around his feet were crushed boxes of tissues and paper towel rolls. "You have a wicked left." That last bit came out with another long groan.

"Remember that the next time you start thinking about grabbing any piece of me." I picked up a paper towel roll from the floor and thrust it into his hand.

"I needed to get your attention." He put some paper towels on his nose. They didn't do much to stop the blood.

"So you've said." I planted my hands on my hips and fought the urge to go looking for some ice. "Why did you need my attention?"

"Is Jody still out there?" he asked instead of answering.

"Last I saw, she was drinking her second cup of hot chocolate and talking with your brother."

"You need to get rid of her. Now."

"Why? Hey, wait a sec. How did you get in here if you didn't come through the front?"

"Used the back door."

"No, you didn't. I locked it."

"Sorry to tell you this, but that lock has been broken for years."

"I know." And now I also knew he had the knowledge of how to wiggle it just right to get it to open. "Why do you need me to get rid of Jody?"

"Because she's toxic. Haven't you noticed that yet?"

"She might be a little high strung, but she seems nice enough. She just told me she thinks of me as the sister she's never had."

"She *has* a sister, Penn."

"That doesn't make sense. Why would she say that if she already has a sister?"

"Because she's nuts," he said, but quickly added, "She hasn't been on speaking terms with her own sister for nearly five years. It bothers her. If you don't believe me, ask her. No, don't ask her." He lowered his voice. "I'm worried, Penn. I'm worried she's in over her head with this development venture she's been spearheading. And I'm worried she might have killed Skinny."

"You think she killed her ex-lover, you mean? Or was he her current lover?" I asked.

"So you know about that already?" He didn't sound happy about it. Not one bit. "Small towns have big mouths."

"I know you threatened to kill Skinny on the night he died. Are you ready now to tell me what the two of you were arguing about?"

Still cradling his bleeding nose in a blood-soaked paper towel, he shook his head. "This isn't about me. Well, it is, kind of. I'm the reason Jody moved to Camellia Beach. She followed me when I moved out here from Atlanta. She came here to make my life hell. And things have gotten out of hand. She's gone off the rails. Lost her mind."

I tilted my head. "Most exes perceive their 'worst half' as toxic or evil or even downright dangerous. I've seen it happen time and again. And it's rarely reality."

"You have much experience in this arena?"

"I have three ex-stepmothers. None of them has ever claimed me as a stepdaughter, but that doesn't make them monsters. Well, stepmother number two might actually be a demon from hell. But the other two have been unfairly vilified. Just tell me what's going on."

"I'm trying to tell you. It's Jody. I think she's the one who's been trying to hurt you."

"Really? Do you know she's been telling me the same thing about you? Why should I believe you over her when you're the one who's been stalking me? You're the one who owns a black sedan. And you're the one who attacked me and dragged me into a dark storage room."

"I know on the surface things look bad. But that's partially her fault. She lives to make me look like the bad guy. And she gets upset with anyone who won't go along with hating me."

I crossed my arms over my chest. "You didn't answer my question." I repeated it slowly, "Why should I believe *you*?"

"Because Jody has something to lose if you decide to keep the shop. I don't. That's why. Mabel has been blocking her redevelopment plans for over a year now."

"And you and Skinny had a nasty history."

"This isn't about me or your friend and what he did with Jody!" He abruptly stopped himself and sucked in several deep breaths. "You should hear the voice mail she left for me when she found out you were opening the shop this morning. No, you shouldn't hear it. It'll only scare you. Let's just say it's made me worried enough to go to that idiot Byrd."

"You mean the police chief who claims there's no crime in Camellia Beach?"

"That's the one. He wrote up a report but said the message sounded like Jody was only 'venting her spleen' or some such nonsense. He refused to take her threat seriously."

"She wants me to meet her at the Low Tide tonight," I said.

He grabbed my arm. "Whatever you do, don't go!" I tensed. He immediately released me, throwing his hands up. "Sorry. Forgot about the no-touching rule."

I couldn't watch him stand there dripping blood all over the floor a moment longer. The paper towels weren't nearly absorbent enough. "Hold on a sec." I darted down the hall to the kitchen, where I knew I'd find a clean dishcloth hanging from a rack. I then dumped ice into the dishcloth from the freezer.

"Mama and I have been looking all over for you," Althea said as she breezed into the kitchen. She'd dressed in a simple winter-white silk tunic and matching flowing pants. Her mandala pendants tinkled like tiny bells as she rushed across the room toward me. "I can't tell you how thrilled I am to see the shop open."

"It's just temporary," came my rote reply.

"I know, I know. Mama told me. But still, I can feel it in the air. There's been a shift—"

"Don't talk about that magic stuff with me." I tried to squeeze past her to get back to Harley. What I hadn't anticipated was that she'd doggedly follow me down the narrow hallway to the storage room where I'd left him.

When I arrived, I found the storage room door shut, the light turned off.

I flung open the door and flipped on the light, expecting to find him cowering like a whipped dog in the corner. The room was empty. All signs that he'd been there—the blood on the floor, the smashed napkin boxes and paper towel rolls—were gone. Wiped away as if he'd never been there, as if I'd dreamed the entire strange encounter.

"Did you see Harley when you came in?" I asked Althea. She must have passed him in the hallway.

"No. I haven't seen him all day." She frowned at the empty storage room and then rescued the icy dishcloth from my strangling grip. "What's wrong?"

Since I wasn't sure who to trust, I simply grumbled, "Nothing. Just thinking about going to the Low Tide tonight."

"That dive? Why in the world would you want to go there?"

"It was the last place Skinny was seen alive."

"Oh. Right. I'd better come with you then. I don't think it's safe for anyone to go there alone. By the way, Mama wanted to let you know she sold the last of the hot chocolate, which is amazing. I saw the size of the pots the two of you brewed."

"That's great news," I said, although my mind was still reeling over what Harley had said. I should have demanded he play the phone message for me. I should have demanded he take that phone message, if it actually existed, to the county detective who was investigating Skinny's murder.

"Mama suggests we close up for the day and help get you moved into Mabel's apartment," Althea said.

"Right now?"

"I'm here to help however I can. That is, if you're willing to let me help." She drew several long breaths. "I am terribly sorry about helping Mabel send you that stupid prize letter. I hope you can forgive me. Mabel should have just called and talked with you. But with her, it was all about the dramatic reveal."

"It seems to be a town trait." I looked back into the storage room one last time before turning off the light. Why was Harley stalking me? And why had he been so worried about Jody finding him if she was the one acting suspicious?

"Before we do anything else," I said while still keeping an eye out for Harley, "I need to put a new lock on that back door."

Chapter 14

As Bertie had suggested, we closed the shop as soon as we were able to persuade the lingering customers to finish their drinks and return to enjoy the island's "winter wonderland." Cal ducked out almost immediately after we'd turned over the closed sign on the door.

Althea started cleaning out the pots and scrubbing down the kitchen. I worked in the front café area, mopping the floor and wiping down the counters. Bertie set about putting the trays of chocolates back into the cooler.

Although we were only open for a half day, by the time we'd finished cleaning, the muscles in my arms and back hurt. I stretched this way and that. Althea was doing the same.

Bertie, on the other hand, moved around like a hyper teen. "The body gets used to the work," she assured me. "I remember how I ached the first week I worked with Mabel. Now let's get you moved into the apartment."

"What about the chocolate in the grinder?" I asked. "Don't we need to do something with that before we leave?"

Bertie sighed. "I'd plumb forgotten about it. We can pour the chocolate into the molds first thing in the morning. It's more important that we get you settled in a more permanent location so you can get a running start tomorrow. Let's go."

"Uh, I guess I should be going too," Derek said.

I nearly jumped out of my skin at the sound of his voice. "Oh! Sorry! I didn't realize you were still here."

He was leaning against the cash register. His eyes looked tired. I doubted he'd slept well last night. Grief was an emotion that stole from the other vital parts of one's life. Like sleep. And happiness.

"Thank you for helping out today," I said to him. "We couldn't have managed without you."

He crossed the room and patted my arm. "Glad to do it."

I remembered how Izzy had told me that Skinny had spent most of his time in Camellia Beach questioning Mabel's children. So I took the opportunity to ask Derek, "Did Skinny McGee happen to talk with you before he died?"

Derek nodded. "Several times. Personable fellow."

"What did you talk about?" I asked.

"Oh, this and that." Not really a helpful answer.

"He didn't happen to ask about—oh, I don't know—the Chocolate Box, perhaps?" I asked, trying to sound casual.

His gaze narrowed as if he knew why I was questioning him. "Not the shop," he answered after his silence had made my heart beat hard for several harrowing seconds. He finally shrugged as if he'd decided telling me what he knew wouldn't divulge anything important. "He wanted to talk mostly about Carolina. Odd, really. Hadn't talked to anyone about my oldest sister in years."

"She's the one who disappeared?" I asked.

Bertie stepped in to answer that one. "She was the one who broke Mabel's heart the most. She not only ran away from her heritage—the walls of this shop—she also ran away from her family."

"And no one has heard from her?" I asked.

"Not a peep in more than thirty years," Derek said.

"It's odd that Skinny was asking about her," I said as the four of us made our way to the back of the building. On the way, I ducked into the office to free Stella. My little dog greeted me by actually wagging her tail . . . a little. She seemed so glad to see us—in fact, she barely growled at either Bertie or Althea. She did, however, jump up and try to nip Derek's unsuspecting hand.

"Stella!" I scolded. Amazingly, she stopped jumping.

Derek chuckled at my dog's antics, but he quickly sobered. "I am sorry about what happened to your friend. He seemed nice, but he also struck me as . . . troubled," he said as we all stepped outside. The marsh beyond the trees looked cold and forlorn.

"He was a troublemaker, stirring up problems where none needed to be." The sharp words seemed to fly like missiles out of Althea's mouth.

"What do you mean?" I demanded as I locked the back door even though the lock didn't work.

"I mean he came here to cause trouble for Harley," she said.

"No, he didn't. I already told you that he came here to—"

"That's what I meant," Derek said, "when I said he was troubled. It was like he had too much on his mind, like he needed to do something. Settle a score or something."

"He was here because I asked him to come here," I said through gritted teeth.

I wish Skinny hadn't muddied the waters with all this trouble with Jody and Harley. And why had he encouraged Derek to talk about a sister who hadn't been around for more than a quarter of a century instead of focusing on finding out why Mabel had sent me that phony prize letter? What had he been thinking? Was he asking about Carolina because of something he'd found in the DNA test?

I hesitated to think the next logical thought. But it came to my mind anyhow.

Could Carolina be my mother?

"Let's get going," Bertie said. She was just about dancing with excitement as she talked about getting me moved into the apartment above the shop. Her enthusiasm mirrored Mabel's.

I reminded Bertie that I needed to replace the back door lock before doing anything else. Derek headed on his own way while Bertie took me to a small hardware store tucked away on the back side of the island where I could purchase the supplies. By the time I'd installed new locks on both the front and back doors, the sun had broken through the heavy clouds and had melted all but a few traces of the scant white stuff that had closed the entire region.

"The airport should be opening back up," Bertie said after I'd replaced the lock and secured the door using the new key. I wiggled the door the same way Cal had done earlier. As I'd hoped, this time the metal door didn't budge.

"You could go back to Madison," Bertie added. "You might be safer there."

I handed her one of the new keys and pocketed the other one. "I'm staying. But just for the festival."

"Child, are you sure?"

"Mama, don't chase her away," Althea said.

"Don't sass me, baby. Penn's life is more important than a festival," Bertie chided. "That's why I didn't let you tell her about it earlier. You know Mabel wouldn't have given her the shop if she'd known the trouble it's caused for her. If Penn needs to leave to protect herself, she should leave."

"I should be okay," I said. Was that true? I hoped so. "I've told everyone I've met that I'm only opening the shop temporarily. So anyone upset over my inheriting it should be appeased."

Again, I hoped that was the case.

Bertie grunted, but at the same time, the older woman looked satisfied. She looked almost as if she felt proud of me, which made my ego get all fluffed up.

Not one to hide her pleasure, Althea hooked her arm with mine and hugged it tightly to her side. I tensed enough that she noticed.

"Sorry." She released my arm.

"No problem," I said, but I didn't let her link arms with me again. As the three of us headed toward the beachfront motel, a wet wind whipped at us, reminding me once again that this wasn't the tropical scaled-down Miami touted in the town's tourist brochure. And yet the breeze didn't feel nearly as bitingly cold as the winds that blew off Lake Mendota during a Wisconsin winter.

Back at the motel, I gathered my bags from where Deloris had stored them behind the front desk. Deloris, after finishing the checkout process, angrily thrust a pile of pink message slips at me. All of them were from Cal. Apparently his calls kept pulling her away from the bridge game taking place in the lobby.

"That boy wants to take you out tonight to celebrate your successful hot chocolate sale," one of the elderly ladies playing bridge at the nearby game table chimed in to say.

"Quite a looker that one," another said.

"Too bad he moved away from town," said a third.

"What?" the first lady said.

"He moved," the third lady shouted. "Out of town."

The first lady clicked her tongue. "Why'd he do a fool thing like that? Thought he was going to take over Billy's practice."

"That's his other son, Harleston. He took over the practice."

"That surfer boy?" She clicked her tongue again. "Can't trust him none. He's a bad seed, that one. Moved away."

"Harleston came back," the third lady shouted.

"Bah!" The first lady tossed down a card and then crossed her arms over her chest. "Came back to surf."

"Come on," Althea said, tugging at my arm. "Let's get you moved in. You can call Cal later."

Stella happily tugged at her leash, barking and growling as she pranced down Main Street. Althea wheeled my suitcase while I carried the bag stuffed with all of Stella's accessories. Bertie hummed a happy tune as she followed along a few steps behind us.

"How well do you know Harley?" I asked Althea, remembering how he had warned me more than once to leave town. He kept saying he wasn't trying to scare me, but that's what he'd been doing. Was that his aim? Was he trying to scare me away?

"I went to school with his brother, Cal," Althea said. "Harley is a few years older."

"She dated him behind my back in high school," Bertie said.

"Who? Cal?" I asked.

"No, Harley," Bertie answered.

Althea stopped abruptly in the middle of the sidewalk. "You knew about that?"

"I'm your mama; of course I knew who you were running around with back then. It was my job to know."

"We were—we were just having fun. It wasn't serious," Althea stammered. "If you knew, why didn't you call me out on it? You never let me put one foot out of line. Never."

"Is that so?" Bertie stepped around her stunned daughter and continued toward Mabel's shop. "Besides, his father never let either of those boys run wild. And the boy had always struck me as a good, hardworking kid. Harmless, even."

"How about now?" I asked as I hurried to catch up with Bertie. "He left Camellia Beach for a long time, and now he's back. He's under pressure from his ex-wife. She cheated on him and now wants to redevelop his hometown. And he's struggling to fill his father's shoes. Is he still harmless?"

"He's still the same Harley," Althea was quick to say as she came up from behind. Was she still in love with him?

"No man is harmless," Bertie warned. "No woman either."

* * *

As soon as we arrived at Mabel's apartment and I unsnapped Stella's leash, the little beastie took off sniffing every corner. Her fluffy tail resembled a wildly waving flag.

She made a beeline to a coat closet right off the kitchen. The door was open. I jogged over and pushed the door closed before she could do more than stick her nose inside. There was no telling what kind of trouble Stella could find within a closet's dark expanse.

"No!" Both Althea and Bertie called out in alarm.

"What?" I asked. "What did Stella do?"

"Not Stella," Althea said. "You. You closed the door."

"The closet door?" I stared at the heavy wooden door that obviously was original to the building.

Bertie shook her head and then produced a toolbox from one of the lower kitchen cabinets. She dropped the toolbox by the closet door with a clank. "The latch sticks. The only way to open the door again is to take it off its hinges."

"Oh, sorry." I added the broken door to the ever-growing list I was making in my head of things that needed to be fixed.

"Nothing to apologize about, dear," Bertie said. "We're so used to never closing that door that I tend to forget to warn others about it. I'll get it open again later tonight. Let's get you moved in."

Althea rolled my suitcase directly into Mabel's room. A simple pale-blue-and-green quilt covered the antique metal bed. A bit of white paint had flecked off here and there from the bed frame. A finely crafted dresser and bedside table, made from a rich teak wood, looked exotic and out of place in the humble room.

"The villagers made these pieces for her grandfather," Bertie said when she saw me running my hand over the dresser's smooth waxed top. "Beautiful, aren't they?"

"Yes," I said. "I love the carvings on the front. Those tiny flowers. They're exquisite."

"According to Mabel, those are cacao flowers."

"Chocolate blooms," I said with wonder as I ran my hand over the raised wood. "Perfect."

"Mabel would be glad that you like them. They're yours. She wanted them to stay here, with the shop."

My knee-jerk reaction was to say no. I didn't want them. Mabel's family deserved to inherit their mother's treasures. Not me. Not a stranger.

But was I a stranger? Or was I a long-lost relative?

Despite my repeated efforts, I hadn't been able to get any information from Hodgkin DNA about the scrap of paper found in Skinny's pocket. I'd even asked Grandmother Cristobel's attorney to make a call to the company, and they still wouldn't budge or even admit to being in contact with Skinny.

I looked at a framed picture of Mabel's children that hung in a prominent location on the wall near the dresser. In the picture, her children were all grown up but looked to be still in their early twenties. It had to have been taken after Carolina had run away since she wasn't in the photograph. I searched their faces, looking for similarities with mine.

They resembled Mabel. But they didn't look at all like me.

I could take a DNA test. But for what reason? No matter what, I planned to sign ownership of the shop over to Mabel's children. In all likelihood, they would sell the land to Jody, who'd already paid someone a large down payment for the property.

I wondered what exactly Jody planned to do with it. Would she renovate the historic building? Or tear it down? That was another thing I needed to ask when I met with her at the Low Tide tonight.

"There's a sideboard in the living room that matches the dresser and nightstand," Bertie said, breaking my silence. She opened the closet door, showing me its empty interior. "I've packed up all Mabel's clothes so you can move right in."

"We want you to feel comfortable here," Althea said. "Like it's your home."

"Your temporary home," Bertie added quickly before I had a chance to say it myself.

"It is just for the week, but thank you. It'll be nice not to have to live out of my suitcase."

Althea and Bertie left me alone to unpack. I'd just started putting my clothes in drawers and hanging up dresses when a rat, naked and wrinkly and huge, scurried out from under the bed. It started advancing on me.

"There's—there's a rat in here. A rat!" I cried. I backed myself into the en suite bathroom. The hairless rat, which had to weigh at least ten pounds, followed, trapping me between the shower stall and sink. And then it rubbed against me.

I shrieked.

It shrieked. And darted back under the bed.

Chapter 15

"You've got a huge rat infestation problem. I mean *huge* huge. That thing is a monster. Call rodent control. Now," I demanded when Althea and Bertie came running to see why I was shrieking. "What—what's so funny?"

"Th-that's just Troubadour. M-m-m-able's cat," Althea barely managed to sputter as she hugged her sides, laughing so hard it clearly pained her.

A moment later, Stella charged into the room, barking her little head off. She stuck her nose under the bed. The naked rat—I mean, cat—growled, low and deep. My fearless little dog whimpered and retreated back into the living room. She stood guard at the doorway, barking and jumping up and down, but she didn't dare cross the threshold back into the bedroom where the cat was hiding.

"That—that's a cat?" I asked, still pressed against the wall, still wedged between the sink and the shower stall. I was also still thinking we should be calling rodent control. "Are you sure it's a cat?"

"Hairless," Althea said, gulping back more laughter.

157

"On purpose?" I opened the slightly rusty medicine cabinet above the sink, only absently noting the line of prescription pill bottles crammed on the top shelf. I angled the mirror so I could keep an eye on the bed and the creature I knew lay beneath it.

"Mabel had allergies," Althea explained.

"So she shaved her cat?" I pulled a dark-colored glass bottle down from the medicine cabinet's shelf. It was a prescription for nitroglycerin, a pill given to relieve chest pains associated with heart disease. "She shaved her cat bald?"

"Dear Lord, no. He was born that way. He's a sphinx. It's a hairless breed," Bertie said. She'd squatted down next to the bed and held out a hand. The ugly cat came out and rubbed against her outstretched fingers.

I shivered at the thought of a whole litter of kittens looking like this huge, wrinkly cat.

"He's sweet as can be," Bertie said. "Sweeter than sweet potato pie, aren't you?"

"I just bet he is." *Just don't let him come near me again*, I didn't say aloud. "Who inherited him?"

"He's a living being. You don't inherit—" Althea protested.

"You can have him," I said quickly.

"I promised Mabel I'd keep him," Bertie said as the cat bumped her hand with its hairless head until she started to pet its wrinkly back. "He's young. Not even two years old."

At least I wasn't going to be stuck living with it. One big-eared monster in my life was more than enough.

"You're more than welcome to take him home with you tonight." I returned the prescription bottle to the shelf and closed the cabinet door.

"I am home." Bertie smiled at the cat, which had started to purr. Loudly. "At least for the week, I mean."

I froze. "You live here?"

"For the past ten years. I've been caring for Mabel. She looked after me too. We were partners."

"You were partners, but you didn't hold official ownership in the chocolate shop? That's not fair."

She lowered her voice. "We weren't partners in the business, although I helped her. We loved each other. We were partners in life. Don't go looking at me like that, like you're shocked or something, Althea. I know you're not. Shocked, that is. And get your mind out of the gutter. We loved our husbands until the day they died. But we loved each other too. We were best friends and partners. We shared this apartment and took care of each other. When you get older, you need someone to go to the doctors with you, who enjoys reminiscing about the old days, and who loves you."

"Mama, I'm here for you," Althea protested.

"It ain't the same. You'll understand when you get older."

"But Mabel didn't leave you the shop. Why?" I asked. "She should have. She should have given you at least part ownership in the building, in the business. Heck, Mabel should have left all of it to you, not me." Was I going to sign the deed over to the wrong family? "I'll give you the property. And the shop."

"I already told you, child. I don't want it. I have property of my own. And besides, I'm looking to retire."

"You have property? In town?"

"She owns my shop," Althea said. "I rent the space. So does Harley, and the small grocery store next to my store, and the CPA whose office is above it."

"The rents provide a modest income." The hairless cat climbed into Bertie's arms. Bertie rose from her crouched position on the floor, cradling the cat like it was a baby. "I don't want to be bothered with more."

"Even so, Bertie, it's not fair," I pressed. "You deserve some part of the shop. Even if all you do is sell it."

"Mabel didn't want it sold," the older woman snapped. She hugged the cat tightly to her breast. "It's been a long day and I'm beat. I'll see you in the morning."

She padded out of the room while shame heated my face. I had to remember that while I had gotten myself all worked up over the mess of inheriting something I never wanted or asked for, Bertie had lost her best friend and life partner. She'd been holding up well all day, but clearly grief had taken a sharp toll. I should have been more sensitive to her feelings.

But at the same time, when all was said and done, I was going to end up breaking her heart. I wasn't going to fulfill her dear friend's wishes. I wasn't going to keep the shop.

"Please tell your mother I'm sorry," I whispered to Althea just before grabbing my purse and hurrying out of the apartment before she could react. I didn't tell Althea where I was headed, since she'd insist on coming with me. Upset as I was at the thought of hurting Bertie, I didn't want her daughter's company. I needed some time alone. I needed to think.

* * *

"You're going the wrong way," Harley said as he fell into step beside me as I marched down Main Street.

"How do you know where I'm going?" I stopped and held my fists at the ready to attack. "And why are you still stalking me? I thought I made it clear that I—"

"I'm not stalking you," he said, but he backed up anyhow. "I was heading home when I saw you running down the Chocolate

Box's back stairs like a pack of hell hounds were chasing you. You looked distressed, and I thought you might need help." He flashed his million-watt smile that was nearly as effective as his younger brother's. "Honest."

There was that charm Jody had warned me about. My fists tightened. "That doesn't answer my first question. How do you know where I'm heading?"

"I know because you told me right after smashing my pretty face." Now that he'd mentioned it, his nose still looked red and puffy. "You told me you were going to the Low Tide to meet with my lovely ex."

"Yes, and you told me not to go."

"Why would you listen to me? You don't even trust me."

"That's true."

"So that answers your question. I know you're heading to the Low Tide, and I also know it's in the other direction." He pointed toward the marsh side of the island.

The Low Tide was a shack built on top of a rickety-looking dock down on the river. Honestly, I never would have found the place without Harley's help. The rusty corrugated building was outside the business district and past several elevated Southern cottages with iconic wide porches. It was on the southern side of the island. To get to it, I had to slog down a rutted, muddy road that wound through thick groves of palmetto trees and scrubby oaks.

Water lapped at the piers holding up the building. A dim light marked the entrance.

"This place is a dive," Harley said. He'd followed along a few paces behind me. His voice floated on the air in the deepening winter darkness.

"But everyone comes here," I said while kicking large clumps of mud off my poor, abused Timberland boots.

"That's true. Everyone comes here."

"It's the last place Skinny was seen alive."

"That's true too."

"He was seen arguing with you," I reminded him.

Harley didn't say anything. I turned around.

He was gone.

A huge black SUV bumped along the rutted road and slowed as it pulled up beside me.

"There you are," Cal said after he rolled down his window. "I've been driving all over the island looking for you."

"And calling around too?" I kept searching for where Harley might have disappeared to.

"Please don't sue me for being persistent." His smile appeared more relaxed, more genuine than his brother's. "Let me buy you dinner."

"They serve food in there?"

"Do they ever! A few months ago, their shrimp po' boys were featured in *Southern Living*. Right now the oysters are in season. We could share a bucket. You know about oysters, don't you?" He waggled his eyebrows in such a funny way I laughed and then accepted his invitation.

The inside of the bar was as dreadful as the outside, with its dark wood-paneled walls, yellow glass and black metal medieval-style lanterns hanging from heavy chains, and a thick haze of cigarette smoke floating in the air. The only redeeming feature was the view of the marsh and the Camellia River beyond. The winter clouds had cleared, and the pale moon reflected on the water. We found a table next to a wall of windows that were actually oversized garage doors. According to Cal, the owners would throw open the doors in warmer weather.

Cal left me at the table and headed over to the bar to order. After a little while, he returned with two frosty beers. "I ordered the oysters and a side of red rice. I hope you don't mind."

"Not at all," I said and took a sip of the tap beer. It tasted surprisingly good.

Soon the food showed up. Fresh oysters were rare in the Midwest. The steaming shellfish piled in an oversized metal bucket tasted fresher than fresh. It was as if they'd been plucked from the surrounding marsh and tossed directly into the steamer. The sweet and salty flavors of the Lowcountry teased my senses with each bite.

"Now I understand why this place is so crowded," I said as I licked my fingers after we'd finished off the large bucket of oysters without any trouble. "Delicious."

Was this where Skinny sat that last night before his death? Had he eaten oysters? Had he flirted with some of the women at the bar? My gaze roamed the room. If I looked hard enough, I imagined I might find some sign of him, a shadow of his life here.

"Looking for someone?" Cal asked when he noticed my wandering attention.

Yeah, my dead friend. "I was hoping I could find someone who might have been here the night Skinny died, someone who saw him, talked with him."

Cal placed his elbows on the table as he leaned forward. "I was here that night. So was Derek Maybank. He . . . um . . . likes to party. So did your friend, by the way. He was a wild one."

"Really? Derek? He seems so . . . bland."

"He does, doesn't he?" Cal chuckled. "Perhaps that's his superpower. Mild-mannered khakis guy by day and animal with an alcoholic drink in hand by night."

"And you like to party too?"

He flashed that innocent, yet somehow sexy, smile of his and rubbed the back of his neck. "Work is demanding. When I have time off, like now, I need to blow off steam. This place is good for that."

"I can see that." It wasn't my kind of bar, although the food was top-notch. I could tell by how the voices were already growing louder that the action was just getting going. In a few hours, after the diners left, I suspected the Low Tide turned into a party place.

If you'd asked me two weeks ago if Skinny hung out in dives like this, I'd know the answer. He wouldn't. He preferred the quiet of early morning waves to the chaos of a rowdy bar.

After hearing how he'd fooled around with Jody, played dirty tricks on Harley, and enjoyed stirring up nests of hornets, I was starting to wonder if I knew Skinny at all. The Skinny the people in Camellia Beach were describing sounded nothing like the Skinny who'd hang out with me in the school library, reading the latest mystery novels and seeing who could solve the crime first, whispering about our hopes and dreams of the future, and complaining about our dysfunctional families. I'd never known him to be a party animal or a barfly.

Some people changed, some people hid their true selves, and some people were afraid to see the truth. I feared I fell into that last category. I didn't see the truth with the Cheese King, and apparently I missed it with Skinny as well.

Steeling myself to hear the worst, I squared my shoulders and said, "Skinny had left a message on my voice mail, saying he knew why Mabel had lured me to Camellia Beach. He'd sounded excited about it. Not worried. He had told me to pack my bags, because I was going to want to see for myself what he'd learned."

"So you think he found out about the will?" Cal asked.

I took another sip of my beer and nodded. "Yeah, I think he must have. But I'm thinking he had to have learned something else as well. It must have been something damning, at least in the murderer's eyes, you know? Just knowing about Mabel's crazy will shouldn't have caused anyone to kill him, right? I mean, other people knew about it, like Bertie and Althea, and they're still alive."

"That's true." Cal seemed to think long and hard before adding, "I hesitate to say anything, but my brother hated Skinny. The night of Skinny's death, I'd never seen Harley so angry with anyone before in my life. It was . . . scary." He quickly waved away the thought. "But he wouldn't have done anything stupid like kill a man."

"Wouldn't he?" I asked.

"He's my brother. Of course he wouldn't," Cal said. But his brows dropped as his forehead crinkled. He looked worried.

I pulled out my phone and opened an app that allowed me to take notes. I named the file "Suspects."

"Okay, for argument's sake, let's say Harley quarreled with Skinny and then stormed off to calm down. So nothing happened," I said even though I wrote Harley's name on the top of my suspect list. "Can you remember anyone else who was here the night of Skinny's death? Perhaps someone who saw Skinny leave? Or someone who might have had a grudge against him? Did he ask someone the wrong questions? Did he sleep with someone else's wife?"

Cal tapped his stubbly chin. "I don't think he hooked up with anyone new. I seem to remember Jody had been flirting with Skinny relentlessly that night, hanging on his arm, whispering in his ear, and kissing him like there was no tomorrow."

"And he let her?" I'd never seen Skinny welcome public displays of affection.

Cal shrugged. "Didn't look like he minded. To be honest, I thought they were going to go home together. But I'm pretty sure I spotted Jody at the bar after Skinny had left."

"Pretty sure" wasn't good enough in my book. I added Jody's name to my suspect list. Not only did she have a rocky history with Skinny, but she'd acted downright hostile when she heard I'd reopened the Chocolate Box. She'd also lied about having a sister. What was that about?

"How about Mabel's kids?" I asked.

"As I've already told you, Derek was here at the Low Tide with me until early morning."

"Oh, right. And he seemed to approve of my taking over the shop," I said. "What about Edward and Florence, Mabel's older children? Were either of them in town that night?"

Cal had to think about that for a moment. "Don't remember seeing Edward that night, not that it would matter. A guy like him wouldn't get his hands dirty with something like murder. Don't get me wrong, I suspect he'd kill a man in a heartbeat if it suited his purposes. It's just he's the kind of guy who'd hire someone to do the deed for him."

"Scary," I said. But then I remembered how he'd acted at the will reading. "He seemed pretty shocked and upset when he heard I'd inherited the shop, which kind of takes him out of the running of suspects. If he didn't know about the will ahead of time, he wouldn't have reason to find Skinny a threat."

"I suppose," Cal said slowly. "Still, he's a pretty nasty piece of work. I'd be careful around him."

While I didn't jot his name down on my list, I made a mental note to learn more about Edward and why he'd gotten so upset about not inheriting a shop he'd considered worthless.

"And what about Florence and her sister—what's her name?" I asked.

"Peach," he supplied.

"Were they around?"

"Not Peach. She rarely comes to Camellia Beach. She's more upscale. Her beach of choice is Sullivan's, the island just north of here where politicians and millionaires keep summer homes."

"And Florence? She was furious at me for inheriting her mother's shop. Had that been shock? Or had she been angry that killing Skinny hadn't prevented me from coming to Camellia Beach?"

"I don't know Florence well. She's married to some Richie Rich who owns several clothing stores in Charleston's historic downtown. Can't understand what she would want with the shop. She'd been bugging her mother for years to sell it and retire to Florida like a normal person. Miss Mabel would laugh and laugh about that. Besides, Florence doesn't need the money since she has her hubby's riches."

"Yet she's furious. She told me after the will reading that I'd get the shop only over her dead body." I wrote her name on my suspect list.

"She's nuts, then." Cal took a long sip of his beer. "Who in their right mind would really want that place?"

That was the key question, wasn't it?

"So that's everyone?" I asked.

"Everyone who?" Jody asked. She'd come up from behind and was standing directly behind me.

"We were just discussing who was around the night of Skinny's murder and making a list of suspects," Cal said much to my chagrin.

My cheeks heated. After all, Jody was the second person on my list. I quickly turned off my phone and shoved it back into my pocket. I hoped she hadn't seen her name on my suspect list.

"What about Florence?" Jody asked. "She was at the bar that night. I remember she'd yelled at Skinny for poking around and asking questions about the Maybank family."

"She did?" Cal asked, raising a brow. "I don't remember that."

"Wouldn't think you'd remember much from that night given the speed you and Derek were slamming shots." Jody pulled up a chair to our table and sat down. She leaned toward me. I edged my chair away when our shoulders touched. "There is someone else to add to that list. Someone no one has seen in ages."

"Who's that?" I asked.

"Carolina Maybank, Mabel's oldest daughter," Jody said. "Skinny said he'd been trying like crazy to track her down."

"Why?" Cal asked. "She ran away when she was a teenager. She's had nothing to do with this town or her mother's shop for decades. My guess is she got hooked on drugs or something and died years ago."

"If she's not dead, she's going to be a very rich woman," I said, remembering the terms of the will.

"That's right. And if she doesn't show up in the next two years, the rest of Miss Mabel's children will get quite the windfall." Cal tapped his chin. "I'd forgotten about that."

"If Skinny found Carolina, that might give one of Mabel's kids a motive for murder. It was a considerable amount of money." I took a sip of beer as I considered what that might mean. "But what would finding Carolina have to do with me? Skinny had left me a message the night he was killed saying that I'd be excited to hear what he'd discovered."

"He left you a message?" In her excitement, Jody grabbed my arm and gave me a shake. "Can I listen to it?"

Since it was too loud inside the bar to hear the message on the phone, we left a tip on the table and headed outside. We had to go to the far end of the crushed-oyster-shell parking lot to escape the music blaring inside the Low Tide. In the near-freezing weather, we stood under a flickering parking lot light as I pulled my phone from my back pocket. It only took a moment to retrieve Skinny's last message.

I'd listened to it scores of times hoping to hear something new—a clue, a hint of who might have killed him.

"Penn, I need to talk with you." He sounded out of breath. A car with a bad muffler drove past. It was difficult to make out what he said next. "I know why you won that fake contest. I know who sent the letter. And it's really cool. No, I'm not going to tell you in a message. Don't want to miss hearing your reaction. I can tell you this—start packing your bags. You really need to come down here and see for yourself." He paused. Then came the clop-clop of his feet. "Look, someone's following me. I've got to go. I'll give you a call first thing in the morning. We can talk then."

Jody pressed her fingers against her lips as she listened. Her eyes had grown large as she turned and stared at Cal, who, even in the soft lamplight, I could see had turned pale.

The wind rattled the palm fronds swaying in the trees above our heads.

"What?" I asked.

"It can't be." Cal shook his head as if trying to chase away the thought that was clearly haunting him.

"It has to be," Jody said.

"What?" I asked again. "What did you hear?"

"The car," Jody said.

"No." Cal kept shaking his head. "It can't be."

"You can't deny it." Jody's voice was sharp. Tears filled her eyes. "I knew it. I knew he was capable. But I had hoped I was wrong. Truly, I had hoped I was wrong."

"It doesn't mean he killed anyone," Cal yelled back, matching Jody's angry tone.

"Really? You heard him that night. He'd threatened to rip out Skinny's throat and dump him in the river."

"But that's not what happened," Cal said.

"You mean Harley?" I asked. "You think he—"

"Yes, Harley," Jody yelled at me. "That's his car you hear in the background. He's neglected to get that stupid muffler fixed for over a year now."

I held up my hands. I needed a moment to pull my thoughts together. Slowly the pieces started to fall into place. Harley had a black sedan with a broken muffler just like the one we could hear in the background on Skinny's message. Also, a black sedan with a broken muffler had tried to run me down on my first day in Camellia Beach. Harley and Skinny had a long history of antagonizing each other. And Harley knew how to bypass the Chocolate Box's back lock.

"I have to report this," I said. My hands shook as I dialed the number for the Charleston County detective who had taken over Skinny's murder investigation.

Skinny's death had nothing to do with illegal drugs. Harley must have planted the marijuana in Skinny's pockets after knocking him out.

I drew a ragged breath. Cal had bent over and was hugging his knees as he shook his head in disbelief. He looked as if he was going to be sick. Jody crossed her arms over her chest. Her expression hardened as she nodded her approval that I was calling the authorities.

Apparently, Skinny's death had nothing to do with Mabel's fake prize letter. Nor did it have anything to do with his trying to find the long-lost Carolina Maybank.

His death wasn't my fault at all. I knew I shouldn't have felt relief at that thought, but I did. My friend, who I apparently didn't know all that well, had gotten caught up in a deadly love triangle. And it had proven fatal.

After several rings, the detective finally picked up. I quickly introduced myself and then breathily said, "I know who killed my friend. It was Harley Dalton."

Chapter 16

"You tried to get me *arrested*?"

That was the angry greeting I received the next morning when I opened the apartment door to go work in the shop downstairs.

The looming figure blocking the door, with fist raised, advanced.

I backed up.

"Harley, you need to leave. Now." We performed a strange little dance as I did my best to keep my distance while he followed me inside. Stella, barking furiously, came to my rescue. She charged at his ankles. Grabbing the cuff of his pants, she tugged and growled using her most menacing voice.

"Stop that," Harley growled back and gave his leg a shake.

Stella's clamped jaws held firm.

"Don't kick her!" I shouted.

"I'm not kicking her!" he shouted back.

I suppose he hadn't actually kicked my little dog, just shaken the leg she'd latched onto. Even so, I had every right to defend her. I knew exactly what this guy was capable of doing. Killing

172

someone by dumping him headfirst into chocolate? That was sick. An evil kind of sick. No, worse—a sick kind of sick.

"I'm sorry you're upset, but you need to leave. Now."

"Not before I get some answers." Harley looked even worse for wear than he had yesterday morning when I'd found him lurking half frozen outside my motel room door. Dressed in the same clothes as yesterday, wrinkled and smudged with grime, his shoulders drooped nearly as much as the dark bags under his eyes. His brown hair stood up in some places and was matted down in others. If I didn't know him, I would have mistaken him for an unfortunate homeless man. I probably would have bought him breakfast.

But he wasn't homeless. He was a killer.

"What's going on?" Bertie emerged from her bedroom. She tugged at the belt of her quilted flowered housecoat and yawned. "Harley, what are you doing here this early in the morning?"

"She told the police I killed her friend." Harley pointed an accusing finger in my direction. "And then she sicced her vicious dog on me."

"Penn?" Bertie had to raise her voice to be heard over Stella's barking. "Is this true?"

"I told the county detective in charge of the case what I'd learned over the last couple of days. He's the one who decided to make an arrest. Hold on a minute—if he arrested you, why are you here and not in jail?"

"He didn't have enough evidence to make an arrest," he grumbled. "Not yet."

By this time, Mabel's cat came slinking out of Bertie's bedroom. It crossed the kitchen and hissed in my direction before making a beeline to Harley, where Stella was still acting like my protector.

With a loud yowl, Troubadour slapped Stella in the face with his razor-sharp claws. Stella yelped and then darted under the sofa.

With a satisfied sniff, Troubadour pressed himself against Harley as if he'd fallen in love. He rubbed against our intruder, doing that figure-eight thing cats do around Harley's legs.

Stella peered out from under the sofa, her eyes wide with shock. Her gaze was fixed on Troubadour, who was still rubbing himself shamelessly against Harley. Seeing that she'd have to get past the cat to get back to my attacker, my fearless dog backed farther under the sofa and let out a long, mournful whine.

"Come inside and sit down," Bertie said to Harley. She moved over to the stove. "I'll fix you some coffee and eggs. It looks as if you haven't eaten in ages."

"Don't come inside." I raised my hands like twin stop signs in an attempt to keep him from getting into the apartment. "Don't invite him in. Don't make him breakfast. He killed my friend."

"No, he didn't," Bertie said. "Sit down, boy."

He obeyed Bertie by stepping around me and dropping into a teal-blue vinyl chair at the vintage Formica kitchen table.

Bertie moved through the kitchen like a force of nature, pulling out a carton of eggs and a package of bacon from the fridge and a frying pan and a loaf of fresh bread from the cupboard.

"Tell me, Penn, why do you think our boy here committed murder?" she asked as she dropped a pat of butter into the pan.

I looked at Harley. He'd raised his brows and had fixed his deep-green eyes on me. Nervous, I grabbed the bacon and eggs and put them back into the fridge. "He threatened to kill Skinny that night. Half the town heard him. We shouldn't be feeding him."

Bertie tsked. "People argue all the time and say stupid things. What else did you hear?" She sliced two pieces of bread from the loaf and dropped them into the toaster.

"Yes, Penn, what else do you have against me?"

My gaze stayed glued on Harley. This wasn't a wise conversation to be having in front of him. What if I said something to anger him? What violence might he do to us? "The detective in charge had promised to keep the source—namely, me—confidential. He shouldn't have told you the information came from me."

"The detective didn't tell me anything. He was like a freaking brick wall, that one. Heard it all from Police Chief Byrd," Harley said.

"He shouldn't have been talking." I hit the cancel button on the toaster and pulled out the half-toasted bread.

"If it makes you feel any better, he didn't actually say your name. He just told me 'that crazy lady' had provided some new evidence."

"That doesn't make me feel better." I crossed my arms over my chest.

"Where did I put those eggs?" Bertie frowned at me. "Penn? Did you move them and the bacon? I can't find the bacon."

"We shouldn't be feeding him," I said again. "He's a killer."

"Not that again." Bertie dropped some more bread into the toaster. "The boy is innocent. And I'm not going to let him go hungry." She retrieved the carton of eggs and bacon from the fridge and pushed down the pedal on the toaster on her way back to the sizzling frying pan. "Now what were we talking about again?" she asked after cracking a couple of eggs into the pan and adding a few slabs of bacon.

"Penn was telling us why she called the cops on me," Harley said. "Please, do go on. What other damning evidence do you have against me?"

"The car," I said.

"My car?" Harley sounded honestly baffled.

"That old thing?" Bertie said at the same time. She carried over a plate piled with a hearty breakfast and set it down in front of our resident murderer.

"Yes, your car. Skinny left me a message on my phone the night he was killed." I cut an angry gaze in Harley's direction. He didn't notice. He was too busy devouring Bertie's breakfast as if he'd been wandering through a desert for several years. "Anyhow, Skinny said he was being followed, and I could hear a rumbling muffler in the background."

"Could be any car," Harley said with a mouthful of eggs.

"No, not any car. Everyone who heard the message identified it as your car," I said.

"Everyone?" Harley looked up from his breakfast.

"Don't be a fool," Bertie said. Her back had been to us because she'd moved to the sink and had started scrubbing out the pan she used for the eggs. She wiped her hands on a towel and turned around. She scowled so fiercely my insides quaked. I wasn't sure if she'd directed that scold toward me or to Harley. Or maybe she meant it for the both of us. Either way, it was intimidating. "Anyone and everyone in town knows Harley keeps the keys to that old jalopy of his under the front seat. He does it so whoever needs to borrow it can."

That didn't make sense. "What do you do if you need to drive somewhere and someone else has driven off with your car?" I asked.

"Oh, for heaven's sake, child, he takes his motorbike."

"You mean to tell me Harley drives a Harley?"

He rubbed the back of his neck, a move I'd noticed his younger brother also did when feeling embarrassed. "Actually, it's a Yamaha."

"You should totally trade it in for a Harley," I muttered. Thankfully, neither of them seemed to have heard me. "So what did you do after you threatened to kill my friend? Leave your car parked at the Low Tide and make nice with the hermit crabs in the marsh?"

"Fiddler crabs," Harley said.

"What?" I asked.

"Fiddler crabs live in the marsh, not hermit crabs. And yes, I did leave the car in the parking lot. After the argument, I walked home to cool off."

"And who saw you 'walk' home?" I asked.

Harley shrugged. "Can't say I remember seeing anyone."

"Boy, what a mess you've gotten yourself into." Bertie came over and patted his shoulder.

"Just like that you're taking his side? What about the evidence? What about the threats? What about the fact that Harley knew about the vat of chocolate and how to get into the chocolate shop through its broken back door? A stranger to the town—as Police Chief Byrd wants me to believe—wouldn't have known about either of those two things. Nor would he have known that Harley always keeps his keys in his car. You can't dismiss all that."

"I've known this boy since he was running around on the beach in his diapers. I know when he's telling the truth. And I know when he's not."

"Thank you." Harley patted Bertie's hand that was still resting on his shoulder. He smiled up at the older woman.

"People change, and not always for the better," I said, thinking about how much I didn't know a lick about Skinny's adult life.

"What about Jody?" Bertie asked.

"You think Jody killed Skinny?" I asked, my eyes growing wide.

"No, that isn't what I'm saying at all," Bertie answered sharply.

"After what happened on Sunday," Harley said, "she's already filed the paperwork to drag me back into court." His frown deepened and his shoulders slumped even lower, nearly touching the kitchen tabletop. "She left a message on my phone last night saying she's going to push to revoke our custody agreement. She even threatened to petition the court to block all visitation rights."

"Visitation rights? For who?" I asked, unable to follow what the two of them were talking about.

"Harley and Jody have a son." Bertie scooped up Mabel's cat and hugged him to her chest.

"A son?" For some odd reason, that news shocked me.

"She uses Gavin as a weapon to hurt our Harley."

He nodded. "One step out of line and I'm back in court fighting to keep what little time I have with him."

"What does she say you did this time?" Bertie asked. "Other than committing a murder, I mean."

"I took Gavin surfing Sunday morning." Harley let out a long, unhappy sigh.

"What's wrong with that?" I asked. "Can't he swim?"

"Of course he can swim." Harley's head snapped up to frown at me. "Both Jody and I made sure he learned to swim even before he learned to walk. He was up on a surfboard by age

178

three. He's nine now and has won the last two surf competitions he's entered for his age group."

"So what's the problem?" I asked. "Why would she haul you into court for taking your son surfing?"

"It wasn't my weekend."

"Your weekend?" I asked.

"I get him every other weekend. And heaven forbid I see him even for a moment when she has him. But he'd asked me to show him a few new carving techniques. What was I going to say, no?"

"I can't believe she'd involve the courts over something like that. Wasn't she the one who followed you here from Atlanta when you quit your high-paying job and moved hundreds of miles away from her and your only son?" I asked. "It sounds like she's the one trying to keep the family together, not keep Gavin from having a father in his life."

"That Jody girl is here for one reason and one reason only—to make our Harley's life a living hell. He wasn't abandoning his son; he was escaping her tirades." Troubadour rubbed his face against Bertie's chin. I shivered at the sight of all that wrinkly skin. The cat's, not Bertie's. Bertie's skin looked radiant, youthful, especially when compared to Mabel's cat, which was now rubbing his head shamelessly against Bertie's cheek.

"After my father passed away, I came here to close up his office, flying Gavin in to visit during my assigned weekends. Living hundreds of miles away from Jody, as you've pointed out, was the breath of fresh air I dearly needed. So I made the decision to stay in Camellia Beach full time."

"That witch couldn't stand that our Harley could offer Gavin something she couldn't."

"I wouldn't call her a witch. She is Gavin's mother," Harley said, even though the situation clearly troubled him.

I'd watched enough of my father's marriages fall apart. I'd seen the deep pain that lingered with both parties, especially when children were involved.

"After I finalized the move," Harley continued, "Jody grew more and more jealous of how much Gavin enjoyed coming to stay with me and surf. She'd call him several times a day. One time when he was staying with me, she told him she'd bought him a kitten; another time it was a puppy. She'd tell him over and over how much she missed him and needed him to come back home. Naturally, Gavin started feeling guilty about coming to visit even though my apartment here is supposed to be just as much his home as mine."

"She dragged our boy into court, accusing him of parental alienation," Bertie said.

"That's a serious charge. What happened?" I asked.

"She lost the case," Harley said. "The next week, she packed up her things and moved to Camellia Beach."

"Things must have gotten better for everyone." I couldn't imagine how it could have gotten worse.

"In some ways it's been better," Harley admitted.

"That woman makes sure nothing is easy for Harley."

"I find it hard to believe Jody could act vindictively like that. She's been nothing but friendly to me." Except for that one time when she thought I was going to keep the chocolate shop open.

Had she really left a threatening message on Harley's phone about me? Quite honestly, I didn't want to know. My father's exes constantly did stupid, destructive things in the heat of an angry moment. Jody was probably no different.

"You have to respect how she's working to rebuild her life, starting a new career here in town and making new friends. A few of my stepmothers haven't done anything other than stay at home and fume."

"She only took the job at the development company because she knew it would get under Harley's skin. What kind of person thinks tearing down our town to build a concrete tourist trap in its place would be a good idea? That's not community. That's not preserving the deep history of our land. That's 110 percent opportunism from an outsider. That's what it is." Bertie had gotten so worked up during her speech she'd accidentally squeezed Troubadour too hard. The cat let out a high-pitched yowl and leapt from her arms. He scooted across the room and disappeared through Bertie's bedroom door.

When Stella noticed her feline nemesis was gone, her ears perked up. It was as if a butterfly was spreading its grand wings. She wiggled out from under the sofa. She charged Harley only to be thwarted by Bertie stepping in the way. "I didn't forget you," she said in a low, calm voice and tossed my pup a small piece of bacon.

With a happy growl, Stella devoured the bacon. She then sat herself down next to Bertie and waited for more. Amazed by her quick turnaround, I decided right then and there to start carrying bacon in my pocket.

Bertie smiled at my dog and then patted Harley's shoulder. "Now if you'll excuse me, there's a store that needs to be opened and Mabel's last batch of chocolate that needs to be tempered. I need to get dressed and ready to get to work."

I stood in the middle of the kitchen, not sure what to do. Harley didn't move from where he sat slumped at the kitchen table. It looked as if he had no plans of leaving anytime soon.

"I'm sorry about your troubles, Harley. Truly I am." I might not trust him or believe him. But I hated the thought of his young son being kept from having two parents in his life. And I hated even more the thought of his son being punished for something his father had done. The scars of my childhood affected every part of my adult life. Those were scars no child should be forced to bear. Unable to keep silent about that, I added, "You need to think before you act, especially considering how you have a son to watch over. Hanging out at bars at all hours of the night. Threatening my friend. You're a father. You can't do things like that."

"I didn't kill anyone." He lifted his head to protest.

"And stalking me. You shouldn't stalk people."

"I'm not stalking you. I'm the one trying to help you."

"Why?" I asked. "Why would you want to help me, a stranger?"

"Because I'm a nice guy." He threw his hands in the air and pushed back from the table. His chair nearly fell over as he stood. "Just because you don't see it doesn't mean it ain't so."

I took a step back as he marched toward me. No, not toward me. He stepped around me and strode toward the apartment's only exit.

He was halfway out the door when I chuffed a breath and said, "Wait."

He stopped but kept his back to me. His shoulders tensed. "What?"

"Can you prove it?" I asked.

He turned around. Anger sparked like lightning in his green eyes. "That I'm a nice guy? I thought I'd been proving that all along. I stood out in the snow because you told me you didn't feel safe in our town."

"No," I said quietly. "No, not that. Can you prove you didn't kill Skinny?"

He closed those stunning eyes of his and drew a deep breath. "No, I can't."

Of course he couldn't. He had the means, the motive, the opportunity, and no alibi. Yet Bertie's faith in him seemed to be rubbing off on me. "What time did you take your son surfing?"

"What?" he asked gruffly.

"What time did you take Gavin surfing last Sunday? The surfing excursion that got you in trouble with Jody? What time was that?"

He closed his eyes and thought for a moment. "I got in the water around seven. You saw me."

"And when did Gavin arrive?"

"Around eight, I think."

Eight? That was too early.

"How long did you stay in the water with your son?" I asked.

"We finished up at 10:36. Jody put the time in her petition to the court. She'd stormed out onto the beach and practically dragged Gavin out of the water to get him away from me."

"10:36?" I repeated.

He nodded.

The wheels in my head started churning. A car with a loud muffler had tried to run me down on my first morning in Camellia Beach. Was the car Harley's black sedan?

My near miss with the fender of that car had occurred a little after ten o'clock, which meant, if both his son and an ex-wife who clearly distrusted him could back up his story, he had an alibi for the attempt on my life.

If evidence against him for one murder attempt fell apart so easily, how long would it take before the evidence against him for Skinny's murder started to fall apart too?

If Harley didn't kill Skinny in a fit of mad jealousy, who did?

Could it have been one of Mabel's kids angry over not inheriting the shop? Or had Jody retaliated against Skinny for rebuffing her advances? But that didn't explain the attempt against my life.

Could the murderer be someone who lusted after Mabel's special chocolates? Did he—or she—kill Skinny in an attempt to keep me from finding out . . . *what*? What was Skinny going to tell me about Mabel?

I sighed.

If I eliminated Harley as a suspect, the shop was really the only motive I had left.

Chapter 17

The velvety-rich and nearly otherworldly scent still surprised me when I walked into the Chocolate Box. The scent pulled at something deep inside me. I supposed some people experienced something similar when walking into a church or returning home after a long absence.

And yet no matter how much I loved Mabel's chocolate, the experience I felt walking into the store was bitingly bitter-sweet. Skinny had died within these walls, killed in the very same chocolate I had come to love. Mabel had died upstairs only a few days after I'd met her.

Death and chocolate. Grief and anticipation. A mishmash of emotions swirled in my heart like ingredients in one of Mabel's stainless-steel mixing bowls. I wondered what Mabel would have said if I could tell her about the conflicting thoughts I had toward her shop.

It's the salt that brings out the sweet in life, she'd told me during one of our cooking lessons. The memory came to me almost as if she were whispering it from beyond the veil. I swiped at the salty tears I hadn't even realized had fallen and smiled.

She hadn't left me the shop with no one to help me run it. Bertie, Althea, Cal, and even Derek had all promised to help me get ready for the festival. And despite the heaps of salt that had brought me to this shabby little beach community, I did find the challenge of running the chocolate shop, even for one week, pretty dang sweet.

It took some effort to put aside the questions that still surrounded Skinny's death as I walked through the shop, flipping on lights. If I was going to make this weekend's chocolate festival the success Mabel had dreamed it would be, I needed to focus.

Among other things, I had ad copy to write, newspapers to contact, ingredients to buy, and mouthwatering chocolates to make.

But first things first: I needed to get the shop ready for its nine o'clock opening and then check on the chocolate beans that had been grinding away in the kitchen. I opened the cooler to fetch the trays of beautiful truffles and stood there . . . dumbfounded.

The shelves were empty.

Okay. Don't panic. Perhaps I'd misremembered that Bertie put the trays of truffles in the cooler. I hurried to the front of the store and peered into the glass display case.

Those shelves were also empty.

"What are you doing standing around gaping at the chocolates like that?" Bertie asked. She'd showered and dressed in a worn pair of blue jeans with an elastic waist. A long-sleeve purple T-shirt printed with the Chocolate Box's scrolling logo and the word "Chocolate" was neatly tucked into her jeans. "Go ahead and eat one," she said as she dropped her apron on over her head.

"The chocolates," I whispered. "They're not here."

"That's because you haven't gotten them out of the cooler yet." While she tied her apron, she turned back around and headed down the hallway toward the storage rooms.

I followed her. "They aren't there, either."

"You must have looked in the wrong place. I put them away myself last night." She swung open the cooler's door and looked inside. "Where's our stock? Where'd you put it?"

"The cooler was empty when I got here," I told her.

She shook her head and hurried back out to the display case. "Where are they?"

"That's what I've been trying to tell you," I said.

"What's going on?" Derek asked from across the room. He'd settled into a café chair, sitting with his legs stretched out and crossed at the ankles. Like yesterday, he was dressed from head to toe in utterly forgettable beige.

I jumped at the sight of him. "How in the world did you get in here?"

"The back door." He pointed in that direction. "It was unlocked."

"I left it unlocked?" I didn't remember doing that, but then again, my mind had been on other things.

"The door was unlocked when I came in too, but never mind that." Bertie tossed her hands in the air. "We've been robbed!" She pulled out a key and opened the register. She gasped at what she saw there. "They took all the money too."

"How much are we talking about?" Derek asked as he lurched up from his chair.

"I'd guess nearly a thousand dollars from yesterday's sales," Bertie said as she rushed down the narrow hall to the kitchen. She frantically dug through the pantries. I chased after her.

"This is bad. This is bad," she was saying as she tossed opened one cabinet door after another.

"What? What is bad?" I asked.

"Our supplies are gone."

I peeked over her shoulder into the pantry door she'd pulled open and spotted a few bags of old Halloween candy and nothing else.

"We'll have to reorder everything," she said.

"Which will cost money," I said.

"And we'll have to put a rush on the order."

"Which will cost even more money," I said.

She turned toward me. "It has to be done. We need to start rebuilding our stock for this weekend's festival."

"And the money in the cash register has been stolen. Please tell me Mabel kept a fat bank account for the business."

"It's not exactly fat," she said.

"All accounts will be held up in probate," Derek said as he followed us into the kitchen. "You won't have access to any of it until, well, I'm not sure how long it's going to take to get access to anything, since Edward plans to contest the will."

My heart dropped. I'd failed even before I'd begun.

That's when I noticed the silence. The melangeur should have been grinding away, changing the Amar chocolate beans into something as dark and mysterious as the shadows in the Amazon jungle.

Not only was the grinder silent. Like everything else, it was gone.

"What are we going to do? How can we salvage this?" I asked. Both Bertie and Derek shook their heads.

"We'll have to report the theft to Byrd," Bertie said. She sounded about as excited to talk with the police chief as I did.

"I suppose so," I agreed. "Would you mind calling him? I'm not sure he'd come if I did."

She nodded and left the room to make the call using the business phone next to the cash register.

"I can't understand how this could have happened." I paced the hallway that connected the kitchen to the front of the shop. Derek, far too calm for the situation, followed along like a happy puppy dog. "I replaced that back lock last night precisely so something like this wouldn't happen."

"I wonder who has a key," Derek said as he tapped his cleanly shaven chin.

"No one," I snapped. "I changed the lock."

"And you gave a copy of the key to no one?" Derek leaned toward me as he asked the question. He reminded me of an old-fashioned sleuth with his slow speech and the way he watched me as if searching for answers in my expression.

"Bertie has the only other copy," I said.

"And she wouldn't want the festival to fail . . . or would she?" Derek tapped his chin again.

"I can't imagine what you're talking about." I returned to the kitchen and tossed open the pantry doors again, hoping against hope that this was all a mistake and if I'd only take a second look, I'd find the supplies right where they were supposed to be.

"Think about it. Bertie wants you to keep the shop open . . . forever, right?"

"She wants—"

"Seems a little convenient to me," he said, not giving me the chance to defend her. "I know." He snapped his fingers. "The two of you work night and day to make up for lost time and barely manage to pull off the festival. But by this time, you're completely committed. How can you walk away from the shop after putting in so much work, after using so much of your own money to make the shop and the Sweets on the Beach festival a success?"

"Bertie?" I emphatically shook my head. "You think Bertie would do something like that?"

"Her, or perhaps that sneaky daughter of hers."

That was when I remembered something important, something that blew a huge hole in Derek's theory and ruined any chance of us salvaging the Sweets on the Beach festival. If the robbers had taken everything, that would also mean they'd taken Mabel's special chocolate. No amount of money could get that back.

I raced across the room and found the ancient cask where she stored the rich and wonderful chocolate bars. I lifted the lid.

"It's just as I feared." It felt as if my stomach had crashed onto the floor. "Mabel's chocolate. It's gone too."

Chapter 18

Police Chief Byrd pressed his lips firmly together as he jotted down notes in his casebook. He leaned against the empty display case as if the act of standing on his own caused him too much work.

Even though I let Bertie do all the talking, his angry gaze kept traveling over to me. After he'd listened to her account of the theft, he examined both the front and back locks. He then violently snapped his casebook closed.

"There's no sign of a break-in. Whoever did this must have had a key," he said, echoing Derek's thoughts.

"That's impossible. I changed the locks yesterday afternoon. The only two people who have keys are Bertie and me."

"Did you lock the door?" he asked.

"Yes! I tested it myself."

"I was there. The door was locked when we left for the night," Bertie agreed.

"Then it must have been someone with a key," he repeated.

"We didn't rob the shop." Hysteria was beginning to fizz in my head like champagne bubbles. "We didn't rob our own shop."

He nodded. "I know Bertie wouldn't do anything foolish like that. Yet neither the front lock nor the back lock was jimmied." The look he gave me, like I was something nasty that had gotten stuck to the bottom of his shoe, made me want to squirm. "We didn't have trouble here in Camellia Beach. This was a peaceful town before you and your troublemaking friend came into town, Miss Penn."

"This isn't my fault." I hugged my arms to my chest in an effort to keep my body still and my emotions in check. The fizzing in my head got louder. "I'm not even keeping the shop."

He hooked his thumbs on his belt loops and hitched up his pants as he stepped toward me. His voice deepened. "I don't know what your game is or why you decided to play it here in my town. During these past two weeks, starting with your friend's murder, every bit of trouble in this town has involved you in some way. And I don't like it. I don't like it one bit."

"I don't like it either. I didn't ask for any of this," I protested.

He unlatched a thumb from his belt loop so he could wag his thick finger beneath my nose. "So you say. So you say. Well, missy, let me make this clear so you'll understand it: you don't have to stay in our fair town. In fact, the sooner you leave Camellia Beach, the better."

*   *   *

It wasn't until Chief Byrd had said it himself that the idea hit me like a frying pan to the head. Everything bad that had happened since I'd arrived in Camellia Beach (and even before I'd arrived) revolved around me *and* the chocolate shop. Sure, the police chief had been insinuating that I had somehow brought the trouble with me. I knew that wasn't true. But until that moment, I hadn't thought about Skinny's murder, or the rogue car coming at me, or the attempted break-in, or even Mabel's will as pieces of a larger picture that I couldn't quite get far enough away from to see in its entirety.

Instead, I'd kept trying to cram the pieces into small, simple theories. Mabel's children want the shop? I tried to shove the pieces into there, even though killing Skinny didn't cause Mabel to change her will. Harley had threatened Skinny's life? Then he must have killed him. I tried to shove the pieces of the puzzle there too. But why would he steal Mabel's letter from himself? And why try to run me down with his car? Those were questions that desperately needed to be answered.

Since we didn't have any inventory to sell, I pushed Bertie and Derek out of the shop's front door and locked it behind me. I even turned off the lights so no one would bother me.

I needed to find the larger picture. To help me, I called Granny Mae on her cell phone because, quite simply, she possessed the most logical mind of anyone I'd ever known. It was a little after ten o'clock on a Sunday morning. If she followed her regular Sunday morning schedule, she would be leaving church and walking home with her girlfriends.

I was right. After I briefly explained why I needed her help, she begged off coffee with her friends and then, despite the freezing cold January Wisconsin weather, sat down on a park bench so she could concentrate.

"You're telling me there's now been a robbery, dear? And you don't have any idea who might have stolen both the money and the chocolates or why?" she asked after I told her about what I'd found that morning.

"I have a feeling all this is connected to everything else that has happened, but I can't pull it together."

"Penn, what you need to do is sit down and concentrate on one thing at a time." How she knew I was standing up and pacing I couldn't even guess.

I settled in one of the café chairs and stared at the small, round metal table in front of me. "My mind is spinning. I honestly don't know where to start."

"Have you read the articles I've been sending you?"

"Um . . ." I hadn't. "I keep meaning to."

"Make a point to read the articles. I think they'll help you. I even sent one on how to train unruly dogs."

"Do you mean now? I should hang up and read them now?" I started to panic. I didn't want to read articles about the chocolate industry or dog training or whatever else she'd sent my way. What I wanted to do was sort out the thoughts I already had in my head, not add to them.

"You should read them, and read them carefully, but I can hear in your voice that you're too nervous to concentrate on that right now. So let's look at what we know and expand our knowledge later."

"Yes. Yes. Let's do that." Unfortunately, I still didn't know how to start.

Luckily, Granny Mae did. "That lawyer fellow who the police had arrested, didn't you tell me he'd warned you about how inheritance laws work in South Carolina? Didn't he tell you something about that if something happened to you within five days of the will reading, Mabel's family inherits the shop?"

"You're talking about Harley. He did tell me that. Since I'm not a blood relative, the state law has this weird provision that says if I die by this coming Wednesday, anything I've inherited from Mabel will be split evenly among her legal heirs."

"Wednesday," Granny Mae said thoughtfully. "That doesn't give us much time."

"But why would anyone want to stop me from inheriting now? I've told anyone and everyone that I'm going to sign the shop over to Mabel's family."

Granny Mae seemed to chew on that thought for a moment. "Last night Bertie had the only other key to the shop. And she wants you to carry out Mabel's wishes. Could she have stolen everything in a desperate move to force you to invest in the Chocolate Box? Is she trying to get you to become both financially and emotionally attached to the shop so you'll stay?"

"That's what Derek suggested." I started to tap nervously on the tabletop.

"Derek is Mabel's youngest son?"

"He is." Granny Mae had an impressive memory.

"He's not a reliable source, then. Who else could have broken into the shop?"

"Althea, Bertie's daughter, could have stolen her mother's key and robbed the shop," I said. "Derek suggested her as a suspect when I told him Bertie would never steal from me."

"And again, he's not a reliable source," she said.

"I don't know. He's been a big help. He even came in this morning to lend a hand in getting ready for the festival."

"Why? Why would he do that?"

"He told me he wanted to help with the festival because it was important to his mother."

"Ah-ha!" Granny Mae clapped her hands. "You've caught him in a lie."

"I have?"

"Yes, you have, dear. Don't you see? If he cared that much about what was important to his mother, he would have made her a happy woman and agreed to take over the shop."

"But he said he didn't know how to—"

"It doesn't matter. You don't know how to make chocolates either. But you're trying to fulfill her wishes at least with the festival. So the question is, why is he really hanging around the shop?"

I thought about that for a moment. "I have no idea."

"Could he have broken into the shop last night?"

"He didn't have a key, and there's no sign of a break-in."

Granny Mae fell silent again. She finally asked, "What do we know about Derek other than the fact that he's Mabel's son?"

"Cal told me last night that Derek likes to party."

"Hmm . . . could mean nothing or it could mean everything. What does he do for a living?"

"I don't know."

"Find out."

I nodded.

"You're nodding, aren't you, dear?"

"I sometimes think you can see through phone lines," I said.

"Maybe I can, Penn." She chuckled but quickly grew serious again. "And you're sure neither Bertie nor her daughter would have a reason to rob the shop, not even in a twisted attempt to convince you to stay?"

"The thief took Mabel's special chocolates. It's not something that can be purchased. Without it, and with me making the chocolates, oohhh . . ." I groaned. "What a disaster. Bertie wouldn't do that. Althea wouldn't either, at least I don't think she would."

"You need to talk with Althea."

"I do," I agreed. Despite the fact that her belief in crystals and woo-woo magic made my skin crawl, I needed to find out more about what she knew. I hadn't forgotten how she had hated

196

Skinny and had clearly lied when I'd asked her why she didn't like him.

"I think we've made some progress here, dear. And my fingers are starting to turn blue, so let's wrap up by summarizing what we do know. You received a letter, which you now know was a ruse to lure you to Camellia Beach so she could teach you about the shop. Skinny was killed because he was asking about Mabel and her family."

"He was asking mostly about Carolina, the missing sister," I added.

"Interesting. I think that's an important clue."

"I do too," I said somewhat shakily. "What if—"

Granny Mae didn't let me continue that thought. "The letter Mabel sent you is now missing as well as Skinny's phone, but they found on him a fragment of a letter from a DNA testing company."

"You don't think I could be—?" Was Carolina Maybank my mother?

"Let's stick to facts right now. We can speculate later. So after Skinny is killed, you take the lessons and a few days later inherit the shop."

"According to Harley, I would have inherited whether or not I came to town."

"That's interesting as well," Granny Mae said. "I'll have to think about that for a while. What else do we know?"

"Jody," I said. "Don't forget that she's desperate to buy the building so she can redevelop this part of town into high-rise condos and shops. She told me the other day that she'd already paid someone a large down payment for the land."

"Who did she pay?" Granny Mae asked.

"I don't know. I meant to ask her last night, but then we got all wrapped up in accusing her ex, Harley Dalton, of murdering Skinny. And everything else just kind of, well, got forgotten."

"Understandable, dear. But it sounds as if you don't think he could have done it?"

"He didn't use his car to run me off the road on my first full day in Camellia Beach."

"He has an alibi?" she asked.

"He does. He was with his son at the time, which means someone else must have been driving his noisy sedan. And if someone else had been driving his car to run me off the road, couldn't that same person have also used Harley's car to follow Skinny while he was making that last phone call to me?"

"But didn't Harley have a motive to kill your friend?" Granny Mae asked.

"He did. Half the town heard him threaten to kill Skinny. He won't tell me what the argument had been about. But it clearly has something to do with Skinny's relationship with Jody. Harley has no interest in the chocolate shop, at least none that I can find. So he wouldn't have a reason to be trying to hurt me."

"So you think. I wouldn't cross him off your suspect list yet."

"I'll leave him on but move his name to the bottom," I said. "I can't shake the feeling that everything that's happened is connected to Mabel's shop and her chocolate."

"And your DNA?"

"Yes. And my DNA."

Chapter 19

The DNA discussion got quickly tabled. Beyond the fragment of a letter found on Skinny's body, there was no evidence that I was at all related to the Maybank family. Granny Mae made me promise to read the articles she'd sent and to call again that evening before we disconnected.

I then called my half sister, Tina, who had threatened to hop on the first available plane south if I missed even one of my daily check-ins with her.

I lied beautifully, telling her how I was up to my elbows in chocolate while busily ensuring the upcoming Sweets on the Beach turned into a smashing success. She fell silent for a while, perhaps picking up on the panic I couldn't quite chase away from my voice. After I told her several more times how much work I needed to get done, she reluctantly wished me well and ended the call.

With that accomplished, I went in search for a piece of paper to jot down everything I'd discussed with Granny Mae before I forgot anything. On a shelf underneath the shop's front counter, I found a legal-sized yellow pad and a pen.

I started to make a new list of suspects, along with my thoughts and action plans. I'd barely written more than a few words when I noticed the impression of someone's notes from the previous sheet of paper above it. The writing was bold and had formed deep creases that had transferred to several pages below even the top sheet.

I turned the legal pad this way and that trying to make out what the list said. It looked like a to-do list.

What if Mabel had created a to-do list for the festival? That was definitely something I could use. Time was running out for us. It was already Sunday, and the festival started on Thursday night. Finding a copy of Mabel's festival notes would save us loads of time.

So instead of jotting down notes from my conversation with Granny Mae, I dug around for the eyeliner pencil I kept in my purse. Using the superspy skill every child learns by age six, I lightly rubbed the side of the pencil along the paper to bring the words pressed into the page into view.

At the top of the page, someone had written the date: the day before Mabel's passing. Below it in all caps read, "To Do."

As I'd suspected, the list detailed things to be completed in advance of the festival, such as who needed to be contacted, display tables that needed to come out of storage, and a list of chocolate truffles Mabel planned to make.

She'd also started a shopping list, but it contained only a handful of items, such as caster sugar and pecans.

Below the incomplete shopping list, someone with a light hand and tight-looped, sloping letters had written, "Mabel, you are out of your nitro pills. Refill ASAP."

I placed both my hands on the sales counter as I reread the note on the bottom of the page. Nitro? Nitroglycerin pills? For her heart? I chewed my bottom lip and tried to remember if I'd seen a bottle of nitroglycerin pills in Mabel's bathroom.

Bertie had cleared out Mabel's clothes and belongings from the bedroom, but she'd left the attached bathroom untouched. In the cabinet below the sink, I'd found stacks of towels and assorted cleansing creams. In the medicine cabinet above the sink, I'd found prescription bottles lined up like loyal soldiers. I thought I remembered seeing a glass bottle of nitroglycerin pills. A nearly full bottle.

Had Mabel gotten her new prescription filled before she'd died? I didn't remember seeing a date on the label. And I wasn't sure why it mattered, but the back of my neck tingled.

When Harley had told me that Mabel had died, the first thing I did was to ask him how she'd been murdered. But that had been the wrong question to ask, since she'd died of natural causes. Unless . . .

If Skinny had been killed for what he'd found out about the Chocolate Box, wouldn't it also make sense that Mabel might also be killed for what she knew?

My heart started beating a little faster. Could this be about that fragment of a DNA results letter the investigators had found in Skinny's pocket? DNA results that possibly linked me to Mabel's family?

If a relationship between me and Mabel was proven, killing me by Wednesday would have no effect on the will. Her children wouldn't get the shop. My heirs would. I'd call that a motive for a murder, or perhaps two murders.

After locking up the shop, I jogged back upstairs to the apartment to take a closer look at Mabel's medicine cabinet. The prescription bottles were all still crammed in there. The glass bottle of nitroglycerin, as I'd remembered, was nearly full of pills.

I squinted at the date the prescription had been filled. The bottle was several months old.

And she wasn't out of pills. Not by a long shot. So what did the note scrawled on the bottom of Mabel's to-do list mean?

"Have you managed to pull your thoughts together about what's going on?" Bertie stuck her head in the bathroom to ask. She'd pulled a black cable-knit cardigan sweater on over her purple T-shirt.

"I thought I had," I said. "But then I found this."

I handed her the to-do list I'd uncovered using my eyeliner pencil.

Bertie reached into her cardigan's pocket and pulled out a pair of reading glasses with purple polka-dot frames. She frowned as she read the page. "Yes?"

"Did you write the note at the bottom of the page?" I asked.

Her frown deepened. "Yes? Why?"

"Because of this." I handed Bertie the glass bottle.

She read the label and nodded. "That's Mabel's nitro. She must have gotten it refilled. Sometimes she needs to be reminded, but she's generally good at refilling her prescriptions."

"Look at the date."

Bertie squinted at the bottle again. "That's impossible. Two days ago this bottle was empty. She took the last one on the second day of your cooking class. She told me she'd suffered a slight 'episode.' She'd never admitted to having heart trouble. She'd only say she had episodes." She gave the bottle an angry shake, causing the pills inside to rattle. "This isn't empty."

"No. It's not. Do you think she reused her old bottles?" For Bertie's sake, I hoped the thought tugging at me was wrong. Dead wrong.

"Why would she reuse it? The pharmacy always gave her new ones."

"Because if you noticed she was out of pills and now there are pills in the bottle, that means someone must have refilled it. Did she always keep the bottle here in the medicine cabinet?"

"No. She carried it with her everywhere she went in her purse. She only put it away at night. I don't understand what this could mean."

"I think someone might have tampered with her pill bottle," I said.

Her hand started to shake. "I gave her a pill from this bottle the night she died. It-it didn't alleviate her pain. It didn't help her at all. Despite her objections, I called an ambulance." She shook her head. "It didn't arrive in time. She told me if the pill didn't work, it must mean it was her time. She told me that she was ready to go. But-but what if . . ." Her voice trailed off.

"What if the pills in this bottle weren't nitroglycerin? What if someone put placebos in her bottle to make sure they wouldn't stop a heart attack?" I finished for her.

Bertie squeezed the bottle so tightly I thought it might shatter. Her voice trembled with red-hot rage. "We-we-we-we need to get these tested. We need to find out what's in this bottle."

I nodded. "And we need to call the police . . . again."

*   *   *

"I'm sure it's not what you think it is. I'm sure it's not murder." Detective Frank Gibbons, from the Charleston County Sheriff's Office, wore a crisply pressed suit with a black wool overcoat. His black shoes had been polished until their sheen reflected like a mirror's. He stood nearly a foot taller than the potbellied

Police Chief Byrd, who nodded vigorously at the detective's declaration that Mabel hadn't been murdered.

Both men carried extra weight around the middle. Detective Frank Gibbons actually had more girth. The difference between the two men was that Gibbons knew what to do with the extra weight—like how to buy properly fitting clothes, how to stand up straight instead of slumping down into a puddle of flesh, and how not to use his expansive waistline like an additional appendage to punctuate a point.

"I told them not to bother you." Chief Byrd turned to glare at me. We were all crammed into Mabel's small bathroom. He stood so close, his nose nearly touched mine. "Ms. Penn has been nothing but a bee in my bonnet since the day she's arrived in my quiet town. If I've told her once, I've told her a million times that the case concerning her friend's murder was all but closed. Drugs. Nothing but an unfortunate illegal drug deal gone wrong."

"Skinny didn't use drugs," I said for the millionth time even as Detective Gibbons calmly stated, "The case is nowhere near close to being closed. There are far too many questions here that still need to be answered." His Southern accent produced a deceptively lazy manner of speech, drawing out his vowels as if each held a separate but important meaning. "It'll be a while before I'm satisfied with the current results of our investigation."

"Harley didn't do it," I mumbled.

"What did you say, Ms. Penn?" The detective leaned in closer to me. I pressed myself into the corner next to the shower to get some breathing room. "Who didn't do what?"

"Harley Dalton didn't kill anyone." I'm not sure why I suddenly felt so certain. I mean, just because he had an alibi for the time someone had run me off the road didn't necessarily mean he should be cleared of all wrongdoing. And yet despite the logical evidence to the contrary, in my heart, I believed what I was saying was true.

Maybe I'd changed my mind about him because I was now convinced Mabel had been murdered. And Harley didn't have a motive for wanting her dead. At least none that I could figure out.

"So now you're a detective, Ms. Penn?" Detective Gibbons asked. "And you're conducting your own investigation?"

"No, of course not. I'm simply saying that last night when I called you, I didn't know Harley let others borrow his car. He leaves the keys in it so anyone can take it. Apparently, half the town knows about this and makes use of his generosity."

"That's what I've been telling her all along." Byrd exerted the effort to pull himself to stand a little taller.

"Let the professionals do the detective work, okay, Ms. Penn?" the detective said to me.

"That's also what I've been telling her," Byrd said.

Detective Gibbons held up his large hand to silence his local colleague. "Ms. Penn, I cannot tell you how much I appreciate your willingness to report both the message on your cell phone and this troubling pill bottle. If you hear or learn of anything else, I do expect I will be the first person you contact. I assure you, your concerns will be taken seriously."

"Thank you," I said.

"Detective, you will let us know right away what you find out about those pills, won't you?" Bertie asked.

"I will, ma'am." The detective carefully placed the medicine bottle into a paper bag. "Now if you'll excuse me, I have quite a bit of work to do." He started to leave but paused long enough to turn back toward me. "Please, Ms. Penn, do heed my advice. Stay safe. Let the professionals do their work."

Chapter 20

Since Hodgkin DNA wouldn't give me any information, I decided I needed to perform my own DNA test. But how? That was the question.

After Detective Gibbons had left, Bertie had disappeared into her room and I'd sat myself down on Mabel's bed, feeling stunned.

Someone had killed Mabel? Because of me? Because of my DNA?

If Skinny had been killed because the information reported in the Hodgkin DNA test proved I was related to Mabel through her missing daughter, Carolina, then that would mean one (or more) of Mabel's children was involved in Skinny's murder. It would also, chillingly, mean her children were involved with their mother's murder.

Asking one of her kids to give a DNA sample might put my life at an even greater risk. But at the same time, the more I thought about it, the more I needed to know. Was Carolina Maybank my mother?

"Are you ready?" Bertie called to me from the living room. Stella barked and zoomed around my legs like a blurry black-and-white cloud. I grabbed her leash, figuring I might as well take her with us. She only halfheartedly nipped my finger when I snapped the leash to her collar.

"I'm ready," I said as I emerged from Mabel's bedroom.

Bertie's eyes looked red and teary. This new information about how Mabel might have died had hit her hard, but she nodded in my direction with determination. I linked my arm with hers and gave her a quick hug. We had decided earlier that we needed to head back down to the chocolate shop. If we were going to have any hope of making the first-ever Sweets on the Beach festival a success, we were going to have to get creative—supercreative, considering we didn't have any chocolate.

"I heard what happened," Cal said breathlessly as he jogged up the steps to Mabel's apartment while I fought with getting the key to turn in the apartment door's rusty lock.

He took one look at Bertie, her ashen skin tone and pained expression, and pulled her into a tight hug. "I can't believe it's true. I can't. The police are going to find out what happened. I know it."

I shook my head. "News sure travels lightning fast in this town. Detective Gibbons left no more than a couple of minutes ago."

Cal lifted his head from Bertie's shoulder to tilt his head in my direction. "Detective Gibbons was here? Just now? Why?"

"Because of Mabel's nitro pills, why else?" I answered as I finally managed to wiggle the key from the apartment's lock.

Cal's gaze narrowed. He unwound his arms from around Bertie's middle and took a step toward me. Stella gave a warning growl before starting to bark again. "Nitro pills?" he asked, raising his voice to be heard above Stella's racket. "What are you talking about? I'm talking about the break-in."

"Oh, yes, the break-in," I said and tossed Stella a piece of bacon from my pocket to get her mind off barking. "Or I suppose I should call it a robbery, since the police chief couldn't find any evidence of anyone actually breaking in."

"Nitro pills?" Cal asked again. "What-what are you talking about?"

"Mabel's nitroglycerin pills had been tampered with," Bertie said in a voice so sharp it could cut glass. "That county detective is investigating to determine if she was murdered."

"Murdered?" Cal shook his head. "Mabel? No, not Mabel. That doesn't make a lick of sense."

"Doesn't it?" I asked. "If Skinny knew something about Mabel's will, something that the killer didn't want anyone else to know, wouldn't it make sense that Mabel, who wrote the will, knew this tidbit of information as well? Perhaps that information, whatever it could be, convinced the killer that he needed to silence Mabel too."

He shook his head again. "No. It doesn't make any sense. If she knew anything, she would have said so right off."

"Not necessarily. Not our Mabel," Bertie said as she headed toward the stairs. "She was all about the dramatic reveal. She didn't warn Penn about the will and had asked me not to tell her about it either. She'd said she wanted it to be a happy surprise."

"It was a surprise all right." Just not a happy one.

"Still, it doesn't seem right. Why would Harley want to kill Mabel? He knew what was in the will, and it didn't affect him. Unless he thought he deserved to get the shop," Cal reasoned.

"Why in the world would he think that?" I asked.

Cal shrugged. "How should I know? He lives in the other apartment. Perhaps he thought that gave him some kind of ownership right. Or perhaps he simply needed the money. He needs money, you know? The divorce and moving here cost him more than he could afford."

I tripped over my own feet and tumbled a few steps down the back stairway when I heard that first part. "Harley? He lives in the other apartment?" I'd moved in next door to a potential killer?

No, he wasn't a killer. Despite what his own brother thought about him, I no longer believed Harley could be responsible for Skinny's death.

Bertie seemed to agree. She shook her head. "Harley didn't do this. He couldn't."

"My brother, the boy you once knew, has changed, Miss Bertie," Cal said as he followed us down to the chocolate shop's back door. "Something happened to him during the divorce. He's turned darker and more secretive. It's been worrying me for the past year. I don't think moving back here did him any good."

Once inside the shop, Bertie grabbed the same yellow pad of paper I'd used to uncover Mabel's to-do list. She gave me a hard look and then shifted her gaze to Cal, who was peering into the empty display case. Her brows raised. "I'm going to make a detailed inventory of anything I can find in the kitchen and storerooms. Why don't you talk with Cal?"

She wanted me to talk with Cal? About what? My confusion must have shown clearly on my face.

Bertie moved closer to me and whispered, "I know, despite what that detective said, you're still going to investigate." She gave a gentle nudge in Cal's direction. "So go and do some investigating."

Cal had straightened and was staring at us. "What can I do to help?" he asked.

"You wouldn't happen to have any of Mabel's Amar chocolates squirreled away somewhere," I said, only half joking.

"Is that all?" He flashed one of his devastating smiles, the kind that made my knees feel kind of wobbly. "Actually, I do. Remember I used it to make your hot chocolate yesterday?"

"You have some? Really?" Even a small amount could prove invaluable. "Could we have it for the festival? I'd offer to pay you for it, but the robbery . . ."

"Of course you can have it. And don't worry about payment. I'm relieved there's something I can do to help. Come on." He held out his hand. "I left some at the beach house."

He led me to his dad's old beach house a block off Main Street.

"I know it's not much to look at," Cal said with a slight shake of his head. "The house has been in the family for a couple of generations. My grandfather built it as a summer house. My parents added indoor plumbing, insulation, and a heating and cooling system so they could live at the beach year-round and raise a family in Camellia."

I looked at the newer mansions on either side, with their large windows and cement board siding. They ate up nearly all the space allotted to them. What was left was mostly paved over for parking. Lanky palm trees that didn't look anything like the native Palmettos stood in regimented lines within thin planting strips along the property line.

In contrast, the Daltons' house sat back from the street. Sand dunes rose and fell all around the home. The yard was teeming with tall sea grasses and random clumps of palmettos that leaned this way and that. Orange and yellow wild flowers bloomed despite

the cold weather. There was something stunningly beautiful about the wildness of the yard and the understated white
board-and-batten cottage. An oak tree that had to be at least
one hundred years old hid half of the house behind its twisting
trunk. But I could clearly see the home's wide front porch, with
its weathered, unpainted boards. It called out for someone to
linger in one of the rocking chairs that were scattered about.

"I don't know," I said while practically running up the steps
of the welcoming porch. "I think it's lovely."

"Really? You think so? If I had complete control of this
place, I'd tear it down and let Jody build one of her company's
stock beach houses."

"Like next door?" I asked.

"Yeah. Nice, aren't they? So modern and spacious. But Harley is part owner, and he doesn't want anything to change. Ever."

My gaze traveled back to the large homes dwarfing the Daltons' home and tried to picture an island filled with houses and
condos that were too big for their modestly sized lots.

The buildings in town would be sleek and modern instead
of the aging shacks that currently populated the island. But that
kind of progress would also wipe out the forest of ancient oaks
with their wind-sculpted limbs and the wild palmettos that had
grown where nature had planted them, many in thick clumps.
Worse, those darling orange and yellow flowers that bloomed
despite the cold would probably be deemed weeds and pulled.

Had I, as the president of the business association had
warned, started to fall in love with the island as it was?

I shivered at that thought. "Let's get that chocolate of yours,"
I said.

Cal led me inside the cottage. Dark pine paneling domi-
nated every room. An African mask frowned at me from the

living room wall. Exotic wooden statues stood in proud poses on side tables. A colorful tapestry hung on the wall leading to a dark hallway.

I ran my hand over the head of one of the statues. "This isn't the kind of decor I'd expect to find in a beach house."

He lifted the figurine I'd been caressing and placed it on the fireplace mantel. "It's just junk I brought back from my business travels."

"Junk?" None of it looked like junk. They weren't the plastic, touristy gewgaws my first stepmother used to bring back from her overseas trips. "It looks like authentic African artwork."

Cal shrugged. "Don't know why I bought any of it. Hell, I don't remember buying even half of it."

"You don't seem like an impulse shopper," I said.

He laughed. "We all have our faults."

Despite the eclectic decor and well-worn furniture, I liked the house. It felt cozy. "Why doesn't Harley live here?"

Cal just looked around, as if that was answer enough.

"But if he doesn't want to let you tear it down, he must like the place," I said as I followed him into a kitchen that looked like it hadn't been renovated since the 1970s. "You'd think he'd want to live and raise his son here, where he grew up."

"You'd have to ask him," Cal said with a shrug. "Ah, here's the chocolate."

I couldn't believe my eyes. Cal opened a cardboard box lined with parchment paper. Lying inside the box were nearly as many chocolate bars as had been stolen from the Chocolate Box.

Chapter 21

"This is the Amar chocolate? Mabel's superspecial chocolate?" My voice quivered. This couldn't be her chocolate. Not this much. She'd said over and over again how precious it was, how rare. Why would she give so much of it to Cal?

"You tell me." A playful smile creased his lips. He handed me the box. "Take a whiff."

I breathed in the chocolate bars' deep, earthy aroma. A touch of espresso scent teased my senses. "This is it!"

In my excitement, I nearly dropped the box. Cal lifted it from my hands. "It is," he said.

"But how? Why? Why did she give you so much of her special chocolate?"

His smile grew a little wider. "Because she liked me."

"She must have liked you a whole bunch," I said.

"Almost as much as I think I like you," he said and kissed me.

I kissed him back, not because I felt anything special toward him, although I supposed I might one day develop an attraction for the younger Dalton brother. He was certainly easy on the eyes, and his hording of Mabel's chocolates may have saved the Sweets on the Beach festival. From what I'd learned from the other business owners who were helping with organizing the events, without Mabel's chocolates, there really wasn't much of a festival.

When we broke apart, Cal apologized. "I shouldn't have done that."

"Um, um . . . probably not," was my brilliant reply. But honestly, after what had happened with the Cheese King and with all the other disastrous relationships before him, I wasn't ready to get involved with anyone, not even someone who looked like the hero from a blockbuster action movie.

The walk back from his family's beach house started out silent and awkward. At least I felt awkward. He seemed his usual unflappable self, the kind of guy who was always comfortable in his own skin. Finally, he looked at me and asked, "I suppose you're investigating the break-in, your friend's death, and now Mabel's death?"

"I suppose I am," I said gloomily. It wasn't something I wanted to talk about. "And I'm trying to figure out how to pull together the Chocolate Box's booth for the festival with absolutely no budget. At least we have chocolate, thanks to you."

"Do you think they might be connected? The break-in and the murders, I mean?"

"Who knows?" Wanting to change the direction of the conversation, I asked him, "Do you know what kind of work Derek does?"

Cal looked at me and smirked.

"What?" I asked.

"'Derek' and 'work' are two words one never hears in the same sentence. He might be old, but he still acts like a trust-fund baby. He flunked out of law school and then out of business school.

Even though he lives in a bachelor's apartment in Charleston, he spends most of his time warming barstools out here in Camellia Beach."

"So his inheritance provided him with enough money to support that kind of lifestyle? Must be nice."

Cal shook his head. "I think he ran through his inheritance years ago. He's constantly hitting up anyone he can find for a loan. Since you're new around here, I'm sure you'll be next."

"Really?" That put Derek's admonition about how money corrupts into a new light. Instead of warning me to take care around money, perhaps he was—in his own twisted way—confessing to the horrible things he'd done to feed his own lust for money.

If Skinny had found a way to prove I was Carolina's long-lost child, Derek wouldn't inherit the obscene amount of money his mother had left for Carolina. If she couldn't be found, Derek and the rest of his siblings would get the money, which would be a strong motive for murder.

But, dang it, he had an alibi. He'd been slamming drinks with Cal the night Skinny had been killed.

"After you give the shop back to Mabel's family," Cal said as if choosing his words very carefully, "what are you going to do with Cabruca?"

"Cabruca? You mean Mabel's cat? Um, Bertie's keeping him."

"Not Troubadour. Cabruca is the South American village where the Amar chocolates are grown exclusively for the shop, remember?"

"Oh, right. I honestly hadn't thought about the village," it embarrassed me to admit.

Mabel, and her father and grandfather before her, had supported the villagers, making sure they were paid a fair wage for the chocolate they produced. She even went without luxuries a woman in her position could afford so she could build the village a new school.

Obviously, Mabel had been interested in my money. And my father's money. She'd picked me to carry on her legacy because my family had the means to support a Brazilian village located deep in the Amazon rainforest.

Of course I could do that kind of charity work from anywhere, as long as I could convince my grandmother to give me greater access to my trust fund.

"If you'd like, I might be able to use my contacts through my business to try to sell the chocolate contract," Cal said slowly. "The right company would be able to not only bring modern conveniences to the town, but it could also help the village increase production of their rare chocolate bean."

"That's very generous of you," I said as we approached the shop. "After we survive the Sweets on the Beach festival, I'll have to give it some serious thought."

I hugged the box of chocolates to my chest. "Thank you for this. And for everything. Bertie will be thrilled too," I said as I jogged up the steps to the Chocolate Box, eager to tell Bertie that we'd be able to make at least part of the chocolates on the festival menu.

Cal didn't come with me. And when I turned to look for him, he was gone.

I wasn't sure how I felt about that.

*   *   *

Bertie was happy to see the chocolate, though equally confused about why Mabel would have given Cal so much. "She tended to hoard it, rarely using much in our chocolate recipes," she said,

216

frowning at the chocolates stacked within the cardboard box. "That was one thing that was going to be so special about the festival. For the first time, she planned to make several of her 100 percent Amar chocolate recipes to offer for sale to the general public. It's not something she'd hand out to anyone."

"Maybe she was grateful to Cal for visiting the Cabruca village and bringing news of the school's progress?" I suggested.

"Or maybe he stole it," Harley said as he emerged from one of the back rooms.

I shook my head. "You Dalton boys sure are quick to accuse each other of wrongdoing. What are you doing here?"

"Bertie asked for my help with inventory." He crossed his arms over his chest and stared at me as if daring me to kick him out.

I merely asked, "Don't you have a law firm to run?"

"It's Sunday. And"—he cleared his throat—"considering what you found this morning . . . you know . . . with the pills, I thought Bertie shouldn't be alone."

"She wasn't alone."

"You weren't here," he countered, his arms still crossed.

I crossed my own arms and took a step toward him. "I'm here now."

He took a step toward me. "Are you telling me to leave? Will you call the cops if I don't?"

"Children, children!" Bertie clapped her hands. "I don't have the energy for your bickering. So, please, let's get back to work. We have too much to do and not enough time already."

"Yes, ma'am," Harley said.

"You don't really think Cal stole this chocolate?" I asked.

"I don't know what to think," was all Bertie would say.

As we worked, I asked Harley why he didn't live in his family's beach house.

"Because of Jody," he said as he stirred a pot of melting chocolates.

"Jody?" That didn't make sense.

He nodded. "If she thought I had control over the beach house, I'd be back in court with her suing me for half its worth in a skinny minute. I don't have the cash to pay her for half, so the lawsuit would force me to sell it."

"To her development company?"

He nodded.

I wasn't sure if I believed that.

"That Jody woman has tried to get her greedy hands on it before," Bertie said as she poured heavy cream into the pot Harley was stirring. "Our boy has kept ownership of the house in his father's estate so she can't touch it."

"Something like that," Harley said. "Bottom line—if I live there, it causes trouble. So I let it stay empty."

"Cal stays there," I said.

"Sometimes . . . when he's in town."

"Which isn't often," Bertie added.

Since none of that seemed pertinent to the murders, I decided to ask them about Derek and his finances. Harley didn't have much to say about Mabel's youngest son, and Bertie was like a hurricane focused only on pulling together enough basic ingredients to start making chocolate truffles by the afternoon. Neither provided me with any new information.

Harley left around three that afternoon, which was probably a good thing. Bertie and I were mixing up a batch of the hazelnut chocolate truffles Mabel had taught me to make when Jody knocked on the shop's door.

I wiped my hands on a towel before letting her in.

"I was hoping we could talk," she said, "about the Chocolate Box's future."

"I'm not keeping the shop, remember?" I said.

"Just hear me out," she said. "Please."

I invited her to sit down at a café table and poured her a cup of coffee from the pot Bertie and I had been refilling throughout the day.

She took a sip of the coffee before whispering, "I'm in a terrible fix."

"How so?" I whispered back.

"Remember I told you I'd already made a large down payment on this building?"

I nodded.

"Edward claims that since he wasn't a party to the deal, I'm going to have to renegotiate after you sign the land over to him and his siblings. And even then, he said he can't promise they'd sell to my company. He went on and on about the highest bidder and that another company has already talked with him about purchasing the shop."

"Really?" I sat back and steepled my fingers. "But didn't you tell me you'd already made an agreement with Mabel? Do you have anything in writing to prove it?"

She stared into her coffee mug as if it held the answer. "Not exactly," she finally said. "Derek had assured me he was acting as his mother's financial agent. Since he was always hanging around the shop and sometimes working the cash register, I believed him. I signed the agreement with him. I gave the deposit check to him."

"Derek?"

She gave me a miserable look. "He can be very persuasive."

"But he had no authority to sell the shop."

She shook her head. "Edward made that crystal clear when I met with him. He told me his younger brother couldn't be trusted with any amount of money."

Even his own brother distrusted him with money? That would give him one more motive to make sure no one found the DNA report Skinny had with him the night of his death—that is, if the report proved I was Mabel's granddaughter. But Derek couldn't have killed Skinny. He had an alibi the night of his murder.

Didn't he?

Jody should know. "The night of Skinny's murder, were Derek and Cal hanging out together the entire time?"

She jerked back, apparently surprised by my sudden change of topic. "What does this have to do with the sale of the Chocolate Box?"

I leaned forward. "It could have everything to do with it." Not exactly a lie, but also not exactly the truth.

Nodding gravely, she closed her eyes. "They started out the evening together. But then, later, I spotted Cal sitting in a corner of the bar all by himself." She opened her eyes and frowned. "I can't see what this has to do with me. How does it help solve my problem?"

"Um . . ." I didn't have an answer to that.

Derek's alibi had just fallen apart. He had a strong motive to silence Skinny if the Hodgkin DNA report said what I suspected it said. Derek had said it himself—the possession of money led to an insatiable need for it, especially when it was gone. Had that been a confession?

He needed money, and someone had robbed the Chocolate Box. He was there when we'd left to buy a replacement lock for the broken back door. Heck, we'd left him standing there at the back door as we'd headed to the hardware store. It would have been a simple thing for him to walk back in and empty out the cash register and the pantries. Which would mean I'd put a lock on an empty shop.

While I understood why he'd steal the money, why did he also take the chocolates and the supplies? Was he trying to encourage me to give up and leave town?

Oh, heck, the reason really didn't matter. I needed to get this information to Detective Gibbons, but Jody remained planted in her chair, glaring at me.

"What do you want me to do?" I asked.

"I want you to sell the shop to me instead of signing it over to Mabel's family. I'll give you a good deal."

Mabel's smiling face popped into my mind. She'd given me the shop because she'd thought—hoped—I'd preserve what her family had built. Because I was part of her family? Maybe. "What are you going to do with the building? Are you going to renovate it?" I asked, hoping she'd save it.

It was, after all, more than a hundred years old.

"Renovate it? This place?" She barked a laugh that was so loud it brought Bertie hurrying out from the kitchen. "The only renovating I'd do in this place would involve a bulldozer."

Sure, I'd thought that myself. Many times. But hearing Jody say it sounded horribly wrong. I thought about the newer houses on the beachfront that her company had built and how out of place they looked on this wild beach island. "But what about the building's historic value?"

That only made her laugh harder. "Not everything old has historical value. If we never tore down existing buildings, we'd run out of places to build new ones. You wouldn't want to expand out into the natural areas of the island. If we're going to preserve nature, we're going to have to focus on redeveloping the existing areas."

That made sense. But still, this was Mabel's heritage we were talking about. She had loved this place and had resisted selling it to anyone, especially to Jody and her bulldozer.

"If you look at the other beach islands in the area," Jody said, "you'll find million-dollar houses and upscale boutiques. There's no reason in the world why Camellia Beach shouldn't enjoy the same riches. It's colonialism at its worst at work here. The rich, like Mabel and her ancestors, come in and keep progress from happening in order to preserve the 'way of life' of the natives. But what they're really saying is that they don't want those 'natives' to enjoy the same economic progress that they do."

"Let me think about it," I said as I rose from the table. I had more important things to do, like call Detective Gibbons.

"Don't wait too long to do the right thing," she argued. At least she'd followed my lead and stood as well.

"I'll give you an answer after the festival."

"You do that." With an angry snap of her head, she stomped out of the shop and slammed the door closed behind her, which was surprising, since the door had one of those gadgets on it that forced it to close slowly.

"What in blazes was that Jody girl doing here?" Bertie asked as she wiped her hands on a towel.

I shook my head. "I think she just helped me solve a murder—I mean, two murders."

Chapter 22

I immediately called the number on Detective Gibbons's card and got his voice mail. In one long, excited sentence, I told him everything I had learned about Derek and asked him to call me immediately.

So Derek had killed Skinny. And even more disturbingly, if test results came back positive, he may have also killed his own mother. And he'd done it all because of money.

I checked the time on my phone. How long was I going to have to wait before Detective Gibbons returned my call? Unable to get anything productive done in the shop, I grabbed the shopping list Bertie had helped make and headed to the island's only grocery store to pick up some of the essentials while we waited for a rush order from the shop's wholesale distributer to arrive.

Bunky's Corner Pantry wasn't the brightly lit, abundantly stocked supermarket I was used to. It looked more like a hole-in-the-wall convenience store. My knee-jerk response had been to turn up my nose at the store and leave. This place was just another symbol of Camellia Beach's decay. The community couldn't even support a decent grocery store. I'd simply have to find a ride to a chain supermarket on nearby James Island.

I was in the process of returning the miniature shopping cart back to its corral when I spotted a framed picture hanging next to the banana display. The black-and-white photo was of the store during what must have been the town's heyday. A half-dozen ridiculously large cars were parked out front. All but one of the cars had at least one long surfboard strapped to its roof. A pair of teenaged surfers with their arms thrown over each other's shoulder's had tossed their heads back and laughed just as the cameraman captured the moment.

Someone had used a permanent marker to boldly handwrite on the photo, "Bunky's, family owned and operated in Camellia since 1948."

The island's history lived and breathed within these walls. I drew a deep breath of my own and remembered the comparison between the newer beachfront houses and the humble but welcoming home the Dalton brothers owned together. If you had asked me a few days ago which house I would have preferred to stay in, I would have picked one of the newer mansions.

But the more time I spent in this town, with residents who were doggedly set in their ways, the more I was starting to see things with a new set of eyes. Bigger and newer didn't always mean better.

Sure, shopping for supplies might be easier in a sleek supermarket. But how often would I get a chance to shop in an authentic family-run corner grocery store? Did these even still exist?

Feeling as if I'd stepped back in time, I started searching the crammed shelves for the items on my shopping list.

I'd rounded what appeared to be the nuts and chips aisle when I spotted Harley pushing a half-full shopping cart toward me. The same young boy I had seen with Jody when I'd first visited the Chocolate Box was walking alongside him. The boy grabbed an oversized bag of chips and tossed it into the cart. Harley said something—I was too far away to hear him—before he returned the bag of chips to the shelf.

That boy must be Harley's son, I thought to myself. I found myself watching the two together.

Harley bent down to listen to what his son, Gavin, was saying. His son pouted about not getting to buy the bag of chips he'd wanted, but it didn't look as if he was going to throw a tantrum like any one of my younger siblings sometimes still did whenever they didn't get their way. Father and son must have been negotiating, because a few moments later, Harley plucked a bag of baked chips from the shelf and handed it to his son. The boy smiled before dropping the slightly healthier version into the shopping cart.

As they continued to banter back and forth, it struck me how Gavin looked nothing like his father. His nose was slightly pudgy. And when he smiled, his cheeks made a cute pair of dimples.

I was amazed how a child could resemble one parent and not the other. And I suppose some children could look like neither parent. Gavin's face had neither Jody's sharp edges nor his father's square features. Perhaps the boy still needed to grow into them.

I was still shamelessly watching father and son when Gavin wrinkled his nose and jutted out his chin in an act of stubborn willfulness.

All of a sudden, it felt as if the bottom had fallen out of my world. I abandoned the shopping cart and hurried out of the store.

Oh, no. No, no, no. It couldn't be true. It couldn't.

I leaned against the grocery store's painted brick wall and forced myself to take several slow, deep breaths. But no matter how many deep breaths I took, I couldn't stop my mind from putting two and two together and coming up with four.

I needed to make sure what I suspected was true. And I knew just the person who could tell me.

* * *

Early the next morning—a bright and sunny Monday—I carried two mugs of hot chocolate from Mabel's small kitchen into the living room, where Althea had already made herself at home on the comfortable sofa. I chose the armchair across from her. Stella barked at Althea until I tossed her a bit of the bacon Bertie had set aside in the fridge.

"I'm pleased you called me," Althea said after she took a slow sip of her drink. Bertie had already made her way down to the Chocolate Box to sort out the supplies I'd purchased yesterday. "I do want to be your friend. What is it you want to talk about?"

"Skinny McGee," I said. My hot chocolate remained untouched.

She set her mug on the coffee table next to mine. Tension creased the skin between her brows. "He was your friend," she said with care.

I nodded. "You've said more than once that Skinny had come into town to stir up trouble. I need to know what you meant by that."

"I don't—"

"Harley won't tell me what had him so upset that he would threaten Skinny's life. It can't be Skinny's relationship with Jody that stirred him up. It can't be because he saw Jody with Skinny

226

at the Low Tide the night of his death. I've been around Harley enough to know he wouldn't go back to Jody even if she begged him. So it has to be something else that Skinny had threatened—something else Harley cares about deeply."

"Even if this was true, why are you asking me?" Her large brown eyes seemed to plead with me to let the matter drop.

I leaned forward. "I'm asking because you are close to Harley."

"We're just friends," she said quickly.

"Are you just friends? Or are you still in love with him?"

She smiled sadly. "I do love him, but not romantically. Not anymore. We've been friends since forever. He's always been my rock through difficult times. And I try to be the same for him."

"So he trusts you? He talks with you?"

"Penn, I don't—"

"I need to know what he told you. I need to know why he threatened to kill Skinny."

She pressed her lips together and turned her head away with such speed the brass mandala pendants hanging around her neck clanged an unhappy tune.

"Please, Althea. I need to know the truth."

"I can't." She leaned her head against the sofa's cushions and closed her eyes. Was it a signal that she wouldn't help me?

I was about to give up on getting the information out of her when she whispered, "It would kill Harley if it got out."

"It's about the DNA test, isn't it?" I prayed she'd say no.

Her eyes flew open. "You already know?"

I shook my head. "I know the police found a fragment of a letter from a DNA testing company in Skinny's pocket. I had hoped it had something to do with me. But it isn't about me. Please, tell me. What was in that letter?"

"Oh, no. Oh, no. The police have the letter? Then that means they're already in contact with the testing company. No, no, no. It's motive. Don't you see? It's a damned good motive for murder."

"Which is why Harley threatened to kill Skinny?" I grabbed both her hands in mine. "You have to tell me what you know."

"Harley's not Gavin's father." Her quiet, whispering voice trembled ever so slightly. "Skinny is."

"Skinny was a father?"

Although I'd suspected it, the truth crashed into my chest like a powerful tidal wave. I covered my mouth with my hand and sat back in the chair. Yes, the armchair was still underneath me, even though it felt as if someone had yanked it away and I was falling.

I had hoped I had found my mother. I had hoped I'd found a loving grandmother who'd reached out to me because she'd wanted to share her legacy. But that wasn't what had happened. Instead, I'd simply been the dupe in yet another con.

My cell phone rang. Hands shaking, I pulled the phone out of my pocket. I started to send whoever was calling to voice mail. But the caller ID stopped me.

"Detective Gibbons," I said as I answered the call.

"You can't tell him," Althea whispered. "You can't tell anyone."

"Don't worry," I mouthed before saying to the detective, "Thank you for returning my call. I have some important information—"

"*Please*," Althea hissed.

"Ms. Penn, I just got off the phone with the police lab, and I'd promised both you and Bertie Bays that I'd let you know what we learned right away," Gibbons said, not giving me a chance to talk. "We don't usually get results back this fast. Actually, we never do. But our lab tech smelled the powder inside the pills we took from Mabel's medicine chest and recognized it right away."

"What was in the pills?" I asked.

"Chocolate."

Chapter 23

"I'm sorry to tell you this." Detective Gibbons spoke slowly, his voice grave. "I've opened a new case file to investigate Mabel Maybank's suspicious death."

I drew a deep breath. "You're saying she was murdered?"

"We're not ready to say that, but her death is definitely going to be investigated further." He then explained what needed to happen next. He would need to formally interview both myself and Bertie. He also mentioned that he'd need to question Althea and anyone else who was around the chocolate shop in the days leading up to her death.

"Well, I have a suspect you need to question regarding her death," I blurted out.

"No!" Althea cried. "He's my friend. I know he didn't kill anyone."

"I won't—" I tried to tell Althea that I wasn't planning to tell Gibbons the secret she'd shared with me. But she wouldn't listen.

"Don't you understand? Talking about it will only hurt Gavin."

"I'm not telling him!" I shouted, which caused Stella to start barking again.

"Hello? Hello?" Detective Gibbons's voice boomed. "Is everything okay over there?"

I jumped up from the chair, which got Stella barking even louder. Between my dog and Althea, I could barely hear the detective. "Wait a minute," I shouted into the phone.

Hoping to get a little peace and quiet, I closed myself into Mabel's bathroom. Stella continued to bark as she scratched at the door.

With one finger pressed against my ear and crouching down on the toilet seat, I said, "Sorry about that."

Detective Gibbons was quiet for a moment before asking, his voice slow and careful, "Are you safe?"

I nodded and then remembered that only Granny Mae had the ability to guess I was nodding when on the phone.

"I'm safe. I think."

"You're not investigating, are you?"

"No, not really. I'm just—"

"I hope I don't have to remind you that there's a killer who may have murdered two people close to you in the last couple of weeks. You need to be careful."

"No, sir, you don't have to remind me. But I did discover something interesting when talking with the residents about the upcoming festival."

I told him all about the break-in, even though he'd already heard about it that morning from the police chief. I then told him everything I'd heard from both Cal and Jody about Derek Maybank's problems with debt and how I suspected he'd robbed the shop to both discourage me and get his hands on the large amount of money we'd left in the cash register when we'd closed the shop the previous day.

Detective Gibbons made small grunting noises as he listened. I could hear a pencil scribbling in his notebook. Since it seemed like he was taking me seriously, I also told him about the hole in Derek's alibi. On the night of Skinny's death, he hadn't been with Cal the entire night as everyone had believed.

My heart started to thump against my chest. "He needs money. He's told me that himself. I think he killed Skinny and Mabel. I think it had something to do with that fragment of the letter from Hodgkin—"

But the information I'd thought I'd find in that letter—my missing mother and a connection to Mabel—wasn't true. It wasn't true.

If what Althea said proved true, that letter established that Skinny was Gavin's father, which would make Harley the prime suspect again.

"Penn? Are you still there?" Detective Gibbons called out to me. His sharp voice startled me.

"Yes. Yes, I'm here." I drew a deep breath. "Have you been able to follow up on the letter from the DNA company you found on Skinny's body?"

He was quiet for a long time. "You shouldn't know about that," he said.

"Then you should tell Camellia Beach's police chief not to shove confidential reports under my nose."

Gibbons growled. "That man is a . . ."

"Yes?"

"A thorn. Do me a favor and forget you saw any of that, okay?"

"Sorry, I can't do that. Were you able to get a copy of the letter from the genetic testing company? I tried, but they wouldn't give me the time of day."

"Nor should they. You're not a cop. They have to respect privacy laws." Papers rustled on his desk. "Look, I can tell you we've sent a search warrant to the company. We should have a copy of what they had sent to Skinny McGee by the end of the day tomorrow."

"So you think the information you're going to get from the DNA company will provide you with a motive for Skinny's murder? Is that why the rest of the letter is missing?"

"I don't know, Penn. We are following up on several leads, including the ones you've provided for us." He heaved a deep sigh. "If some of these last pieces of evidence pan out, I hope to make an arrest by the end of the week."

"It sounds like you know who that might be."

"I can't discuss—"

"I know, I know. I'm just saying that it sounds as if you're homing in on one suspect."

"We might be. Thank you for letting me know about Derek Maybank's money trouble. I'll pass that information on to Chief Byrd. I'm sure he'll want to question Mr. Maybank in connection with your recent break-in."

I started to ask another question, but Gibbons didn't give me the chance. "Call me if you hear anything else," he said, his voice beating sharply against my ear. "And, Penn, stop playing detective. It'll only get you hurt."

* * *

Althea fell uncharacteristically silent after I told her what the county police detective had told me. Mabel's nitroglycerin pills had been replaced with chocolate-filled placebos. But what really hit her hard was learning that the detective was also in the process of getting a copy of the DNA report they'd found on Skinny's body.

"That's it, then," she said as she sank back down on the sofa. "That's it. Everyone in town is going to know Harley is not Gavin's father. Can you imagine what that'll do to that sweet little boy? Not to mention that Harley will likely go to jail for a crime he didn't commit."

I returned to the chair I'd been sitting in and finally took a sip of my now-chilled hot chocolate. "Are you sure Harley is innocent? I mean, I know you're his friend, but you have to face facts. He has a pretty strong motive for the murder. He was trying to protect his son. He even publically threatened to kill Skinny."

"Harley might threaten someone in the heat of anger, especially if Gavin was in danger. But hurt someone? Never. I'm sure he wouldn't."

"Not even to protect his son?"

Her frown deepened as she seemed to ponder that question. "What about Mabel?" she suddenly blurted out. "Why would he kill Mabel?"

"There might be two murderers running loose in your perfect little beach town." But even as I said it, I didn't believe it. What were the chances that two separate murderers would both use chocolate to kill their victims?

It had to be the same person.

Was it Harley?

As Althea had already pointed out, why would he kill Mabel? Unless . . . did she know about Skinny's relationship to Gavin? It could be a motive.

And what about Derek? I'd been banking on that DNA letter being about me. With that off the table, Mabel's son really didn't have much of a reason to kill Skinny.

So who else was there?

Jody? She had a motive—two motives, really. If she, like many of the others in the surfing community, didn't know about Skinny's riches, she would resent Skinny popping in from nowhere and telling people Gavin was his son. Had he threatened to sue for custody? Such a move might have sent Jody, who needed to be the one in control, over the proverbial cliff.

She also desperately needed Mabel to sell the shop to her development company, since she needed that land in order to start construction on their expensive condos and high-end shops.

Did she have an alibi? I couldn't remember if I'd even asked her about one. She'd been so eager to tell me what everyone else was doing at the time of Skinny's murder that she'd completely deflected my attentions whenever they'd focused on her.

I swallowed the rest of my not-so-hot chocolate in one gulp and jumped up from my chair. Stella started running around my legs, barking. Since she hadn't been outside for a while, I snapped the leash to her collar.

"I'm sorry to run off like this, Althea, but I just remembered something I need to do."

"What?" She jumped up from her chair as well. "I can tell by that look in your eyes that you've thought of something, something important. What is it, Penn? Where are you going?"

With Stella at my side, I hurried across the room to put the hot chocolate mug in the kitchen sink and grab my purse. I swung open the door. "I have to go talk with a lawyer."

"Which one? Harley or Edward?"

I groaned. "Probably both."

"Penn"—Althea rushed across the room so she could cradle my hands in hers—"thank you."

I slid my hands free. "For what?"

"For not telling that detective what I told you just now."

I clasped my hands behind my back so she wouldn't be tempted to grab them again. "I don't know why you're thanking me. He's going to find out about it soon enough."

"Yes, but *you* didn't tell him. Which means you bought us some time to figure out what really happened that night. So thank you."

Chapter 24

Miss Bunny shook her head. The movement made her blue beehive jiggle. "Harleston isn't available. Won't be available for the rest of the day."

I could hear the low rumble of his voice coming from his adjoining office. "But he's here. Could you at least tell him that I need to talk with him? Please? I'm willing to wait."

To prove my determination, I planted myself on the waiting room's Naugahyde sofa and crossed my arms over my chest. Stella, acting surprisingly tame, plopped down at my feet and wagged her tail at the older lady.

Miss Bunny's beehive hairdo did another little dance as she had a quiet discussion with herself about what she should do about me. Her matching blue eyebrows scrunched together when she looked up and glared in my direction.

I smiled.

With a huff, she rose from her desk and tapped on Harley's office door. She'd knocked so lightly, Stella didn't even lift her head from where she'd laid it on her paws.

"See?" Miss Bunny whispered. "He's too busy to talk to anyone. Even me."

"I can wait," I answered loudly. Miss Bunny glared again.

Inside the office, Harley's low rumble came to a halt. After a short pause, it started up again, but only briefly before the door swung open.

Miss Bunny suddenly found herself standing nose to nose with her employer. "I tried to tell her that you're too busy to see anyone," she protested.

He rose up on his toes and craned to one side so he could see over Miss Bunny's shoulder.

"Penn?" Half his face smiled, while the other half frowned as if he wasn't sure if he was glad to see me or not. I supposed I deserved that reaction, considering how I'd been the reason Detective Gibbons had picked him up for questioning in the middle of the night. "What are you doing here?"

"I told her you didn't have time to meet with anyone today," Miss Bunny repeated, louder this time.

"It's okay, Miss Bunny." He stepped around his bulldog of a secretary, patting her shoulder as he did so. He stopped several feet from the sofa where I was seated, remaining well out of hitting (and biting) range. "I can spare a few minutes. Is this about the will?"

"Maybe," I answered as I rose from the sofa. I glared back at Miss Bunny, who was still giving me a wickedly sharp stink eye. Stella jumped to her feet and started barking at him. "Can we talk in your office?"

He gave Stella a hard look before finally saying, "Of course, of course." He stepped back, giving me plenty of space as he motioned for Stella and me to precede him into his office. "Please, have a seat," he said as he closed the office door behind him.

I couldn't sit down, not now that I was finally in Harley's office, having a face-to-face conversation with him. My body hummed with energy. I felt as if I was this close, and I mean *this* close, to solving Skinny's murder. I simply needed to get a few things straight in my mind. With Stella's leash hooked around my wrist, I laced my fingers behind my back and started to pace. My pup followed along. Her long, silky fur flowed gracefully around her, making her resemble a white cloud sailing around the room.

"I just had an interesting conversation with Althea," I said. "The two of you are close. You share almost everything with her, don't you?"

He shrugged. "I've known her since grade school."

"And you secretly dated her when she was in high school," I added. I turned and paced in the other direction.

He dragged a hand through his already unruly hair. "She shouldn't have told you that."

"Her mother told me. Apparently, she knew all along that the two of you were sneaking around."

"She did? She knew? Bertie knew? In all my born days, I don't know how I'm going to be able to face her again."

I nodded, which made him grimace. "That tears it. I am not going to be able to face Bertie again. I'm going to have to move. Thank you for coming here to tell me. If you'll excuse me, I have some packing to do."

I wasn't sure if he was being serious or not. He looked serious, but he didn't open his office door. Instead, he went over to his desk chair. "Please, Penn, have a seat," he said. "My mama raised me to remain standing until the lady is seated. And I have to confess, I'm operating on very few hours of sleep. If I don't sit down right now, I am going to fall over."

Now that he'd mentioned it, I noticed how he was listing alarmingly to the right. So I did him a kindness and sat my anxious body in the wooden guest chair directly across from his desk. As soon as I did so, he dropped into his own chair and heaved a long, exhausted sigh. "Thank you. Now tell me why you're really here."

Stella clearly wanted to continue pacing. She tugged on her leash and made such distressing choking sounds, I set her loose in the office.

Harley lifted his legs. He frowned as he watched my tiny beastie running around near his toes, which was silly. His well-shod toes were safe within his leather loafers. After a few tense moments, in which he watched Stella while clearly holding his breath, he shrugged and turned his attention back to me.

Stella, on the other hand, ignored both of us. She was much more interested in licking the office's ancient carpeting.

Not sure how to broach a subject Harley had been so keen on not discussing, I decided the ripping-off-a-bandage method was the way to go. So I sat back in the chair, drew a deep breath, and said, "I know why you threatened Skinny the night of his murder."

He gave me a patronizing look. "You mean you think you know."

Obviously the bandage had failed to come off. So I tried again. "You didn't want Skinny telling everyone that Gavin is actually his son. You didn't like that he was waving a DNA report around."

He jerked back as if I'd sucker-punched him in the nose again. "I suppose Skinny told you that. I suppose he bragged to everyone how he was going to sue for the right to raise my son."

"Skinny said that?" A heavy weight landed in the pit of my stomach, reminding me once again that I didn't know my friend nearly as well as I'd thought I had.

Instead of answering, he turned his head away.

"Skinny didn't tell me anything." The bitterness in my voice surprised me. "I convinced Althea to tell me."

His gaze spun back toward me. "Althea? Impossible. She wouldn't—"

"She did, because I convinced her that if justice was going to have any chance at prevailing—for both you and me—I needed to know the truth. It wasn't easy to pry the information out of her. She's extremely protective of you and Gavin."

"You think Althea killed—?"

"No!" I was surprised I had never really suspected her, even though she was the one who'd sent me that phony prize letter and had helped Mabel to try to con me into taking over the Chocolate Box. "Should I suspect her?"

"No! She would never . . ." He bit his bottom lip. He shook his head as if trying to shake away the thought that his friend might have killed to protect him. "I hate how this investigation is turning everyone in this community against each other."

"Detective Gibbons said he'll be making an arrest soon."

"I suppose you told him about the DNA report?"

"No, I didn't need to."

"I don't see how. Althea isn't going to tell him."

He shook his head as I told him about that tiny scrap of paper and how the detective had issued a warrant to Hodgkin DNA to get copies of the files. "They'll have the report by the end of the day tomorrow."

"Thank you for letting me know. You can go now," he said without looking in my direction. He rose from his desk chair. "And please take your little dog with you."

He walked over to the door and pulled it open. Stella darted out and headed straight to Miss Bunny. While she sniffed the older woman's legs, I stayed put. Harley might be done with the conversation, but I wasn't. I'd come to get information, not give it away.

"Does Jody know?" I demanded.

He finally looked at me. "You're not going to leave it alone, are you?" His cheeks had turned red, and his mouth had tightened into an angry line.

"No," I said. "Not if this proves you're innocent."

My statement made his brows shoot up into his hairline. "Proves it to whom?"

"To me." I held up my hands to keep him from dismissing me before I had a chance to explain. "The killer took great pains to dip Skinny into a vat of chocolate. There are many easier ways to kill a man. He could have just hit Skinny one more time over the head and finished him off, but he didn't. He'd taken the time to heat up a huge vat of chocolate and use it as a murder weapon. Is that the action of a man passionate about protecting his son? Or does it sound more like a plan carefully executed by someone who is coldly calculating and methodical?"

Perhaps someone like Jody?

I didn't think he'd appreciate the direction of my thoughts on who committed the murders, so I kept them to myself.

He pushed the door closed before answering me. "I don't want it to get out that I'm not Gavin's biological father. Especially now that Skinny is dead, I don't want Gavin to ever wonder about his family. But I suppose it's too late for that. When it's entered as evidence, it'll become a public document."

"Does Jody know?" I asked again.

"Yes, Jody knows. I'm pretty sure she's known all along."

"But you didn't?"

He didn't answer right away. And when he did, it was explosive. "I was there when Gavin was born. I wept as I held his tiny, warm body cradled in my arms. I was there for midnight feedings, diaper changes, first steps, first days of school, and his first surf competition. Skinny wasn't there for any of those things. I was. I don't care what a piece of paper says. That boy is *my* son."

If only all fathers felt so passionate about their children.

"Did Mabel know about this?" I asked quietly.

He looked taken aback by the question. "Mabel? No. Why would she know about it?"

"No reason she would," I said with a shrug. "I just had to ask because Mabel was murdered."

"She wasn't murdered," he countered. "I was there when she died. She had a heart attack. Her pills didn't help her."

"Someone tampered with those pills to make sure they couldn't save her. She was murdered. And I think it was for the same reason Skinny was killed."

"And what would that reason be?"

"Chocolate."

Chapter 25

*C*hocolate?
I don't know why I said that. Jody didn't want the chocolate. She wanted the right to tear down the chocolate shop and build a massive housing and retail complex.

Derek didn't want the chocolate either. If what Cal and Jody had told me about him proved to be correct, he lusted after money. Not chocolate.

I supposed if I used my imagination, I could picture Derek using his mother's beloved chocolate to kill both Skinny and Mabel as a way of jamming the very chocolate his mother had used to alienate her own children down Mabel's throat. A poetic punishment? I wasn't sure Derek had that kind of imagination in him.

And yet he was one of the few people who knew when Bertie and I had closed the shop the day of the robbery. He also knew we were going to change the locks.

Althea also knew about the locks, a voice in my head reminded me. But she had no reason to kill Mabel or to rob the shop. None at all.

As far as you know, that pesky voice returned to say.

In reaction to my pronouncement that Mabel's special chocolates were at the heart of the murders, Harley leaned on the edge of his desk and frowned at me.

Since we really didn't have much else to talk about and the awkwardness between us crackled like static electricity in the air, I decided to leave him in peace.

"Penn," he said as he followed me to the door. His brows furrowed with a look of true concern. "Be careful. You do realize there are only two days left."

"Two days before the festival starts? You don't need to remind me about that." There was so much that needed to be done, I truly didn't know how we could possibly get ready in time.

"I'm not talking about the festival. I'm talking about Mabel's will and that quirky piece of law that says if you die by Wednesday, Mabel's children automatically inherit everything she left to you."

I nodded. I hadn't forgotten.

"If someone is trying to kill you in order to change the inheritance, they'll need to do it before midnight on Wednesday." He put his hand on my shoulder. "Please, be careful."

*   *   *

Stella's growls grew louder and louder as we climbed the back staircase that led to Mabel's apartment. I scanned the adjacent marsh, trying to figure out what had spooked my little dog. All I could see in the muddy flat was an army of black fiddler crabs with their claws held high as they performed a funny little dance in the pluff mud.

The cold front had moved away, taking its biting winds and its freak snowstorm with it. The winter sun, hanging high in the clear sky, provided a surprising amount of warmth to the air. Even though it was still January and the deepest part of winter back in Wisconsin, here in this tiny Southern island, it felt like spring.

"Calm down, Stella," I said to my growling pooch and tossed her a treat. She ignored it. That was odd. She never refused a treat.

I paused on the top step and leaned my elbows on the porch's rickety handrail. I took a slow, deep breath of the clean salty air.

"I could get used to this," I said to myself.

"Not if I have anything to say about it," a gravelly voice replied.

I began to turn to see who had spoken when something smacked me in the side of my head—something brutally hard.

I vaguely remember hearing Stella barking. Luckily, I had enough sense to drop her leash. I threw my arms out to my sides in an attempt to stop myself from taking a deadly nosedive down the steps, but whatever had hit me had scrambled my brain to the point that I didn't know up from down. My head slammed against the side of a splintery tread. After that, I tumbled down, down, down into a deep, black hole of unconsciousness.

*　　*　　*

"Penn?" a soft voice whispered from a distant shore. "Penn? Can you hear me?"

"She's breathing," someone else said.

Stella barked. It was higher in pitch than usual. She sounded panicked. I needed to go to her, to reassure her. I tried to get up, but none of my limbs worked.

"She's twitching," someone said. "Does that mean she's having a seizure?"

"I think it means she's trying to wake up." The voices were starting to sound closer. "EMS is on its way."

That was good to hear. My entire left side felt as if it was on fire.

"She must have tripped and fallen down the stairs, the poor dear."

"Pushed," my voice rasped.

"What did she say?"

It took a Herculean force of will, but I managed to pry open my eyes. Cal hovered over me. His wide-eyed gaze mirrored the concern I'd seen in his brother's not ten minutes earlier. Bertie stood behind him, wringing her hands. Althea stood a few feet away with her cell phone pressed to her ear.

"Pushed," I tried to say again. It came out kind of garbled.

"Don't strain yourself," Cal said and laid a strong hand on my shoulder. "You fell down the stairs. You're bleeding."

The thought of blood made the world spin back into tones of gray. I fought like the devil to keep my wits about me.

I drew a slow, steady breath in an effort to gather every ounce of strength I could muster so I could say as clearly and loudly as possible, "Who pushed me?"

"You were pushed?" Cal squinted as his gaze shifted from me to the landing. "Are you sure?"

"Something . . . slammed . . . side of my head. That's why . . . fell. Not . . . not an accident. There was . . . a voice."

"A voice?" His frown deepened. He kept his gaze glued on the stairs. "I was passing on the street and heard you call out. I arrived in time to see you land at the bottom of the stairs."

"I came running from the back door of the shop," Bertie said. "When I saw what had happened, I ran back inside to get Althea and her phone."

By this time, all three of them were studying the flight of steps. And all three of them were frowning.

I followed their gazes and, blinking hard to chase away the blurriness, fixed my eyes on the wooden stairwell.

Those half-rotted steps provided the only access up to the second floor. The only access. (I applauded my badly rattled brain's ability to make such an important realization.)

Despite everyone's protests, I sat up. The world spun only a little bit. Upon seeing my movement, Stella's barking grew more urgent.

"Bertie, could you get my dog? I've never seen her so stressed."

"I'd better go instead," Cal said. He jumped to his feet and practically vaulted up to the second floor.

Stella let him grab her leash, but when he tried to lead her down the stairs to see me, the little dog laid her huge butterfly-shaped ears flat to her head and, crouching, backed away from the steps.

"She must be afraid she'll fall too," he called down.

I never knew Stella to be afraid of anything. She seemed to enjoy ruling over everyone in her noisy, autocratic way, biting and nipping anyone who dared to defy her.

"Take her into the apartment and give her a piece of bacon to help settle her down. You'll find some in the fridge," Bertie called back up to him.

Cal nodded. His mobile gaze kept a careful watch on the second-floor landing as he headed toward the apartment door and disappeared from view.

Sirens blared in the distance.

"The ambulance will be here soon," Althea said.

I nodded, which wasn't the best thing to do. It only made the world wobble.

Stella, growling and tugging on her leash, reluctantly followed Cal into the apartment.

"Wait a minute," I said and tried to stand. I needed to go after Cal. I ended up landing on my rear just as a pair of EMTs came running toward me. "Cal's up there. And whoever pushed me could still be up there."

Althea blinked several times before rushing toward the stairs after him. "Mama, call the police."

"Not again," Bertie groaned.

The two burly EMTs knelt down beside me. One took my pulse. The other pressed something cold to the side of my head as he questioned me about what had happened, asking my name and other kinds of nonsense, like what day it was and what year.

"Harley had warned me. Not ten minutes ago, he'd warned me to be extra careful. He was afraid that because of Mabel's will, the killer would strike again, and strike soon. But I don't understand it. I've told everyone that I was going to give the shop and the property to Mabel's kids. So why would killing me solve anything? What do you think is going on?"

"Honey, I don't know," Bertie said, her eyes fixed on Althea as she climbed the stairs. Her daughter had just stepped foot on the second-floor landing.

Not a heartbeat later, a deafening blast crackled through the air.

Althea screamed.

Chapter 26

"He ran at me with a look of murder in his eyes." Cal shook his head with dismay. A handgun, presumably Cal's, lay on the ground. "I had to protect myself. I had to."

Althea hugged herself. Fat tears fell from her large brown eyes.

By this time everyone had made it up to the top of the landing. The EMTs were the first to run up the stairs, taking two at a time. Bertie had nearly knocked them over in her haste to get to her daughter. Holding the icepack to my bleeding head and fueled by a jolt of adrenaline, I managed to make it up to the back porch not that long after everyone else.

We found Cal standing in the open doorway to Mabel and Bertie's apartment. His arms hung limp at his sides. Behind him, fully inside the apartment, was a man sprawled out facedown on the floor. My gaze latched onto the soles of the man's feet.

"What? Who?" I stammered. I dropped the icepack and scooped Stella into my arms.

My traumatized little dog looked ready to bite anyone who came anywhere near her. She snapped at the air several times before tucking her muzzle into the crook of my arm. She shivered so hard, I slipped her inside my jacket.

For a moment, no one moved. No one spoke.

A distant heron shrieked *tik-tik-tik*.

Harley's apartment door flew violently open and bounced against the wall with a crash. I jumped. It couldn't be Harley. He was still in his office.

I prayed it wasn't his son. No child should be witness to this.

Luckily the person who emerged from the apartment was Jody.

"What's going on?" she demanded.

Since I happened to be standing closer to her than anyone else, I answered. "Someone pushed me down the stairs and then attacked Cal. He defended himself. What are you doing here?"

"Gavin had left his school notebooks the last time he stayed overnight. He needs them to finish a project that's due on Friday." She had two loose-leaf notebooks tucked under her arm. "Who attacked you? Was it . . . Harley?"

"I don't know." I supposed that if Harley had wanted to do me harm, he could have rushed back to his apartment ahead of me. It wasn't as if I had been in a hurry. Stella had stopped several times to sniff and to do her puppy business. If Harley had taken one of the side roads, he could have made it back to the apartment without me seeing him.

Jody stood with her arm nearly pressed to mine as we watched the EMTs nudge Cal aside. They knelt down next to the man lying on the floor. My heart thumped in my chest. Maybe he wasn't dead.

"Who is it?" Bertie asked.

"Is it Harley?" Jody demanded.

Althea swallowed hard several times but only managed to shake her head.

"He ran at me, like he was going to hurt me. He'd already kicked Stella," Cal explained to no one in particular. His voice shook. "I had no choice."

One EMT made a call using the radio attached to his uniform. The other rolled the body over. He looked up at his partner and shook his head much like Althea had.

Althea started crying harder.

Bertie whispered a silent prayer.

Both Jody and I squeezed our way through the crowd around the door to see for ourselves. There, on Mabel's ancient Linoleum kitchen floor, was the man who must have attacked me. His limp arms were flung wide. His sightless eyes were fixed in a staring contest with the ceiling. A bloody wound stained the white polo shirt he'd worn beneath his tan blazer.

"Well, I guess I don't need to visit Edward Maybank anymore," I said, because stupid things pop out of my mouth whenever I feel nervous or stressed.

But it was true. The dead man on the floor wasn't Harley. It was Edward's youngest brother, Derek. I hated being right about him. He seemed like such a nice guy, coming to help us out with the shop and suggesting we sell Mabel's special hot chocolate during the snowstorm.

Of course, he'd probably only offered to work at the shop so he could rob us after we had closed up for the night.

And he'd tried to kill me . . . why? Why would he want me dead?

I'd told everyone I was going to give Mabel's children the shop as soon as the festival ended. So Derek didn't have any reason to want to hurt me. None at all.

And yet, instead of talking with me, instead of telling me what was going on in that thick head of his, he'd hit me in the head and had sent me tumbling to what he'd probably hoped would be my demise.

Had he also driven Harley's car and tried to run me over?

And the attempted break-in at the motel, had that been him too? Why? Why would someone do that to a fellow human being? Why?

The world seemed to spin faster and faster as the questions kept coming at me, questions Derek would never be able to answer, like how a man who professed to love his mother could put chocolate in her pills.

"I need to sit down," I said. My voice sounded thready.

Bertie took one look at me and grabbed one arm. Althea grabbed the other. Their strength and determination were the only things that kept me from falling on my face.

They helped lower me to the porch floor. Bertie pushed my head between my knees. Stella growled a reminder that she was still nestled within the folds of my coat. I sat up to give her more room.

A second later, her little black nose popped out of the coat. She turned those big puppy eyes toward me. I held my breath, thinking she might feel grateful that I had rescued her and had comforted her when she was frightened. I half expected her to lick my nose when she moved closer to my face.

Silly me.

She bit my nose and then wiggled and growled her way free from my jacket.

"Is it bleeding?" I asked as I cradled my nose.

"No," Althea said, but she winced. "Not much."

"Althea, you'd better go catch her before she gets too far," Bertie said as my ungrateful dog bound down the stairs.

"Yes, ma'am." She paused only long enough to wipe her eyes dry with the back of her hand before she followed after Stella.

"What's happening to this town?" Bertie found the icepack I'd dropped and handed it to me to press against my nose. "Violence. Murders. In my own apartment. It's never been like this."

"At least it's over," I said as I looked over at Cal. He'd left the open doorway and propped his elbows against the railing as he gazed out over the wintry brown marsh grasses. "Thanks to him, it's all over."

Chapter 27

Unfortunately, it wasn't over. Not by a long shot.

The Sweets on the Beach festival was slated to begin on Thursday . . . in just two days. Because of my tumble down the stairs, I woke up early on Tuesday morning with several bruised ribs, a concussion, and a sprained ankle. What I didn't have was the money Derek had stolen from the shop. I was sure it was long gone. Nor did I have Mabel's chocolate that he'd pilfered.

Feeling depressed at the state of things, I found myself in bed staring at the ceiling when someone knocked on the apartment door. I hobbled into the living room only to find Bertie welcoming Detective Gibbons inside. He looked larger than life, dressed in a crisply pressed dark brown suit. An oversized envelope was clasped in his hands.

He reluctantly refused Bertie's offer to whip him up some eggs and sausage. "I have to get downtown for an early precinct meeting, but I wanted to bring this by, and I also wanted to talk to you about what happened yesterday." He placed the envelope on the kitchen table and came and sat down on the sofa. I'd managed to hobble that far before plopping down next to him with my sprained ankle elevated on several throw pillows.

"What's in it?" I asked, indicating the envelope. It wasn't nearly big enough to hold the store's worth of chocolates Derek had stolen.

"It's a copy of the DNA results your friend had ordered shortly before his death. They arrived yesterday afternoon."

Which meant the envelope contained the paternity results for Harley's son. I nodded. "Why give them to me?"

He gave me a hard look. "Because after everything you've been through, I thought you deserved to see them." He gently patted the sofa next to my propped-up leg. "How are you faring?" he asked with a long sigh.

"I've been better. I'm supposed to stay off the ankle for several days, but I don't know how that's going to happen. The festival starts on Thursday. And we hardly have any chocolates made. Are you sure you can't release the truffles your officers found in Derek's apartment?"

Looking decidedly uncomfortable, he shifted on the sofa. "As I already told you on the phone, even though the man is no longer living, we still have to move forward with the investigation. I'm sorry, Penn. The chocolates are evidence."

Bertie looked up from the eggs and sausage she was busy frying. She'd been cooking in the kitchen all morning. I'm not sure who she thought she was going to feed with all that food. "It's a sorry way to end things," she said.

Detective Gibbons rubbed the back of his thick neck. "Uh, that's one of the reasons I'm here, ma'am."

"What's going on?" I asked. I couldn't imagine he had any more questions for us. The police had questioned everyone for hours last night. After I'd been released from the hospital, a cop had driven me directly to the county sheriff's office located on the outskirts of the city of Charleston so the detective could take my statement.

"It's not over," he said. He frowned so deeply his entire face seemed to droop.

"But you said—" I started.

"He didn't do it," Gibbons snapped. He then punched a fist into his hand and swore. "Derek Maybank had an alibi for your friend's time of death."

I shook my head. "He didn't have an alibi. Sure, he was with Cal for most of the night. But Jody told me that she clearly remembers seeing Cal drinking alone at some point in the evening."

"That's what we thought too." He ground his teeth for a few moments before continuing tightly, "Late last night Derek Maybank's sister comes flying into the precinct, shouting and raving like a madwoman that they killed the wrong man, that her brother was innocent."

"Which sister?" Bertie demanded.

He ground his teeth some more as he pulled a little notebook from his jacket pocket. "A Florence Corners. Her husband is some bigwig business owner in the area."

Bertie made a sucking sound through her teeth. "The woman can screech."

"But she couldn't be right. You found the chocolates when you searched his apartment, right? He robbed the shop."

The detective tilted his head to one side. His gaze slipped away from mine to stare at a far wall. "He may have robbed the shop. It's true that we found the shop's chocolates in his apartment."

Last night the police had sounded certain that they'd caught their man, that they'd be able to quickly close all the cases: the robbery, the murders, and the attacks on me. Now he didn't sound certain about anything.

"What about this?" I pointed to my leg. "Are you going to tell me you don't think he pushed me down the stairs? That you don't think he attacked Cal? What was he doing hiding in Mabel's apartment if he wasn't responsible for all this?"

Gibbons held up his hands. "We have to follow the facts. We have to gather the evidence. He may have robbed you. And he probably did push you down the stairs. However, his sister, once we got her to calm down, provided an ironclad alibi for her brother for the night of Skinny McGee's murder."

"Impossible." I crossed my arms over my chest. "What's this alibi?"

"She picked him up at the island bar and drove him straight to a rehab center. We called the facility. The time he was checked in lines up with when she said she picked him up. In fact, she must have exceeded the speed limits in order to have gotten him to the facility so quickly."

"He was in rehab?" I asked, unable to believe it.

"Not for long. He checked himself out a few days later."

Bertie nodded. "That must have been the day he showed up suddenly at the shop. Mabel enjoyed his company, but . . ."

"But—?" Gibbons prompted.

"But the cash register never added up at the end of the day whenever he was around. I mentioned that once to Mabel, and she refused to address it. She'd said he was still her baby and that if he needed someone to take care of him, she'd do it."

"She wasn't the only one taking care of him," I said. "He'd told Jody that he had power of attorney over Mabel's affairs and convinced her to pay him a large down payment for this shop."

"Is that so?" One of Gibbons's bushy eyebrows popped up. He started writing in his notebook.

Encouraged by that, I continued. "I don't know how, but he killed Skinny and poisoned his own mother. With his constant need for money, he had the most to lose with Mabel's new will. He needed the money, so he had to make sure the land and the shop went to his family and not to some stranger from the Midwest."

Gibbons shrugged. "He didn't kill your friend. I don't know about Mabel. The two deaths might not be related at all. As I said, the cases are still open, and we'll keep investigating. Oh, crud, look at the time. I need to get going."

On his way out, Bertie asked Gibbons if he was going to make it to the funeral on Wednesday afternoon. He said he'd try.

The funeral.

Mabel's funeral.

It was just one more item on a growing list of things that desperately needed to be done, and a particularly unpleasant one at that. After the chilly reception I'd received from Mabel's children at the will reading, I dreaded the inevitable confrontation. Would they blame me for their youngest brother's death? Would they think I had somehow besmirched his name by accusing him of murder?

My initial thought had been to skip the funeral. But Bertie used her special brand of charm to guilt me into accompanying her to the historic church in downtown Charleston.

With the thought of confronting Mabel's family weighing heavy on my mind, I spent the rest of the morning down in the Chocolate Box kitchen with Bertie and Althea. The three of us used the time to experiment with various recipes.

First, we used the bags of the leftover Halloween candy in the pantry to make chocolate-covered candy bombs that were startlingly hard to bite into.

Next, we tried to make something with the inexpensive ingredients I'd picked up at Bunky's Corner Pantry. We dipped nuts and figs into a milk chocolate. We could sell these to the children who came to the festival. But nothing seemed good enough for the food critics who were coming from all around the region just to taste Mabel's gourmet chocolates.

By lunchtime, my swollen ankle was throbbing, my concussed head felt as if a metal band was squeezing the life out of it, and my bruised ribs made breathing feel like shredded glass had found its way into my lungs.

"Let's take a break," Bertie suggested as she washed her hands in the sink. "We're out of heavy cream anyhow. We can't make the truffles without it."

"And you need to eat something, Mama," Althea added.

Bertie nodded, but the way she jutted out her chin made me suspect she was just going through the motions in an effort to avoid a confrontation with her daughter on what was already turning into an emotionally charged day.

"How about we run over to the grocery store to pick up more supplies, Mama? On the way, we can grab one of those freshly made crab cake sandwiches at the Dog-Eared Café that you love so much."

Her mother's harsh expression seemed to soften a bit at the mention of a crab cake sandwich. "I suppose we could do that. We do need to get busy if we're going to accomplish anything before tomorrow's service."

The kitchen suddenly felt as if it were missing its heart without Mabel's vibrant presence. She was going to be sorely missed.

I hobbled over to settle into the nearest chair to give my throbbing ankle a break. There was so much that needed to be done for the festival, and even with Bertie's expert assistance, the chocolates we were making were going to be a pale imitation of the adventures in flavors Mabel would have produced.

Perhaps it was a good thing I was planning on signing everything over to Mabel's children instead of indulging my wild fantasies of taking over the business. It would be better to close up than to create chocolates that were less than perfect.

"Penn?" Althea had apparently been talking to me while my thoughts wandered. "Penn? Are you okay?"

"Sorry," I said. I leaned down and rubbed my ankle, which was a mistake. I hissed at the searing pain that shot up my leg. "What were you saying?"

"When was the last time you took something for that?" she asked instead.

"This morning?" I asked while I tried to remember the exact hour.

"I reckon it's high time you took another one. You're turning green," she said.

While Althea rushed upstairs to get my prescription bottle, Bertie pulled a second chair over. Using extraordinary care, she eased my pulsating ankle onto the chair. "You need to keep it elevated, dear. Why don't you head upstairs and rest? Let me finish making the chocolates for tomorrow."

"No, I couldn't let you do that. It's too much."

Bertie laid a comforting hand on my shoulder. "Honey, it's you who has done too much already. Don't get me wrong, I'm grateful for the effort you've put in, but Mabel wouldn't have wanted this." She indicated my ankle and bruised body. "She wouldn't want to see you hurting."

"But—"

"At least take a rest while Althea fusses over how much lunch I manage to eat today. Do it as a favor to me."

"A favor to you?" I asked incredulously.

"Yes, to me. You'll be giving me one less thing I need to worry about."

She seemed so sincere I actually gave in and let her help me hobble upstairs. After downing the pain pill Althea had gotten for me, I crawled into bed and slept for a solid hour before waking with a start.

The killer was still out there.

I needed to call Granny Mae. She might have some new advice on what I needed to do. I started to dial her number when my cell phone rang.

It was Tina, my half sister.

"You didn't call yesterday," she said in place of a greeting.

"With the shop and upcoming festival, I've been awfully busy."

There was a long pause on her end.

"I called Granny Mae late last night," she said quietly. "She told me what happened. With the stairs. The murder attempt."

"Oh." I didn't know what else to say. She'd caught me in a lie, and it shamed me. "I didn't want to worry you. Honest, that's the only reason I didn't tell you."

She fell silent again. This time it went on for so long, I wondered if she'd hung up on me.

"Tina? Are you there?"

"I'm here."

"Do you really want to hear the truth about what's going on?" I asked.

"I do. I want to help you, Penn."

"You do?"

"Truly."

"I don't want you flying here. It'd just . . . complicate things, you know?"

She sighed. "I know."

I didn't intend to tell her everything. She'd worry. She'd get on a plane and fly to my rescue. And yet the words fell out of my mouth. I told her everything that had happened, everything I'd kept from her. I even told her that the reason I'd lied about the situation in Camellia Beach was because I was worried that she'd come and put herself in danger, which would only make Grandmother Cristobel hate me that much more. I ended my rushed speech, telling her how I needed to talk with Granny Mae.

"You already know what Granny Mae is going to tell you," she said.

"And what is that?"

"She's going to tell you to read the articles she's been sending you. Have you read them yet?"

"Um . . . how do you know about the articles?"

"I had a long conversation with Granny Mae yesterday, remember? She told me everything."

"She must have."

"She also told me what the Cheese King did to you. What a jerk. You aren't really going to keep the vicious dog he gave you? Daddy is going to be livid when he finds out."

"You think our father will be upset when he finds out about Stella? That doesn't make sense. Why would he care?"

"No, silly, when he finds out about how the Cheese King is dragging your name, and our family name, through the mud up in Wisconsin. Grandmama is livid. She's already trying to figure out how to get a message through to him even though he's instructed everyone that there's to be no outside contact until he's completed his travels."

When I heard that, it suddenly felt like my heart had started pumping ice through my veins. Grandmother Cristobel could make life awfully hard for me. She'd done it before . . . many times. My father, who has never truly stood up to her, only compounded the trouble by agreeing with everything she did and scolding me for the trouble I brought on myself.

"I don't need this kind of difficulty now," I whispered.

"I know you don't, Penn. But I couldn't sit by and let you get blindsided by it either."

"What is the Cheese King doing?" I supposed I needed to know.

"He's saying you tried to seduce him. And when he rebuked you, you started a smear campaign against him and his company. He's threatening to sue."

"I haven't done anything!" I shot up in the bed, causing all sorts of aches and pains to go ballistic. Groaning, I quickly laid back down. "I haven't done anything," I repeated in a tight whisper once the blinding pain receded.

"Of course you haven't done anything, silly bean," she said, using her childhood nickname for me. "I know that."

"I wish the rest of the family did."

"Yeah, me too. They never act much like a family to you. It makes me want to scream sometimes."

"What did you say just now?" I asked.

"That I wanted to scream. Look, I—"

"No, that other part, the part about family."

"What? That our family never acts like a family when it comes to you? Well, it's true. Instead of supporting you, they like to jump to the worst kinds of conclusions, like thinking you'd actually try to seduce someone who refers to himself as a 'Cheese King.' I mean, come on. That's not how a family is supposed to act. And that's not how they act toward the other members of the family, except for the exes. But that's an entirely different set of problems, isn't it?"

She kept rambling like that for several more minutes while my mind raced.

Family. That had been a vital clue I'd been ignoring. Well, not really ignoring; it was something I didn't really understand. Most of my family treated me like I was something gross that needed to be scrubbed from the bottom of their shoes.

But not all families acted like that. Althea and Bertie supported each other, even when they didn't agree with each other. They took the time to see the best in the other instead of finding ways to tear each other down. Camellia Beach worked like one large family too, protecting their own while shunning outsiders who might disrupt their quaint and comfortable way of life.

So if I was going to find the killer, I needed to start looking where families weren't working. The most obvious dysfunctional family was Mabel's own children. She had pushed them to take over the shop. And all her children had rebelled against her. Some, like Derek, had even conspired against her by trying to sell the shop out from under her to support his lust for money.

Then there were Harley and Jody and their extremely broken relationship. Their lives had devolved into a battlefield. But I had a strong feeling that wasn't the clue I was searching for.

What other examples of dysfunction existed in Camellia?

"Penn? Are you even listening to me?" Tina shouted in my ear.

I jumped. "Um . . ."

"I'm trying to help you here."

"I know, I know. And I'm grateful. You have helped me. Tremendously. In fact, I think you solved it."

"Solved what?" She sounded surprised.

"The murder."

"What? How?"

"I'm not exactly sure. I need to think about it. And I need to read those articles Granny Mae sent me. I need to see if they provide any supporting evidence for what I'm thinking right now."

"What? What are you thinking about?"

"The murders, of course. What you said about family is spot on. Families see the best in each other and support each other, except when they don't. Some families, like ours, are broken. That's where I need to look. I need to look more closely at the broken families in town."

"I have no idea what that means. But if I helped you, I'm glad."

"You did help me."

"Once you figure out what's going on there, you're going to have to deal with the troubles brewing up here. Grandmama will insist on it."

I groaned. The sound seemed to satisfy her. She didn't mention the Cheese King again. Instead, she said, "Penn, be careful. You know I love you, silly bean."

I pulled the phone away from my ear and stared at it. She'd never said that to me before. No one in my family had ever said that to me.

Hearing it now must have knocked loose a chunk of that thick wall I'd built up around my heart, because I quickly returned the phone to my ear and said, "Thanks, Tina. I love you too."

Chapter 28

Since Bertie and Althea still hadn't returned from their shopping excursion, I found myself with a few spare hours before I needed to get back to work in the shop. I took Tina's advice and finally started reading the articles Granny Mae had sent.

They covered a wide range of topics. Many were about Camellia Beach, and some others were about the chocolate industry in general. There were even articles on training difficult dogs and dozens of chocolate recipes.

I propped my aching foot up on the sofa and shifted this way and that until I found a comfortable spot where I'd be able to scan through the articles. As I read them, one stood out in particular. The article described a murder. Not Skinny's murder; it wasn't even a murder that had taken place on this continent. But after reading it through twice, the suspicion that started with Tina's phone call seemed to lock into place.

I had a feeling that I was finally getting far enough away from the small pieces of information so that I could see the big picture that had eluded me for so long.

The article described a reporter investigating working conditions on a chocolate plantation in West Africa. The reporter had
been stabbed to death with the same hooked knife workers used
to harvest cacao beans from the trees. The holding company for
the plantation in question had been accused in the past of using
child slave labor to harvest and process the beans. The company
had put out several statements about how they were now enforc-
ing fair labor practices and banning the use of young children
on their plantations. They had even included photos of happy
workers. However, repeated requests to visit the plantation by
news agencies had been denied, which was why the investigative
reporter had gone undercover and, posing as a delivery driver,
had gotten himself onto the plantation.

The last line in the article read, "Although the death has
never been solved, it should be pointed out that the chocolate
industry is a billion-dollar industry. With stakes this high, companies have shown time and again how they will fervently protect both their reputation and their bottom line."

The main similarity between the murder in West Africa
and the murders in Camellia Beach was that they were all committed because of greed. Pure, ugly greed.

Tina's mention of families supporting each other tickled
in the back of my mind. Families that worked held each other
up. They were so different from families like mine. Case in
point: Grandmother Cristobel believed the Cheese King's slan-
der against me without bothering to ask for my side of the story.
The woman would probably literally throw me under a bus if it
made the family look good. And because of it, that's the kind of
behavior I expected in all families.

Had Tina actually said she loved me?

Had I dreamed that?

Thanks to Tina, I now had a really good idea about who had killed both Skinny and Mabel. And why. Unfortunately, I didn't have any evidence I could take to Detective Gibbons.

The most I had was a sinking feeling in the pit of my stomach that I would get whenever I trusted the wrong person. Well, come to think of it, I *had* trusted the wrong person.

I sat back and tapped my chin.

"What's the matter?" Bertie asked as she trudged into the kitchen with Althea following closely behind. Shopping bags, stuffed to the brims, were balanced precariously in both their arms.

"Just trying to figure out my next step," I said and snapped the cover of my iPad closed before either of them could see what I'd been reading. "Let me help you with that." I eased off the sofa and hobbled into the kitchen to help with the bags.

*　　*　　*

While I'd read through Granny Mae's articles, Bertie and Althea had also been busy. Very busy. Not only had they restocked the apartment's kitchen with supplies, but they'd also filled the commercial kitchen downstairs with boxes and bags of sugar, cocoa powder, coconuts, heavy cream, and several varieties of gourmet dark chocolate.

"How did you manage to pay for all this?" I asked as I hobbled around the Chocolate Box's kitchen.

"I maxed out my credit cards," Althea answered with a wide grin.

"You shouldn't have done that. I don't know when the shop will be able to repay you . . . or if it ever will be able to." It wasn't as if I was going to keep the shop open. And since the police had seized the money stolen from the cash register, and Mabel's family was promising to contest her will in the courts, who knew when we'd see a dime from the shop. "I pray the money we make at the festival will cover your costs."

"Don't worry about it, Penn. I'm just happy to be able to help out." She gave me a hug but made it a quick one. "Really, I don't want anything from you. I'm not trying to guilt you into staying or trick you. I promise."

I gave her a sideways glance. She sounded and looked sincere, but . . .

"Thanks," I said tightly. That damaged part of me had a hard time accepting her help—or anyone else's, if I was going to be honest with myself. Yet with only a day and a half to go before the festival started, I needed to swallow my fear and accept all the help I could get. As things stood right now, it was going to take a miracle for the three of us to finish the preparations in time.

We were just starting to get busy with our next recipe when someone started banging on the shop's front door.

Bertie wiped her hands on her apron and went to see who it could be. She returned a few minutes later. Her smile reached from ear to ear. Behind her, a crowd of older men and women ambled into the kitchens. Althea handed out aprons while Bertie handed each of them a hairnet. I recognized many in the crowd from the motel lobby.

"We're here to make sure you don't mess up the festival," a man with a full head of bushy silver hair said as he nudged my arm. I was taken aback by his gruff tone and was about to defend myself when he winked.

"Thank you, I—" I started to say and then remembered how a couple of the ladies in the group were severely hard of hearing. "Thank you," I shouted. "I couldn't do any of this without you."

"Jeez, you don't have to shout," one lady complained while another asked, "What did she say?"

Everyone laughed.

"But how will this work?" I asked Bertie. "We still don't have Mabel's expertise. And without her, we can't begin to reproduce even a fraction of the magic she put into her chocolates."

It wasn't Bertie who answered but another woman I recognized from the motel bunko game. "We all took Mabel's classes. All of us. She insisted we take private lessons where she focused on just one recipe, hounding us until we perfected it."

Each and every one of them had come here because they loved Mabel. They'd come to help.

"Mabel worried this might happen, didn't she?" I asked Bertie. "That she might not be here for the festival?"

Bertie swallowed hard and nodded. "Not just for the festival. She taught her most precious recipes to the community so they could one day teach them to you."

"Why me?" I asked for what felt like the hundredth time.

"Sugar, I wish I knew," Bertie answered.

"We're here, honey, 'cause we know Mabel put her faith in you," one of the ladies said. Everyone nodded. "That Mabel of ours was no fool. If she thought you were the one to fill her shoes, then we support you as if you were born and bred in Camellia."

"You're one of us now," another said.

"You're family," a third said.

Oh, how I wished it were true. But I wasn't family, not Mabel's. And certainly not Camellia Beach's.

Skinny had performed the DNA test to prove he was Gavin's father, not to make a connection between Mabel and me as I'd hoped. But none of that mattered. What mattered was the roomful of volunteers wanting to help.

"Why are we standing here, staring at each other?" I said. "We have chocolates to make."

I stood back and watched in amazement as busy fingers got to work gathering ingredients, each making the special recipe Mabel had so diligently taught them and only them.

"We still don't have enough of the Amar chocolates to make three days' worth of Mabel's special truffles," I said to Bertie. "What are we going to do?"

Bertie thought about it for a little while before shaking her head. "We want everyone to taste her chocolates and to learn about how rare and special they are. If we mix it into other chocolates, its distinct flavor will be muted. So how do we make the Amar chocolate last the entire weekend? I don't know."

"I don't either," I said.

Since everything seemed to be under control in the kitchen for now, Bertie sent me back upstairs. I didn't argue. I wasn't going to be any help anyhow, not with my ankle throbbing like the devil. Besides, my mind was still obsessing over the murder investigation. I needed to continue my research. Perhaps if I looked hard enough, I'd find that all-important piece of evidence I could take to the police.

Chapter 29

It hadn't mattered that I'd given up a night of sleep to scour the Internet and pick through the articles Granny Mae had sent. By the next morning, I didn't have anything other than conjecture and suspicion about the murderer. I couldn't take either of those to the police, which frustrated me to no end. How could I prove what I knew?

Grumpier than a rabid badger, I hobbled around the kitchen, ignoring how much my bruised ankle still throbbed. I dug a piece of white bread from its bag, which I shared with Stella, who followed alongside me, growling at my heels whenever I took too long to toss her a piece.

"It's Wednesday," Althea said in place of a greeting as she entered the apartment. She had a garment bag slung over her shoulder and a paper shopping bag hooked on her arm.

"I don't need the reminder," I grumbled.

Wednesday was Mabel's funeral. It was also the day before the start of the festival. I still had no idea how we were going to serve the rare Amar chocolate to the festivalgoers. Although the chocolate I'd gotten from Cal had seemed like a treasure trove at the time, when I started to calculate how much we needed, I quickly discovered it wasn't enough chocolate to last even a day, not even if we melted down the bars to make superminiature truffles.

If that wasn't enough to worry about, Wednesday was also the fifth day after the will reading. The fifth day was the last day where if I happened to die, Mabel's family would automatically inherit the chocolate shop and everything associated with it. This meant that if the killer wanted Mabel's family to have control of the shop, today was the day to kill me. Not a comforting thought.

But the killer wouldn't try to kill me, right? I'd already promised to hand the chocolate shop over to Mabel's family. Unless—

No. That would be foolish.

"Hello? What in the world is going on in that mind of yours?" Althea asked. She apparently had been trying for quite some time to hand me a steaming mug. I sniffed the drink's fragrant scent.

"What's this?" I asked instead of telling her about the crazy idea that had suddenly popped into my mind.

"A chai latte. It's my own secret blend." Althea smiled slyly as she pressed a finger to her lips.

I preferred coffee to tea. I stared at the oversized mug before taking a tentative sip. A sweet and spicy mixture danced like tiny stars on my tongue. I quickly took another, deeper sip. "This is good. Really good. What's in it? Do I taste chocolate?"

"Ah, you've discovered my secret."

"It's not the Amar chocolate?" I asked, a little panicked at the thought of Althea using any of the chocolate we desperately needed for the festival.

"No, no, don't worry. It's not Mabel's chocolate. Now wouldn't that taste good? We'll have to try it sometime." From a metal thermos, she poured the drink into two more mugs. She then stuffed the thermos back into her huge purse.

"So what else is in the tea?" I asked.

"Nuh-uh. It's a secret." She sealed her lips again. But she didn't keep them closed for long. "I do have good news, though. Last night I came up with an idea about how we can make Mabel's chocolate last all weekend."

Bertie sauntered into the room with her flowered house-coat waving around her bare legs. She moved slowly and was slightly hunched as if she was actually feeling her age this morning. "What's the idea?" she asked with absolutely no emotion in her voice.

"Gorp," Althea said. Or maybe she'd burped. I wasn't exactly sure.

"Excuse me?" her mother snapped as she pulled an egg carton from the fridge.

"Chocolate gorp. We melt the chocolate and mix in nuts, pretzels, cereal, and I don't know what else. With the recipe I have, just a little bit of chocolate will go a long, long way."

Bertie paused from breaking an egg into a bowl. Her tired gaze shifted from her daughter's eyes to mine. "It might work."

"We could test it?" Althea said. It sounded like a question. "See how it tastes?"

She stared at me and seemed to hold her breath, as if waiting for me to either agree or disagree with the idea.

"We've got nothing else," I said. "Let's test it."

So we spent the next hour in the kitchen making a small batch of Amar gorp. While the end result didn't equal Mabel's knock-it-out-of-the-park flavors, it tasted . . . good.

275

"This might work," I said as I ate another chocolate-covered pretzel. "If nothing else, it'll give the visitors a small taste of what makes the Amar chocolate so special. I've never tasted a chocolate that even comes close to its depth of flavors. We can sell small cellophane bags of the mix. Of course we're going to have to call it something more palatable than 'gorp.' How about 'The World's Rarest Trail Mix'?"

Althea clapped. No, she didn't just clap. She clapped and jumped up and down like an overzealous teenaged cheerleader. She jumped around the kitchen until she'd wrapped her arms around my shoulders. "It will work. You'll see. It'll work. And it's going to be fabulous."

I tensed. No surprise there. I don't like people hugging me. What surprised me was that I didn't ask whether she'd consulted some so-called magical source to come up with the recipe. Instead, I simply wiggled out of her embrace and patted her arm. "I hope you're right, Althea. I truly do."

*   *   *

We spent the rest of the morning in the Chocolate Box's kitchen, melting the chocolate and stirring in an assortment of nuts and pretzels. We then poured the mixture into small cellophane bags, tying them closed with pretty yellow ribbons. By the time we'd finished, my concussed head throbbed and my swollen ankle screamed with pain. But I didn't care, because we'd accomplished something. With Bertie and Althea's help, I was actually going to do this. I was going to be a chocolatier. Though I winced with every step as I climbed the stairs to Mabel's apartment, I was smiling on the inside.

Sure, the fantasy would last only for a weekend. Afterward, I would return to the real world, return to being nothing more than an unemployed advertising manager with a pile of bills to pay. But oh . . . the next few days promised to be delicious.

I simply had to live through today to get my reward.

Mabel's funeral was in a few hours, and we needed to get ready. Bertie, with Troubadour rubbing circles around her legs while he gave me the stink eye, disappeared into her bedroom without saying much of anything.

Althea followed her mother into the bedroom and then returned with the black silk dress she'd generously offered to let me borrow, since I hadn't packed anything appropriate for a funeral. On her, the dress's flowing skirt would have reached her ankles. On me, the hem didn't extend below my midthigh. Thankfully, the rest of the dress, with its naturally loose fit, didn't look too odd on what my grandmother referred to as my very un-Penn-like, awkwardly tall, and manly physique.

I was struggling to get my short hair to stop curling out at the ends when a loud knock sounded on the front door. Althea called out over Stella's barking that she'd get it.

After tossing Stella several treats, I hobbled into the living room just as Althea let Harley into the apartment. He was dressed in a somber black suit that perfectly fit his trim body. "Are you about ready?" he asked Althea.

"My mom is putting on a little more makeup. I picked up some of the waterproof variety at the drugstore this morning. We should be ready soon," she said and then returned to Bertie's bedroom.

"You're driving?" I asked, not sure why it surprised me.

"I am," he answered. He was looking past me instead of at me. "I can't tell you how sorry I am about what happened to you the other day. I should have walked you home. I should have—"

277

"I'm an adult." I bit off the sharp-tasting words. "I can take care of myself, thank you very much. I'm not one of your fictional Southern belles who needs or wants a strong man to rescue her."

"But I should have—"

"Detective Gibbons dropped off that envelope," I said, cutting him off before he could blame himself for not saving me from that tumble down the stairs. Who knew what might have happened if he'd followed me home. Derek might have hurt two people instead of just one. And if Harley had gotten injured trying to protect me, then I would be the one feeling uncomfortable and guilty on top of all the hurts I'd suffered.

"The detective left the envelope," I repeated. "He said it contains a copy of the DNA report that Skinny had ordered. I thought you might want to have it."

The tips of Harley's ears turned bright red as he gazed at the envelope lying on the table. With a quick motion, he snatched it up and, after folding it over several times, stuffed it into his pocket.

"What are you going to do with it?" I asked.

"Destroy it, of course."

"What about Gavin?" Even though I knew I had no right to say anything, Skinny had been my friend, and I felt as if I had to speak up for him, since he couldn't speak up for himself. "Doesn't he deserve to know?"

Harley seemed startled by the question. He leaned back on his heels and appeared to think about it before saying, "I suppose I should tell him, but not today. One day when he's older and ready to hear about it, I'll tell him the truth about his father. And don't worry, I won't make him sound like a monster. Right now, with the uncertainty of the divorce and the animosity between his mother and me, Gavin is already questioning his place in my life and in Jody's life. Could you imagine what it would do to him to be told that a man who was no longer living was his father? I'm already fighting nearly every day to make sure he feels loved and safe."

I nodded. "You're a good man, Harley Dalton."

He bit his lower lip and shifted from foot to foot as if his shoes were a few sizes too small.

Had I forced him into promising to do something he felt he shouldn't? "If you change your mind and throw the results away, I won't say anything."

"No, you're right, Penn. Telling Gavin is the right thing to do. I'll give him the report as soon as he's ready to hear it. I promise. Sometimes, despite the trouble it causes in our lives, we all are called to action not because it's safe or easy, or because it makes us look good, but because doing so is the right thing to do."

The right thing.

My heart suddenly pounded wildly in my throat.

The right thing.

Yes, I was going to go through with it. The crazy idea that had popped into my head early this morning no longer seemed *that* crazy anymore. In fact, it felt like the right thing to do.

I was going to catch a killer.

Today.

Surprisingly, the thought of baiting a killer wasn't what had my body suddenly shaking. No, it was the thought that I needed help. Asking for help meant I needed to put my trust in someone. And that, quite frankly, terrified me.

I drew a deep breath. And then another one.

279

"This isn't easy . . ." I said. But what needed to be done needed to be done.

"The funeral?" Harley asked. "No, it's not going to be easy. Mabel is going to be fiercely missed by everyone who knew her." He patted his jacket pocket. "I have a box worth of tissues squirreled away in every available pocket."

"No, not that. Though I am dreading the service. It's going to be hard to say good-bye to her and even harder to face her family after everything that has happened. I'm afraid they're going to blame me."

He started to say something. I cut him off. If I didn't speak now, I would lose my nerve. And unless I wanted to put myself in grave danger, I needed him. "What I'm finding hard to do right now is to ask for help. And I need help. I need *your* help."

"My help?" He wiggled his finger in his ears. "Did I hear that right?"

I hoped I looked sincere as I nodded. "You heard right. I need your help."

"Doing what?" he asked. "Wait, don't tell me. You want me to drive myself back to the police station to save you the hassle of calling your detective friend to have me picked up and arrested again."

I could tell by the exasperated tone of his voice that I had some work to do to win his trust. Fine. I could do that.

"I know who killed Mabel and Skinny." I held up my hands and quickly added, "I know it isn't you. At least I hope it isn't. But I don't have any proof that I can take to the police."

"That hasn't stopped you before," he cut in.

"If I'm going to do this right, I need to get proof. There's no way Detective Gibbons will believe me otherwise. Not again. But I can't gather the proof I need alone. Not safely."

He chewed on that thought for a moment before asking with a laugh, "You want *me* to help *you*?"

"I do." I sighed. "Besides, this involves you as much as it does me." I then told him everything I knew about the events leading up to the murders.

After listening, he nodded gravely. "So what do you need me to do?"

Chapter 30

The church, located in the center of historic Charleston, was one of many significant houses of worship that gave the place its nickname, "the Holy City." Its ancient stone spires reached up toward the fading blue sky. For the last part of her life, Mabel had driven into the city from Camellia Beach every week to attend Sunday services. And now the church was holding a special Wednesday service in her honor.

Upon entering, I recognized many faces from Camellia Beach in the pews. The nave was so crowded, overflow seating had been set up in an adjacent courtyard.

Great, I thought. This was my chance to avoid Mabel's family altogether. However, when I moved toward the chairs in the courtyard, Althea caught my arm. Keeping a tight grip on me, she ushered me up the aisle to a row of pews at the front reserved for Mabel's family.

"I shouldn't be here," I protested in a harsh whisper, tugging at Althea's iron grip. "I'm not family."

"None of us are," Althea pointed out. "Not by blood. But this is where Mabel wanted us to sit. And since you're with us, you'll need to sit here too."

I tried to wiggle away one more time, but people were starting to stare. To keep from embarrassing myself and everyone around me any further, I sat down and then slid as low in the seat as possible. But then I remembered the impossible plan I needed to set into motion. So I put some steel in my spine and sat up straighter.

This was where the unveiling of a murderer was to begin.

Harley, who was sitting next to Bertie, leaned toward me and gave a nod as more familiar faces took their seats. Jody sat directly behind us. Cal squeezed into our row and sat next to Althea. Detective Gibbons and Police Chief Byrd chose seats in the back row. I glanced around, suddenly feeling as if I were a character in an Agatha Christie novel.

But this wasn't a book with a guaranteed happy ending. This was real life. I needed more than clever words and wobbly evidence. I needed proof, the kind the police could take into court. So while wringing my hands, I reviewed each part of the plan over and over and hoped everything went as intended.

The church bells started to ring just as an organ began to play. Everyone rose for the procession.

The memorial that followed was a lovely remembrance of Mabel's life. I dabbed tissue after tissue to my eyes as her family and friends talked about how Mabel loved her community and the chocolates she made. Those two things had been her passion and her life.

What if, like Mabel, I devoted my life to chocolate? What if I kept the shop and started learning everything I could about crafting the perfect chocolate bar? Would that give my life more meaning? Would it make me happier?

Perhaps Mabel's shop was exactly the kind of passion that was missing in my life.

It was a crazy thought. Certainly I would change my mind as soon as I got away from Camellia Beach and the temptation of Mabel's chocolate. Besides, I didn't have time to think about such fantasies. I had a plan to put into motion and a killer to catch.

After the service, as we ambled down the aisle toward the back of the church, I blurted out to Bertie and Althea, "Don't get your hopes up too much, but I think I'm going to keep the shop. That's what Mabel would want."

Althea squealed with glee and gave me another one of her tight hugs. "You won't be sorry."

"Won't I?" I quipped.

Jody, who was standing just a few feet behind both Bertie and Althea, gasped as if in pain. She gripped the nearest pew. Her wide eyes looked at me in horror, the kind of horror someone would display if I'd just stabbed her cat. I expected her to explode into a tirade of foul language or perhaps try to claw my eyes out.

Instead, she abruptly turned away from us and pushed through the crowd toward the nearest exit, rudely shoving aside several of Mabel's children as she went.

"Keeping the shop is a lovely idea, dear," Bertie said as she took my hand in hers. "And you know I'll be around if you require any help."

I nodded and patted her hand. "I know. But it's just a crazy idea that popped into my head just now. I might not do it," I warned. "I'll probably change my mind by tomorrow."

"But you might not," Althea said brightly.

Harley winked at me before moving away to talk with Mabel's son Edward.

Wait a minute. That hadn't been part of the plan. He was supposed to stay and watch my back, not wander over to chat with Mabel's family. Suddenly, I panicked. Trying to trap the killer was the stupidest idea ever. No, believing I could trust someone to watch my back had been an even stupider idea. I had no reason, no reason at all, to expect anyone to be there for me when I needed help.

My mother had left when I was less than a few hours old. My father had left again and again to start family after family, shuttling me off to whatever fresh hell Grandmother Cristobel had arranged for me. Even the Cheese King, who I once thought had cared for me, was currently launching a campaign to ruin my reputation. No doubt his goal was to make sure I'd never work in advertising again. As Tina had warned a few days ago, I needed to deal with that mess as soon as possible.

Walk away, I told myself. *Forget your foolish plan and get the hell out of there before anything bad happens. Like getting yourself killed.*

I started to do just that when a sharp finger tapped my shoulder. I turned around and found myself standing face-to-face with Mabel's daughter Florence Corners.

"He didn't do it," she whispered. Her voice, gravelly and soft, was so very different from the screech she'd used when accusing me of stealing their inheritance from them. "He didn't kill your friend."

"I know," I said, my shoulders tensing. "Detective Gibbons came and spoke with me yesterday morning. And I'm sorry.

285

You've suffered too many losses. No matter what Derek did, he was still your brother."

I tried to walk away. She gripped my arm like a falcon grabbing onto its prey, her talon trapping me. "You don't understand. He was working to change his life. He was working to . . ." Tears swam in her eyes as she shook her head. "Because of you, he's dead. It's your fault he's dead."

"I'm sorry," I said, even though what I really wanted to say was that he robbed from his mother's shop and then had tried to kill me. And he'd tried to kill Cal too. But she was Derek's sister. Despite his flaws, she clearly loved him. I had no right to deny her anger or her grief. "I'm truly sorry for your loss. Please, let go of me."

I tried to twist my arm free, but she only tightened her hold. She pulled me closer. "I'm not going to let you get away with it," she spat in my face.

"Excuse me. I need to have a word with Ms. Penn. It's urgent." Cal did a little dance with Florence. I'm not sure exactly what the moves were, but he managed to smoothly slide my arm out from her pinching clutches.

With his hand planted on the small of my back, he quickly ushered me out of the church and onto the wide sidewalk. Had Harley sent Cal over to me? Or was Cal acting on his own?

I stood on the sidewalk, shifting the weight off my sprained foot while trying to figure out my next step in the plan and if I even wanted to continue what I'd already started.

The late-afternoon sun had settled behind the city buildings, casting the sky into shades of deep reds and blacks. Cars, with their bright headlights creating spotlights on the blacktop road, passed by. A harbor breeze caressed my face with its cool breath, reminding me that winter still had a grip on this part of the country.

It took less than a second for me to take notice of these things. They were everyday things, yet they were things my troubled mind clung to because I was tired of trying to figure out what to do next. I was tired of trying to force the wheels of justice to turn. I was tired of mourning the loss of loved ones. And I was tired of lies, of murder, of disappointing those closest to me. I simply wanted to stand on this street in the middle of this Southern city and think about the weather.

But then I remembered Cal had said that he'd desperately needed to talk with me. "What's wrong?" I demanded. "What's the emergency?"

I hoped Harley was okay. I didn't see him on my way out of the church. He'd disappeared into the crowd. Had he found trouble of his own?

"There's no emergency," he said as he wrapped his arms around my waist. "You simply looked like you needed rescuing."

"Really?" I smiled up at him. "I did need rescuing," I had no trouble admitting. "Thank you."

He pulled me a little closer, close enough that his lips could easily brush against mine if I wanted them to. "Would you like to go back to my place?"

I thought about it for a moment. He lived in downtown Charleston, so his place would be convenient. "No." My voice quivered from a sudden burst of nerves. My heart slammed against my chest. "No, I think I'd rather go back to the Chocolate Box and Mabel's apartment. There's the festival that starts tomorrow morning and . . ." I sighed. "I know it sounds silly, but I want to be close to where Mabel lived, close to the things that were hers. Perhaps I'll be able to feel her spirit lingering in her belongings, you know?"

We unwound from our embrace and walked down an alley-way, past long, narrow clapboard houses that had witnessed the Revolutionary War. The silence between us unnerved me so I blurted out, "With all the work I've been doing with the shop, I'm thinking about changing my mind. I'm thinking about keeping it."

He stopped in the middle of the alleyway. "Keeping what?"

"The shop."

His mouth dropped open as he stared at me. "You . . . you're going to keep the Chocolate Box? Really?"

Butterflies danced in my stomach as I nodded. "Crazy, I know. But for whatever reason, it's what Mabel wanted. And to be honest, I think I'd enjoy the challenge."

"Wow." He shook his head. "Wow. We should, I don't know, celebrate. Mabel would be so happy to know that her legacy will continue."

I held up my hands. "It's probably too early to celebrate. I'm still just playing with the idea. It came to me during the service just now. We'll see how this weekend goes before I make a final decision."

He stopped beside his black BMW SUV. It was parked in front of a skinny moss-green house that looked to be one room wide. The house was just about the same width as the double porches that ran along the entire left side of the structure. "Yep, that's where I live," he said. "I travel, so I don't get to spend a lot of time here. And I don't need a lot of space."

"It's"—*Small?*—"charming," I said.

He opened the car's passenger door and, like a true Southern gentleman, waited for me to climb inside. I was glad to be able to get my weight off my sore foot. He then rushed around the car and jumped into the driver's seat. "I don't care if your idea is crazy or not, we should celebrate it tonight. You know Mabel would like that."

I leaned across the center console and impulsively planted a playful kiss on his lips. "Yes, I'd like that too."

Chapter 31

I had no idea where Harley had gone. He hadn't followed me back to Camellia Beach. I would have heard his car's broken muffler from more than a mile away.

Unfortunately, alone or not, there was really no going back. I'd already told everyone who would listen that I planned to keep the shop. By now, the entire town should know. Ready or not, all I could do was to wait for the plan to unfold. I hoped it wasn't about to unravel.

After putting my purse down on the kitchen table in Mabel's apartment, I hooked Stella's leash to her collar. Cal accompanied me while I took Stella out for a short, hobbling walk (I hobbled, Stella walked) down to the end of the block and back. Instead of trying to bite my companion's toes, my normally fearless dog whined and tugged, keeping herself as far away from him as her leash would allow.

"Maybe she's reacting to the trauma from the other day," I said, puzzled by her odd behavior. She'd never shied away from Cal before—of course, she'd never witnessed him kill a man before either. I took a piece of bacon from my coat pocket and held it out for Cal to give to Stella. "Bertie makes it for her every morning. She's a huge fan."

Stella, with ears nearly twice as big as her head, heard the movement of the bacon coming out of my pocket. She whirled around and wagged her tail at me. When I didn't immediately give her the treat, she gave an aggravated bark.

Cal frowned at the slightly greasy treat and then at my naughty dog. He lifted the bacon, holding it gingerly between his forefinger and thumb, and quickly tossed it at Stella, who by now was barking full force. She gobbled the bacon but still avoided him for the rest of the walk.

After we returned to the apartment, my little beast started to bark like crazy. "What's wrong with her?" Cal asked. "She didn't make this kind of fuss a few minutes ago."

"I don't know what's up with her," I said, frowning. "If I didn't know her better, I'd think she was scared."

Stella whirled around in circles, poking her nose under the sofa, the coffee table, and wherever else she could put it. With a growl, Troubadour darted out from under the china cabinet and swatted Stella across the nose. Stella yelped.

Troubadour, his gaze narrowed with scorn, hissed first in Stella's direction and then in mine. Apparently satisfied that he'd properly put us in our places, he sauntered into the kitchen with all the pride and self-importance as the Emperor with No Clothes.

I knelt down on the floor and coddled Stella, fussing over her without actually holding or hugging her. I also gave her several treats. As soon as she looked her feisty self again, I led her into my bedroom and locked her in. She barked and scratched at the door for a few minutes before finally settling down.

"Wow, sorry about that. I'm still working on training her," I said to Cal, who'd been patiently waiting in the kitchen. "Can I offer you some dinner? Bertie has been cooking as if expecting several hungry armies to drop by."

He looked around. "Shouldn't we wait for her to get home?"

"She's going to stay with Althea tonight. It was Althea's suggestion. She wanted to be close to her mom. So I've got the place to myself. Well, there's Troubadour and Stella, but they don't take up much space."

His brows rose at the thought that we would be alone all evening. My cheeks heated at the thought as well. Was I ready to be alone with a man so soon after the Cheese King's betrayal? Part of me dearly wanted to be ready. Another part, a much bigger part, felt as vulnerable as Bertie's naked cat.

"Yes, well." My nerves caused my insides to bounce around as if they were balls on a squash court. "Let's see what we can find to eat."

I started taking bowls from the refrigerator and pulling back the foil to peek inside.

"Is that Bertie's chili?" Cal asked as he peered over my shoulder. His hands landed on my hips as if they belonged there.

My breath hitched in my throat. "It-it looks like chili."

"It does, doesn't it? I haven't had her chili in ages. It's fabulous. You know she puts chocolate in it?"

"Chocolate?" I sniffed the chili. It didn't smell like chocolate.

"You don't taste it, but it makes the chili taste amazing." He reached around me and took the bowl from my hands. "This is what you'll want to eat for dinner. Trust me."

Trust him? I barely trusted myself.

While I reheated the chili on the stove, Cal set the table. We talked about the funeral and tomorrow's festival and the weather. Suddenly he looked up at me. "You're not really going to keep the shop, are you?"

I shrugged as I stirred the chili. The steam rising from the pot teased me with its spicy flavors. "Mabel thought I should keep it. She worried about what would happen to Camellia Beach and the village of Cabruca without her and the shop to support them. I got the feeling she thought both places needed a caretaker."

"But why you?" he asked, not meanly. He sounded genuinely curious.

"That's what I keep asking. No one seems to have the answer. Did you know that Mabel wrote me a note explaining it all, but someone stole it from your brother's office?"

Cal grimaced. "More likely Harley misplaced it. I hate to say it, but he isn't a very good lawyer."

"You shouldn't say that. He's your brother."

He lifted his hands. "There's a reason he's no longer working in Atlanta, and it's not because Dad died. That's all I'm saying. With the divorce and everything else that's been going on, he's been having trouble keeping his mind on his cases."

I spooned the reheated chili into two bowls and carried them over to the table.

Cal patted the chair next to his. "Come, sit down. Your foot must be killing you by now."

"You're right about that." I slid into the chair and picked up a spoon.

"Here's to new beginnings, whatever they may be," he said as he lifted a spoonful of chili into the air as if making a toast.

"New beginnings," I said and lifted my spoon as well. When we clinked them together, chili splattered all over both of our clothes. We both laughed as we dabbed at the stains with water from our glasses.

To be honest, I wasn't sure why I was laughing. This wasn't my dress I'd just spilled chili all over. It had to be nerves. I tended to laugh at inappropriate things whenever I felt nervous. And spending this much time alone with Cal and sitting this close to him was turning me into a mess of quivering nerves.

Even my nerves felt like they had nerves.

Who knew what might happen tonight?

He smiled and put his hand on my leg, which only kicked my heart into overdrive. I still hadn't tasted the chili, so I scooped a big spoonful into my mouth.

It was hot. Peppery hot. Fiery hot. Who in the world would make chili this hot? My face heated. And heated. I imagined I looked as red as a sunburned turnip. I chewed as daintily as humanly possible while pretending my mouth wasn't being devoured by a flaming inferno. Sweat beaded on my brow.

Cal noticed. A blind man would have noticed my discomfort. He slid the glass of water closer to me.

"Got one of her peppers, I see," he said, his hand still on my leg and my heart still beating as if it might burst free. "Don't be a hero. Drink all your water and mine too, if you need to."

I drank mine. And his. And three more glasses of water. And I still had to swallow several times before I could form words. "Didn't taste the chocolate," I managed to croak.

He laughed. "Not every bite is like that."

I wasn't sure if serving chili that tasted as hot as the sun was a joke the locals played on newbies like me or if he was telling the truth. He seemed to be enjoying his dish without sweating tears, so I cautiously took another, much smaller bite.

Hmmm . . . the flavors swirled around in my mouth. He was right; you didn't taste the chocolate. Not really. It wasn't a sweet dish. The flavors had a richness, both sharp and subtle at the same time, that made me dig in for another try. I kept a lookout for peppers.

"You know," I said after devouring nearly half the bowl, "I'm not very good at investigating murders. I've questioned people and researched instead of sleeping. And what do I have? I've ended up suspecting nearly half the town. Like I thought your brother was guilty, but he didn't do it. And then I wondered if either Bertie or Althea was behind the crimes. But that's crazy."

"Then it's a good thing we had the police working on it," he said after he swallowed another spoonful of the chili.

"It is. You know, my latest research had led me in two very different directions and to two suspects."

"Really?" He leaned forward. "Who are your suspects?"

"Jody and, well . . . you, actually." I gave a nervous laugh. He didn't laugh with me.

"What do you mean, me?"

"Don't get upset. I already told you I'm no good at detecting." I took a long sip of water.

"I still don't understand it. Why would you think I would want to kill anyone?"

I set down my spoon and looked at Cal—really looked at him. "You see, there was an article about a murdered reporter in West Africa. The poor man had been investigating human rights violations on a large chocolate plantation. This article about his murder kept coming back to me. I'm not sure why I couldn't stop thinking about it. And then I remembered your family's beach house. It was filled with artwork you'd brought back with you from your travels. Much of it was from Africa. With the demand for chocolate being what it is, I started to think that, for some unknown reason, you desperately needed to buy the rights to Mabel's chocolate in order to sell it to some large corporation. Chocolate is a billion-dollar industry, after all. Stupid, I know. Like I said, I don't have the instincts for finding anything. I once lost my keys in my apartment for two months. I'd torn through every nook and cranny, only to find them months later tucked in the very pocket of my purse where I always keep them. How crazy is that?"

He pushed his bowl aside. "One deal out of the hundreds I make every year wouldn't make or break me. The rights to Mabel's chocolate aren't really something I need. I offered to sell the rights as a favor to you. But you've decided to keep the shop."

"I have." I pushed my bowl away as well.

He sat back in his chair and smiled at me. "And none of this matters. We already know the murderer's identity. Derek killed your friend and his mother. Then he tried to kill you and me."

"No, he didn't." I leaned toward him. "Derek didn't kill anyone. At least he didn't kill anyone that we know about."

"Yes, he did. And he also robbed the shop."

"Yes, he robbed the shop. And he also pushed me down the stairs. But he had an alibi for the night of Skinny's murder. The police are still looking into Mabel's murder, but Detective Gibbons told me yesterday morning he didn't think Derek was guilty of either crime."

"Oh, right. Of course he had an alibi," Cal said slowly. "He was with me all night."

"No, that's not his alibi. He wasn't with you." I stood up and carried both bowls to the sink and started washing them. "Which means you also don't have an alibi."

"I don't need an alibi. Why would I—? You think I would . . . for a . . . for a ridiculously small chocolate deal? The village doesn't even grow enough of the Amar beans to fill the shop's needs. Who would want to buy it?"

"You should know the answer better than I would. In fact, you told me just a few days ago that, in the right hands, the bean's production could be expanded. I imagine it could easily become a must-have chocolate for the megarich. A luxury treat for those who could afford it. And the person who sells the rights to the beans might become superrich as well. That sounds like a motive, I think."

He laughed. It was an ugly sound. "And you think I'd commit murder, that I'd kill an elderly woman, just so I could purchase the rights to her chocolate beans? Oh, my goodness, Penn. You weren't lying. You *are* terrible at investigations."

"Horrible, really." I rinsed the soap off the bowls and set them on a dish towel beside the sink before adding, "But in my defense, some of the things you've been doing do look somewhat suspicious."

He carried the water glasses to the sink. And then he stayed, standing so close I felt trapped between him and the counter. "Like what?"

To give myself some space, I twisted around and, after nudging him out of the way, hobbled toward the living room. "Now, don't be mad. I'm simply telling you where my investigations have been taking me." I drew a deep breath. "For example, that first chocolate class I took with Mabel had been a spur-of-the-moment thing. But all the rest were planned. And you attended those classes."

"I like chocolate." He joined me in the living room. He took both my hands and cradled them as if they were precious objects. His stunning green eyes sharpened. His voice deepened, turning all chocolatey smooth. "In case you hadn't noticed, I'm kind of interested in you."

"So you say." It took several tugs to pry my hands loose. "Did you know Mabel had lied to you? She hadn't cancelled that last class. She didn't want you there." I moved away from him and managed to put the sofa between us. The door was behind me, so if I needed to escape, I could. "Why wouldn't she want you there? Perhaps you came to the classes not because you liked me and not because you liked chocolate. You were there because you wanted to make sure Mabel didn't tell me something." I tapped my chin. "But what could she tell me? What didn't you want Mabel to tell me? Was it something about the will?"

He took a step toward the sofa, and toward me, but thankfully didn't come any closer. "I didn't know about the will, remember?"

"Didn't you? Unlike Mabel's family, you didn't seem at all surprised when your brother announced that I had inherited the shop and the Amar chocolate."

"I wouldn't say I wasn't surprised. I simply didn't care."

"And you'd visited the village of Cabruca, a place that according to Mabel is horribly remote and difficult to get to. You visited it not just once but several times."

"What can I say? I'm a nice guy. She enjoyed getting news from the village. So I made excuses to go there."

"A nice guy with expensive taste in clothes. I didn't think anything about it at first. My half sister is a fashion designer, and the first time I saw you, I immediately thought you'd fit right in on one of her runways. It didn't occur to me until today why that was. It's because your clothes are all expensive designer name brands. Even the suit you have on right now, a Zegna suit, costs close to five thousand dollars."

"So? I can afford it."

"Perhaps. Derek had warned me that possessing a little fortune only made a person hungry for more. I had thought he was talking about himself. What if I was wrong? What if he was warning me about you?"

"Don't be silly. Of course he was talking about himself. Derek was an idiot with money. He squandered the trust fund his parents had given him in less than a year. And then he would waste whatever money Mabel would give him. For someone with access to so much money, he was always broke."

"Still, what he'd said to me had felt like a warning. I thought he was warning me against my own failings. But what if he'd been warning me to be wary of someone who might want to do me harm? Someone who lusted for money? You and your brother came from a modest background. You're a self-made man. But now you have a chance to make more money than most people can imagine. But to do so, you'd have to control the rights to the Amar chocolate beans. Chocolate is an expensive commodity. It's something people are even willing to kill for."

"Not me. I'm a business broker, not a killer." His voice tightened. "And even though I don't need an alibi, I have one. Even if Derek wasn't there, I was at the bar the night Skinny was killed. Apparently I was too drunk to even know Derek had left."

"You could have easily left the bar at any time that night after Derek left. He was your alibi, but he wasn't at the bar, not at the time of Skinny's death. You could have left and come back, stumbling around like you'd had too much. You could have easily acted drunk even if you were sober. Heck, you could have left to drown Skinny in Mabel's vat of chocolate, returned, and proceeded to slam down enough shots to prove to everyone how drunk you were."

"Why would I do that? What possible reason would I have to kill him? It didn't stop you from inheriting Mabel's chocolate shop."

"I don't know. Maybe you killed him because he knew something, something that would make me want to keep the shop. He'd sounded excited on the phone. He'd told me to come to Camellia Beach."

He took another step toward the sofa and me. "And yet his death didn't change the outcome."

"Didn't it?" I asked while forcing myself to stand my ground.

"You're keeping the shop and the chocolate. So, no, his death didn't change anything."

Again I had to force myself to stand my ground, not because he'd advanced on me again, but because my confidence in my foolish plan had started to crumble.

What if—?

No. No. I needed to press forward. I needed to hear the truth, even if the truth turned out to be that I was in fact a terrible investigator.

"Why did you kill Derek?" The words popped out of my mouth.

"You're not listening to me. I didn't kill—!" he shouted.

"Yes, you did. You shot him dead. Why? Was he threatening you?"

He shook his head. "You know he threatened me. You were there."

"He threatened to do what? Expose you? Did he threaten to tell the police that he'd left the bar early that night, that you couldn't use him as your alibi? Was he demanding you pay him money in exchange for his silence?"

"No wonder everyone in town thinks you're crazy. You don't know what you're talking about, but you keep saying things anyway."

My confidence slipped a little further. I had no idea what to say to that. Perhaps he was innocent after all.

"If I was working with Derek," he said, his voice low and tight, "why would I help save you? It would have been an easy thing to simply snap your neck after you'd fallen down the stairs. No one would have been the wiser."

"True. You could have." I shivered at the thought. "But at the time, I was still going to give away the shop and let you sell the rights to Mabel's chocolates. Edward had already told Jody that he was going to renegotiate selling the building. Had he told you the same thing?"

Cal sighed again. "You're like your nasty little dog. You don't know when to give up. I'm starting to think maybe I should have snapped your skinny neck."

Only a killer—or perhaps one of my ex-boyfriends—would say something like that.

"Thank you for not snapping my neck," I said.

Since I was fairly certain Harley had abandoned me at the church, I started looking around the room for backup. A misplaced gun. A crowbar. A heavy book. Anything I could use to fend off Cal if he actually attacked me.

"I mean"—I held up my hands and took a step back, edging closer to the door—"let's not argue. I was simply telling you what had been going on in my head. It's not like I ran to the police with these wild ravings or anything."

"You went to the police?" Several red blotches appeared on his face. Apparently he wasn't listening to me.

"No! I just said I *didn't* go to the police. Why would I?"

"Why? Why? Because you called the police when you thought my brother was guilty of the crime."

"I'm sorry?" I said. I'm not sure why I made it a question. And I wasn't sorry. "Today has been an emotional, exhausting day for the both of us. Let's just go our separate ways, okay?"

He jammed his hands in his insanely expensive pants pockets. "It's not that easy." He walked back to the kitchen.

While his back was turned to me, I decided it was time to make my escape. I charged toward the door. With each step, my sprained ankle threatened to collapse under me.

He shouted a curse and ran after me. I managed to peel the door open just as he grabbed my arm.

I twisted sharply and managed to free my arm long enough to land a blow to his chin. He staggered backward. I dove out the door.

I would have made a clean escape if not for my sprained ankle. It twisted as I ran toward the stairs. I stumbled and would have taken yet another tumble down the stairs if not for Cal grabbing me from behind. He wrapped an arm around my chest, trapping my hands.

I tossed back my head and screamed. He slammed a hand over my mouth as he dragged me back inside. A flock of startled herons took flight out of the nearby trees. Otherwise, the chilly night was silent.

Cal kicked the door closed behind us and then removed his hand from its bruising grip over my mouth.

"What-what are you doing?" I gasped. He dragged me into the kitchen. "Let me go. Now."

When I struggled against his hold, he kicked my sprained ankle. The pain nearly blinded me.

"Getting this." With his free arm, he pulled down Mabel's intricately carved wooden cask.

"How did that get there?" I'd left it in the shop. I know I did.

"I put it there." He put the cask on the kitchen counter and stroked the top of the box. "Beautiful, isn't it? And what's inside it is worth more than gold."

"I don't care what it's worth. You can have it. Just let me go."

"Too late for that. Today is the last day."

"What?" I twisted and turned but could not break loose.

"That idiot Derek had worried you would go back on your word," Cal explained. "Damn if he wasn't right. I really should have snapped your neck when I found you at the bottom of the stairs. But the only reason the fool wanted you dead was so he could get his brother to demand more money from *me*. The greedy bastard wanted his share of the money and more. You were right about one thing. He was blackmailing me because he knew I'd used him as my alibi. Then he pulled that stupid stunt of trying to kill you. After that, I knew the fool had to go. He was a money pit hungry for his next high."

I tried again to twist away from Cal. I'd taken more than a dozen self-defense classes and considered myself proficient at escape maneuvers. But unlike the instructors in the class, he moved like an octopus. Whenever I'd managed to kick or punch away one arm, he seemed to already have another one on me. Plus he kept hitting me in my bruised ribs or kicking my sprained ankle.

"You want to kill me?" I shouted, hoping against hope that Harley or anyone might hear me. I hoped like I'd never hoped before that Harley was hiding somewhere in the apartment and waiting for the right moment to jump out and save me.

I could hear a knocking sound coming from somewhere in the apartment. Was that Harley? The plan had been for him to wait in the other room with a recorder and to intervene if needed.

But that knocking was probably just Stella. The poor nervous puppy had started barking like crazy again. I could picture her throwing herself at the door.

"Haven't you been paying attention? Of course I want to kill you. And it has to happen tonight, baby." Cal's breath felt hot on my face. "If you die tomorrow, your heirs will inherit the shop and the rights to Mabel's chocolate. But if you die tonight, Mabel's greedy family will get their hands on everything she wanted you to have. I might have to pay their inflated price, but they've already agreed to sell the chocolate to me."

"How-how can you do this? I-I thought you liked me," I cried as his hands encircled my neck.

"Don't be stupid, Penn." He didn't look attractive anymore. I wondered why I'd ever thought he looked like an action hero or a fashion model. He was ugly through and through. "You're about as likable as a porcupine. Only an idiot—a blind idiot—would want to be with you. Even your own dog hates you."

Cal's hands closed even tighter over my throat—so tight, I couldn't even wheeze.

Why had I trusted Harley or anyone to help me? I should have known better. I should have known I was on my own with this.

My vision grayed even further. I gasped, but no air could get into my lungs. My chest heaved with distress.

I clawed at Cal's hands. I knew I'd drawn blood, but his hold didn't budge.

"Stop kicking around. It'll be over in another moment. Just another moment and it'll be all over. And then I'm going to stuff Mabel's chocolate down your skinny throat. You should like that." He sounded so calm about my death, like it was something he orchestrated every day.

I wanted to scream at him. But I couldn't because I couldn't breathe. All I could do was flail my arms and kick my legs. And they were starting to feel heavier and heavier. My movements had begun to get slower and slower.

One of my wild kicks landed hard on his leg. He stumbled, pulling me along with him. His hold on my neck loosened just a bit. For one glorious moment, I could suck air into my starving lungs.

Out of the corner of my eye, I spotted the ornately carved cask of chocolate sitting on the counter where he'd left it. If I stretched, the tips of my fingers could just touch it.

Thankfully Cal seemed too focused on strangling the life out of me to care what my arms were doing. I stretched a little more and managed to move the cask forward on the counter. I moved it just enough that my hand could close over the end of the cask.

I then used every ounce of strength I had left and swung Mabel's heavy wooden chocolate box. Although my aim wobbled, I managed to slam it into the side of Cal's head.

His eyes widened in surprise.

His hands slid off my neck.

He landed on the floor with a thud just as a loud crash sounded behind me.

I whirled around and smacked the cask into Harley's face.

His eyes were wide and wild, his knuckles bloodied. He stumbled as he cried out in pain. His arms went around me.

305

He held onto me so tightly, I feared he might crush my ribs as we both tumbled to the ground.

"You're here?" I rasped.

"You broke my nose!" he cried.

"You're here?" My voice sounded like my throat had been scraped with sandpaper.

"I would have gotten to you sooner, but I had to break down the damned door to get out of the closet. It wouldn't open."

"Th-the lock is broken."

"Well, you don't have to worry about that anymore." He nodded toward the closet. Its door lay cracked in several places a few feet from the closet's gaping opening.

"Stay where you are," Detective Gibbons said as he jogged past the two of us. "I've got this."

The detective pressed his knee into the center of Cal's back, halting his attempts to get up off the floor. He then slapped a pair of handcuffs on his wrists.

Harley moaned. I don't know if it was distress at seeing his only brother being arrested for murder or because of his broken and bleeding nose.

"Why-why did you leave me?" I asked. The words sounded like a series of gasps, since I was still unable to pull enough air into my aching lungs. "You-you'd said you'd watch my back, but then you'd disappeared."

"He came and got me," Detective Gibbons explained as he pulled Cal up from the floor. "Good thing too. You shouldn't have attempted to confront a killer on your own."

By this time, even more backup had arrived. Two uniformed officers from the county ran into the apartment. "Sorry we're late, sir. There was an accident that closed the bridge."

Harley, his nose dripping blood, struggled to his feet. He then reached down and pulled me off the floor. Once he was sure I wasn't going to fall over, he marched over to his brother, who was bleeding from where I'd hit him in the head with the wooden cask.

"Are you okay?" Harley asked Cal.

"Do I look okay?"

"No," Harley said and then slugged his brother.

Detective Gibbons shouted a protest and grabbed Harley by the shoulders while his officers grabbed onto Cal, who looked dazed and glassy-eyed. His head dropped to his chest.

"How could you do something like this?" Harley hissed. "Our parents taught us better."

Cal lifted his head just enough to whisper, "They taught us to be poor."

"Poor? What are you talking about? We had—"

"Nothing. We had nothing." Anger flashed in his eyes. "We had hand-me-down bikes and clothes. Even our books came from the used bookstore. While the Maybanks had everything because of that chocolate."

"What are you talking about?" Harley demanded. "Mabel's shop barely ever made a profit."

"Didn't you know? Mabel's grandfather invested the profits from selling the Amar chocolate beans. That's how the family built their fortune. They used those damn beans to get rich. And then Mabel took over the chocolate shop, and she wasted what could have made them ever richer because she was worried about taking care of those uneducated villagers." He spat the last of those words.

"Mabel had principles. I thought you did too. Dad taught us—"

307

"Dad taught us to be poor," Cal mocked. "Look at you, working in his go-nowhere office. You're pathetic."

"No, you're the pathetic one," Harley said and turned away, unable to watch as the officers led his brother out the door.

"Are you okay?" Detective Gibbons asked as Harley dropped to the sofa and buried his face in his hands. "Do I need to call EMS?"

"I'm okay," Harley answered after a long silence.

"And you?" Gibbons asked me.

I felt my throat. It was sore to the touch. It would be covered in all manner of colorful bruises by morning, and my foot hurt like the devil. But I was alive. And I'd helped catch Skinny's killer.

"Did . . . did you get enough information?" I croaked.

Gibbons nodded. "Enough to press charges? Yes. He tried to kill you. I'm sure once we start digging a little deeper into his past activities, we'll find even more damaging evidence and will be able to charge him for the other murders. The ones who think they can't get caught tend to make the most mistakes."

I nodded and then collapsed onto the sofa next to Harley. His fingers intertwined with mine. As we sat there while the police did their business, he kept a tight grip on my hand.

I didn't mind.

Chapter 32

The next morning, Althea loaned me a pretty pink silk scarf to wrap around my neck to hide the rainbow of bruises that had formed overnight. Both she and Bertie took turns hugging me as we stuffed ourselves with French toast drizzled with chocolate sauce. Because I understood why they felt the need to squeeze me periodically, I tolerated their fussing.

Harley had spent the night on the sofa and looked about as stiff and tired as I felt. I tried to talk with him over breakfast about what had happened. I tried to offer him some measure of comfort. It had to be killing him to know his younger brother had committed such horrible crimes. How did he manage to hold his emotions in check knowing Cal had killed Mabel, a woman who had been an important fixture in both their lives ever since they were babies?

Harley stubbornly refused to accept any comfort from me or Althea or even Bertie. He batted away the hugs Althea and Bertie tried to press on him. After downing a cup of black coffee, he stood up. "I have to go find a top-rate criminal lawyer for Cal.

Despite what he did, he's still my baby brother. I have to take care of him," he explained. His voice sounded raw.

"Of course you do." I laid my hand on his arm. He tensed but didn't pull away. "Did he do anything or say anything that explains why he'd suddenly do something like this?" I asked gently.

His shoulders slumped as if the troubles weighing on them were too much to bear. "I suppose I should have seen some sign that there was something wrong with his thinking lately, but for whatever reason, I—"

He turned away from us. "I need to go," he whispered as he made his way toward the door. "With our parents gone, I'm all the family Cal has."

"Child, before you run off into the city," Bertie called out to him just as he started to step outside, "make sure your boy hears about Cal's arrest from your lips."

Harley stopped. "Oh, God, Gavin." His shoulders shuddered. "I don't know what I'm going to say to him. He's suffered too much upheaval already. He doesn't deserve this."

"You don't either," Bertie said as we watched him leave the apartment.

Because this was the first day of the Sweets on the Beach festival, I swallowed several powerful pain pills to keep my swollen foot from bothering me too much. Althea and I then headed down toward the ocean to set up our booth. Bertie stayed to work at the shop.

The sea air felt crisp and clean. The sky glowed a brilliant blue. The ocean sparkled as if diamonds danced just under its surface. While Stella chased sea gulls, the two of us got to work on our beachside booth. A three-sided pop-up gazebo provided protection from the ocean breeze. Two long tables gave us ample space to set up the chocolate display. Oversized photos of the villagers harvesting the Amar beans were set up on easels along with a map showing exactly where the chocolate came from. Brochures detailing the chocolate trade and the importance of buying from reputable fair trade sources were fanned out on either end of the tables.

It wasn't perfect. Many of the chocolates we offered for sale didn't taste nearly as amazing as the Amar trail mix, which sold out almost immediately.

However, everyone from the town who came by, including all the men and women from the Pink Pelican Inn, agreed that the festival and our part in it was a raving success.

Detective Gibbons stepped into the booth toward the end of the day and purchased several truffles. He smiled as he savored one of Bertie's sea salt chocolate caramels.

"Has Cal talked at all?" Althea asked. "Did he explain why he'd kill a man in a vat of chocolate?"

The detective shook his head as he chewed. "Thanks to that brother of his, Cal lawyered up first thing this morning and isn't saying boo to us. But I can tell you this much: by putting Skinny in the melted chocolate, he destroyed any physical evidence that would have helped us identify Cal as the killer."

"I'm not sure that's the only reason he did it. After hearing what he said last night about resenting the Maybanks and their money, I think he wanted to use the chocolate beans against them," I said.

"Or he could have used Mabel's vat of chocolate in an effort to implicate someone else, like my mom, as the killer," Althea pointed out.

"We may never know what he was thinking," Detective Gibbons said as he reached into his bag for another caramel. "All we know for sure is that Cal's obsession with Mabel's Amar chocolate and the fortune he thought he deserved caused him to make some awful decisions."

Several tourists suddenly crowded into our booth and started to ask about the chocolates we had for sale, which put an end to our speculations about what had been going on in Cal's troubled mind.

The detective picked up the bag of chocolates he'd purchased and gave me a hard look. "What you did last night was dangerous and stupid. Don't ever pull a stunt like that again. Come talk to me instead, okay?"

After he left, I had very little time to reflect on what had happened or on anything else. The booth remained busy until the very end of the day.

"So what do you think? Are you going to keep the shop?" Althea asked as she started to pack up the truffles.

"You mean forever?" I asked as I stuffed a handful of brochures back into a box.

"Mama and I know you only told us you were keeping the shop to force Cal to show his hand," Althea said as she folded up the easels. "But we'd really like you to stay."

I was tempted to say yes. Yes, I'd put down roots here in this quirky backward coastal town. Oh, yes, I was tempted.

But I shook my head. "I have a disaster unfolding in Madison that requires my attention. My ex is destroying my reputation. And my family is livid that I haven't stopped him from raking the Penn name through the mud."

"But then you'll come back?" she asked. Her dark eyes sparkled. "We need you here. Look what you've done." She indicated the crowd that wandered up and down the beach.

I shook my head. "This was Mabel's doing, not mine."

"Your last-minute advertising and press releases certainly drummed up interest. I haven't seen it this crowded in the winter . . . ever. Didn't you see the front page this morning? 'Chocolate Shop Murders Solved.' And the reporter included all the details you'd provided about the festival. That was your doing."

Her enthusiasm was certainly infectious. I couldn't help but smile. "I'll miss you, Althea," I said.

"You don't have to. Go get things settled in Madison, but come back. Live above the shop."

Gracious, I was tempted. But I ended up shaking my head. Although I had a mess of a life to put back together in Madison, what I was returning to was my life. It was the life I'd built for myself, not some vision that a misguided—but talented—old lady had foisted on me.

"I'm honored that Mabel picked me as heir to her chocolate shop. And I do plan to protect the village of Cabruca and their amazing chocolates," I quickly added. "The Penn Foundation has some wonderful resources. I hope to convince my father to offer them to the villagers. If I can't do that, I believe I can pull together enough money to create a trust fund. But Mabel's family should have the shop and the land. It's their legacy, not mine."

That last bit physically hurt to admit. It surprised me how much I'd hoped Skinny had discovered a DNA link between Mabel and me. Learning that it hadn't been the case ached like a burning sore in the center of my chest. I rubbed it.

"I came here to find Skinny's killer. Now it's time for me to leave," I said, still rubbing that sore spot on my chest.

"What I don't understand is why Cal killed Skinny. It wasn't as if he had any special information that would have convinced you to stay and run the shop, did he?"

"If he knew something, I suspect that information died with both him and Mabel. Remember Mabel had written me a letter that I was supposed to get at the will reading. And it was stolen."

"Do you think Cal has it?"

I shook my head. "I imagine it's been destroyed by now. It'd be dangerous for him to keep it."

"Well, I wish you'd change your mind. We're going to miss you. *I'm* going to miss you."

And despite that crusty shell I wore like a shield of armor, I believed her. I truly believed she wanted me to stay in Camellia Beach because she genuinely wanted to be my friend.

That felt . . . nice.

"Let's get this stuff back to the shop," I said, picking up a box. "I think I should make some more chocolate truffles to restock for tomorrow."

She picked up a large box and placed it on the handcart we'd used to ferry supplies down to the beach. I set my box on the handcart and started to pick up another when I heard, "Penn! Penn!"

I looked up. Harley was jogging toward us. He waved a large envelope in his hand like a flag. "Penn!"

As soon as he reached us, he thrust the envelope into my hands. I frowned at it while he struggled to catch his breath.

"Ran all the way from your office?" Althea said. "You're getting out of shape."

"I . . . ran . . . from . . . my . . . office . . . via . . . the . . . chocolate . . . shop," he said.

"What's this about?"

I handed him a bottled water, which he gulped down. The envelope he'd given me was the same one Detective Gibbons had brought over. It was a copy of Gavin's DNA report. I really didn't want or need the responsibility of keeping it. Did he want me to give the report to Skinny's family? What kind of trouble would that cause for Gavin?

Yes, Gavin deserved to know the truth. But I agreed with Harley. His son needed to be told when he was ready. Not a moment sooner.

"I was about to stuff this into the back of my safe, but something told me to open it first," he said.

"So?"

He smiled at me. "Open it."

I tried to hand the envelope back to him, but his smile only grew wider. "No, seriously. You need to open it."

I did. Inside, I found a single piece of paper.

My name was on the top right corner.

Thankfully, I hadn't yet folded up the chair. Or else I would have ended up sitting in the sand.

I landed in the lawn chair with a thump as my eyes absorbed the words as if they were foreign and unintelligible.

"What does it say?" Althea demanded.

I read the words through again. "I—I—"

"Harley? I swear, you tell me right now what it says," Althea demanded, stomping her tiny foot.

I looked up from the paper and my gaze met Harley's, and he nodded at me. And then I looked over at Althea, who looked as if she was about to strangle Harley.

That ache in my chest suddenly vanished. Something warm and surprisingly happy started to spread throughout my entire body.

I smiled. "It looks as if I'm about to have a change of heart." Tears sprang to my eyes. "I'm keeping the shop. For real this time."

"You are?" Althea shouted. "You are!"

Skinny, my sneaky friend. I don't know how he'd managed to get samples of my DNA or Mabel's, but he had. The DNA report stated the results were conclusive.

"Mabel was my maternal grandmother."

"She was?" Althea squealed. She then pulled me from the chair and hugged me so tightly, I wasn't sure I would ever be able to breathe normally again. "She was!"

By the time she let go, we all had tears staining our eyes.

"I suspect that's why my brother went after Skinny," Harley said, his voice husky with emotion. "He couldn't let anyone find out. I have a feeling Mabel suspected you were her granddaughter, but I don't think she knew for certain. This piece of paper proves it. It proves you are a legal heir. If Cal had succeeded and you had died yesterday, this piece of paper would have given your heirs, and not Mabel's family, control of the shop and the chocolates."

"But who is my mother?" I asked.

"You don't know?" Harley sounded surprised.

"No. I've never known."

"Then that's a mystery that'll have to be solved another day," he said.

"But you are going to stay? You are going to keep the shop?" Althea asked, wringing her hands. "You have to now."

"I already said I would, didn't I?" I answered. "Oh, I'm going to have a lot to learn about living in a close-knit community like Camellia Beach. And about trust. And chocolate. I think I'll need a lifetime to learn about chocolate."

Thank you, Mabel. Thank you for trying to scam me.

Because of her, I think I've finally found my home.

Recipes Snipped From the *Camellia Current*, Camellia Beach's Local Newspaper

A day without chocolate is like a day without sunlight.
—Bertie Bays, resident of Camellia Beach, South Carolina

Bertie's Sweet and Spicy Comfort Chili

When the weather turns damp and chilly, make a batch of this sweet and spicy chili. It'll make your tummy sing.

Ingredients

1 pound lean ground beef
2 medium onions, chopped
3 cloves of garlic, minced
1 28-oz can tomatoes, cut up
2 8-oz cans tomato sauce
1 medium green, red, and/or yellow sweet pepper, chopped
2 habanero peppers, chopped (optional)
2 4-oz cans diced green chili peppers
2 cooking apples, cored and chopped
3 tbsp. chili powder
1 fair trade dark chocolate bar, chopped
1 tbsp. curry powder
1 tsp. ground cinnamon
1 15-oz can red kidney beans, drained
1 15-oz can black beans, drained
1 14.5-oz can whole-kernel corn, drained
⅔ cup slivered almonds
Cheddar cheese and plain yogurt or sour cream (optional)

In a large skillet, cook beef, onions, and garlic until meat is brown. Drain off fat. In a slow cooker, stir together beef mixture, undrained tomatoes, tomato sauce, sweet pepper, hot peppers, green chili peppers, apples, chili powder, chocolate, curry, cinnamon, kidney beans, black beans, and corn. Cook on high until chili begins to bubble. Add slivered almonds. Reduce heat to low and cook until thick (about 2 hours). Serve topped with grated cheddar cheese, yogurt, or sour cream if desired.

Mabel's Hot Chocolate Shots and Hot Chocolate
(This Is Not Your Childhood Hot Chocolate Recipe)

We can't tell you how we got our hands on this particular hot chocolate recipe. Everyone in Camellia Beach will attest to how carefully Mabel guards her secrets. So be sure to snip it out and hide it in your safe right away, because I can guarantee you won't be seeing this one printed again.

By the by, here's a bit of trivia you can use to impress others at your next dinner party: Hot chocolate and hot cocoa are not the same thing. Hot chocolate is made using chocolate bars. Hot cocoa is made from cocoa powder.

Ingredients

For the hot chocolate shots:
½ cup whole milk
¼ cup heavy cream
5 oz of 70% or higher fair trade dark chocolate
    (about 1½ bars), coarsely chopped
1 tsp. salt

For the hot chocolate:
3 cups whole milk
1 tsp. corn starch

For the hot chocolate shots:

In a medium saucepan, bring the whole milk and heavy cream to a slow boil. Turn down the heat and add the chocolate and salt. Whisk until smooth. Serve immediately in shot glasses.

For the hot chocolate:

Follow the instructions for the hot chocolate shots (above). Add whole milk and corn starch to the mixture. Heat over medium low heat. Whisk until smooth. Serve in mugs. (Optional: top with whipped cream.)

Dark-Chocolate Hazelnut Truffles
(So Simple Even Charity Penn Can't Ruin This Recipe)

So sinfully dark. So easy to make. You'll impress your guests with these bite-sized chocolaty truffles. Make it once, and your friends will return again and again for more. This recipe is guaranteed to become a holiday favorite.

Ingredients

¾ cups powdered sugar
2 tbsp. cocoa powder
1 tsp. of salt
6 tbsp. butter
7 oz of 70% or higher fair trade dark chocolate
    bars (about 2 bars), coarsely chopped
¼ cup heavy cream
About 60 whole roasted hazelnuts
½ cup cocoa powder
(For a little extra crunch, use chocolate bars with nibs
    added or toss a small handful of chocolate
    nibs into the melting chocolate.)

Mix the sugar, cocoa, and salt in a bowl. In a medium saucepan, melt the butter over medium-low heat. Add the chocolate. Stir until melted. Add cream and the sugar/cocoa mixture. Stir until creamy and smooth. Pour into a square dish. Cover and refrigerate for several hours until chocolate is set.

Remove chocolate from the refrigerator. Use a teaspoon to scoop out chocolate. Roll into bite-sized balls with a hazelnut at the center. They might be hard to roll at first, but as the chocolate warms to room temperature, it will become easier to work. If chocolate becomes too soft, return to the refrigerator for a few hours.

Roll balls in cocoa powder. Serve immediately or store in a covered container in the refrigerator.

Acknowledgments

Chocolate! I couldn't have done it without you.

Oh, what's that? There were a few others who helped get this series together? Sorry, I haven't eaten any chocolate yet today, so that's all I can think about right now. Excuse me.

Okay, I'm back. (Licking fingers.)

First, a huge thank-you goes out to cookbook author and all-around fun person Holly Herrick for sharing kitchen stories and helping me brainstorm what could happen in Penn's chocolate shop. Also, I need to thank Michael Hoffman, the bean-to-bar chocolate artisan behind Bitte Chocolate in Charleston, South Carolina, for spending an afternoon teaching me all about the delicious chocolate-making process and patiently answering all of my silly questions. My story is richer thanks to him. If you find yourself in Charleston, buy one of his chocolate bars. Trust me, you'll thank me for it.

A million thanks to my agent, Jill Marsal, for believing in my series with its nutty characters and for becoming one of its biggest cheerleaders. She gave me the best roller coaster ride of my life when selling this book. Also, I cannot give enough thanks to the talented editors (especially Anne Brewer) at Crooked Lane Books for championing my yummy series and for making publishing a book so much fun.

Finally, I'd like to thank the incredible authors in the Lowcountry Chapter of Romance Writers of America, Sisters in Crime, and Mystery Writers of America, whose unflagging support has kept me pounding away at my keyboard, especially Amanda Berry, Nina Bruhns, Amy Fagley, C. J. Lyons, Dianne Miley, Nicole Seitz, Tracy Anne Warren, and Judy Watts for patiently listening and giving advice as I worked out plot problems and tilted at windmills while writing this book. I couldn't have done it without you!